Love Will Out

Love Will Out

A Newfoundland Story

David Michael

Inglewood
PRESS

Cover Design & Art Direction: Oberholtzer Design Inc.
Cover Illustration: Grant Boland
Book design: Alex Bolduc

ISBN 978-1-9992597-5-4

This is a work of fiction.
While this book is based on real events in the history
of the author's family, the names of some of the people,
business establishments, events and locales
have been changed and some events have been fictionalized.

Cataloguing in Publication data available upon request.

INGLEWOOD PRESS
180 Bloor Street West, Suite 1200
Toronto M5S 2V6, Canada
www.inglewoodpress.ca

PRINTED IN CANADA

This book is dedicated to the memory of my parents,
Makoil Elia & Miriam Burnstein,
aka Mickey & Marion Michael.

I learned two things from my parents:
Make the most of what you're given,
and give the most in return.

Contents

If music be the food of love, play on;
Give me excess of it, that, surfeiting,
The appetite may sicken, and so die.

— William Shakespeare, *Twelfth Night*

Main Characters

Ali Abdullah – son of Majedah and Shafeek Abbott

Aiden Abbott – Ali's younger brother

Antonio – Jacob Arenberg's shipmate in the merchant marine

Doc Harrison – unlicensed doctor

Dr. Lindsey – doctor at St. Clare's Hospital

Erin O'Shea – Ali's parents' live-in maid

Hannah Epstein – Joseph Rosenberg's housekeeper

Isaac Schulman – Joseph Rosenberg's bookkeeper

Jacob Arenberg – an English merchant marine

Joe Murphy – Zane's father; Chief Constable

Joseph Rosenberg – Ruth's father and Sarah's husband

Lilly Rosenberg – Ruth's sister; Joseph and Sarah's daughter

Majedah Abbott– Shafeek's wife and Ali's mother

Naseem Farouk – Ammita's father

Rosie Maloof – Ali's first cousin; owner of The Continental

Ruth Rosenberg – daughter of Joseph and Sarah Rosenberg

Sami Abbott – Ali's youngest brother

Sarah Rosenberg (née Feinstein) – Joseph's wife

Shafeek Abbott – Ali's father and Majedah's husband

Skeeter Dunn – school bully and Tommy Chan's henchman

Tommy Chan – bouncer at The Continental Night Club

Zane Murphy – son of Joe Murphy; drummer in the band

Part I

St. John's

Dominion of Newfoundland

1919

I

The Lumber Yard

"See, I told you she couldn't do it!"

"She's just a weakling!"

That was exactly the incentive Ruth needed.

She'd climbed piles of lumber before and was determined that the one she was now tackling in Scanlon's Lumber Yard would not get the better of her. The boys looking up, and their jeering at her only served to strengthen her resolve.

Ali had invited her to join his gang and had set her this challenge. She was determined to see it through.

She felt the strength return to her legs, and her nerves settled down. She mustered her courage and then started to climb again. She knew she couldn't show any further sign of weakness. When she felt the top of the pile, she triumphantly pulled herself up.

Without pausing to consider the consequences, she raced along the pile of lumber, jumped to the next, ran its length and without stopping to see what lay ahead, with arms outstretched, she dove into the void.

She saw the gang gathered in a tight clutch exactly where she hoped they would be. They looked up as she soared off the edge.

Ruth Rosenberg and her father had moved in next door to Ali Abdullah and his parents the year before, as the Great War was finally grinding its way to a halt. Due to the fact that Ruth's bedroom and Ali's faced each other, they had often caught glimpses of what the other was up to.

It seemed to Ruth that Ali's main occupation was being confined to his room. There was a certain routine she couldn't help but notice. First, she would hear yelling and screaming from the ground floor of his house. That would be followed by shouts of "Get up to your room and don't let me catch you doing that again!" Then she would hear a door being slammed and bolted. Finally, she'd see him flop onto his bed and fitfully kick his feet in the air. He would stay like that for a very long time.

It seemed to Ali that Ruth's main occupation was trying on dresses.

The first time they actually looked directly at one another, Ali was as per usual room-bound. Only, this time, he seemed to have been there for much longer than the usual couple of hours. In fact, he'd been there for the entire afternoon. Ruth had no idea what he had done. She couldn't help but feel sorry for him. She decided to take things into her own hands.

From the shelves in the kitchen, she took bread, cheese and an apple and wrapped them in a cloth. Then, she tied the cloth up with one end of a long rope and headed back to her room.

She opened her window and looked to see if Ali's window was open as well. She checked the alley below to make sure her parents weren't watching.

Confident that all precautions had been taken, Ruth grabbed the bundle of food in one hand, leaned out the window and, with the attached rope gripped in the other hand, she threw the bundle towards Ali's window. It only made it half way. She pulled in the rope and tried again.

Closer, but still not close enough. She took a deep breath, gathered her determination, and with a mighty heave, threw it for a third time. It sailed neatly through Ali's open window and hit him squarely in the back of the head.

Startled, Ali rolled over and saw something tied to the end of a rope. It trailed over his bed, down onto the floor and out his window. He opened the bundle, saw the food inside, then followed the rope to the window. Ruth was still holding the other end. He smiled at her. She smiled right back.

Ali nodded his head to the side and gave her a wink. Ruth nodded and winked back.

He was elated. Partners in crime are hard to find, especially when you're only nine years old.

From an early age, Ali Abdullah had made his way with two things: his cunning and his fists. He refused to turn the other cheek when kids called him 'dirty black', 'garlic scum', or 'spaghetti eater'; and, for some reason, 'Syrian'. He often wondered about that one. He was obviously Lebanese.

As he got older, he didn't hide his light under a bushel. Get in his way, and there would be hell to pay. His boxing coach saw to that.

As Ali would remind anyone within earshot, he was never beaten in the ring. He liked to chalk it up to his mighty fists and his ability to take a punch. Others might have attributed it to the low centre of gravity he came by due to his unimpressive stature. Whatever the truth, anyone who could take on all comers had no one to fear.

As famous as he was for his fisticuffs, however, he was even more famous for his booming singing voice.

At twelve, his favourite place to perform was The York Music Hall. The York was situated in a nondescript, featureless, three-storey attached building on a slight curve in the road on the west end of Water Street. The clapboard siding on the facade was in great need of repair, and whatever paint that might have once graced its surface had long since flaked off. Although not much to look at from the outside, the inside teamed with life on Thursday, Friday and Saturday nights.

Whenever Ali was scheduled to sing there, he would be accompanied by his father. On approaching Frank Green, the doorman, Ali's father would start the brief exchange that never failed to bring a smile to Ali's face.

"Hello, Green. Dead yet?"

"You first. Age before beauty."

On show nights, comedy acts, mimes, impressionists and even male and female impersonators would entertain while the audience ate, drank and smoked tobacco. And, there would be music.

In tribute to Al Jolson, one of Ali's idols, he would fall on one knee with arms outstretched, and fill the Music Hall with Jolson's 'Mammy, My Little Mammy'. He was irresistible. At least that was how he would describe himself during his performances. They billed him as "The Boy Wonder".

While Ali was fighting and singing his way around the harbour-front, Ruth was sitting on her father's knee as he read poetry and regaled her with stories of his youth back in Warsaw. As he spoke, her imagination would soar. She'd marvel at the towering peaks of the Tatra mountains, follow the gently flowing Vistula and wander through the multi-coloured Papaver poppies that covered its river-banks.

But her absolute favourite thing was when her father would bring her into their front room, and take his violin case down from the top shelf near their fireplace. He would gently open the snaps and even more gently take out his violin and bow. He would whisper in her ear and she would run off to her room, returning in the very latest fashionable dress that her father, a tailor, had made for her. She would also be sporting her father's straw hat and carrying his stick. He'd motion for her to stand in front of him so that the light could better illuminate her face. Then she would tip her hat, twirl her stick, and soft-shoe dance her way through "The Sidewalks of New York". A smile would come to his eye whenever she sang, "The tots sang 'Ring-a-Rosie', 'London Bridge Is Falling Down' ", and fell flat on her behind. Ruth was at her happiest when she sang.

Roaming the streets and alleyways of St. John's, however, Ruth's wardrobe of choice was dungarees, worn men's shirts and scuffed-up, weather-beaten work boots.

Her stepmother, Hannah, never approved, but her father always smiled when she ran through his shop dressed to play. "My littlest tramp", her father would call her. And, doing her best Charlie Chaplin impersonation, she would bow and tip her hat to him. Then she would penguin-waddle out into the street looking for trouble.

Ruth's real mother and her little sister, Lilly, were back in New York. It had been years since they had all been together. Ruth missed them. But she was happy with her father.

One lovely warm summer afternoon, Ruth found herself in front of Hall's Horse Wagon Repair Shop, on George Street. Her father was having one of the wheels of his delivery wagon worked on. He'd asked her to meet him there at three o'clock. He wanted her to run an errand.

Hall's was a dingy old place. The wagon and wheel repair shop was on one side and the horses were on the other. Bits of rusted metal and broken, spoked wheels were scattered hither and yon. Whenever it rained, water would flow freely from an open wound in the back wall, cover the grease-sodden dirt floor, then pool in the clogged gutter just beyond the front entranceway. If the smell of axle grease and sweat didn't get to you, the horse manure surely would.

When Ruth showed up at Hall's, her father handed her some documents and instructed her to deliver them to his shop's office manager, Isaac Schulman. They were insurance forms he said that he wanted Isaac to fill out and mail. She folded the papers, put them in the chest pocket of her overalls and pinched the snaps closed.

That's how Ali caught sight of her, putting papers into her work clothes. He'd been on his way to meet up with his buddies at Scanlon's Lumber Yard on the other side of New Gower Street, and had decided to take a detour along George Street to check out the horses.

At first, he hardly recognized her. She looked even scruffier than he did.

Feigning absolutely no interest whatsoever, he sidled up to her and bumped her with his shoulder. Much to his surprise, she bumped him right back. She bumped him so hard, it knocked him off his feet. She looked down at him.

"What are you doing down there?"

She gave him a hand up.

"My name's Ali."

"I'm Ruth."

"Let's go!"

Ruth shouted to her father.

"Is it okay if I go with Ali? He lives right next door to us."

"Yes, I know him. Just remember to drop off all those insurance forms to Isaac Schulman for me. Be sure and tell him they have to be filled out and mailed."

"Thanks, Pop."

Ali took her hand and they headed off.

Scanlon's Lumber Yard was the preferred hangout for Ali and his mob of gangsters, which included his two younger brothers, Aiden and Sami, as well as their closest friend, Zane.

Mr. Scanlon liked having them around. In return, the boys would occasionally stand watch to make sure no one ran away with any of the wood.

What Mr. Scanlon didn't like, however, were the dangerous games of dare they would often play on the lumber at the back of his yard. The boys knew this and would wait for the most opportune moment.

When they arrived this time, they were pleased to see that Mr. Scanlon was out in front tending to a customer. They quietly snuck around the back. They had never before had a girl tag along with them. They were, understandably, apprehensive. Ali rustled them all together.

"This is Ruth. She's pretty tough. Do you think she has the guts to join our gang?"

The boys jeered.

"She's just a girl!" shouted Aiden.

"She could never complete the test!" mocked Sami.

"She'd start crying!" taunted Zane.

"Boo-hoo-hoo!" they all teased.

Ali demurred.

"Let's try her out. See how she does."

The gang jeered louder.

Ali ignored them and turned to Ruth.

"Would you like to join the gang?"

"I don't know. I've never been in a gang before. What do I have to do?"

"You have to undergo a test that only the strongest and toughest can survive."

Ruth thought for a minute, then nodded.

Ali led her to the nearest pile of lumber and set out the rules. They were simple. Ruth had to climb the pile of 2x4s using only one hand, and run its length. Then, without stopping to take a breath, she had to jump to the next pile of 2x4s, run its length as well and, with arms outstretched, swan-dive off without looking. Ali swore he and his posse would be there to catch her. There was a lot riding on this.

She made her way slowly around what looked to her like a mountain-high pile of lumber, inspecting it. Her heart was beating so hard she had trouble catching her breath. Finally, she looked straight up and started to climb. One hand pulled her up and the other was tucked firmly behind her back.

Normally, she felt as sure-footed as a mountain goat. But this time, half-way up the pile, her body was letting her down. All her strength was ebbing away. Her legs trembled and her hands were cold and clammy. She stopped to take a breath.

When finally she did soar off the edge, the gang caught her like a penny from heaven.

There were whoops and hollers, hand-shakes and hip-bumps all round. She was now part of 'Ali's Gang'. St. John's finest! Nothing could stop them. They could run and hide wherever they wanted and never get caught. They could control the waterfront, guard the wharves, frustrate the Constabulary and, most importantly, sneak into the Customs House and ferret away the odd cabbage or two for mom's evening meal. They could make every other gang in St. John's cringe in fear.

Most importantly, Ruth now believed Ali was true to his word. He was her friend and would push her to be the best she could be.

Further celebration, however, would have to wait.

The call was familiar and unmistakable. It started on front stoops and was passed from one mother to another along the streets and alleyways and over the backyard fences. "Dinner is ready!" If Ruth, Ali and the rest of the gang didn't get themselves back home in two shakes of a lamb's tail or sooner, there would be hell to pay.

When Ali finally reached home, he avoided the front door. Retribution lay in wait that way. Instead, he entered through the back door. He was seated at the kitchen table when his parents entered. He asked them calmly what was for dinner. Majedah and Shafeek saw right through their son.

———

Ruth also heard the call to dinner. But she still had to deliver the insurance forms her father had given her to Isaac Schulman.

Ruth didn't like Isaac, and she didn't like the area of town where he lived. Isaac Schulman was her uncle and married to her father's sister, Esther. Joseph had brought both of them over from Poland to help with his business. Originally, he had planned to set Isaac up as a salesman who would travel around Newfoundland selling bolts of cloth and accessories to small businesses scattered across the island. Isaac, however, proved to be a huge disappointment.

Although he would traverse the island well enough, he would also rack up substantial expenses. He proved himself incapable of doing what Joseph asked of him. Sales were not Isaac's problem. It was collecting payment for those sales that eluded him. But regardless of how much he cost him, Joseph couldn't fire him because Isaac was the only source of income for himself and his wife.

Joseph sat him down one day and tried to find out what, if anything, Isaac was actually good at. He was surprised to discover that his brother-in-law had worked as an apprentice bookkeeper back in Poland. Joseph had his answer. Isaac would become his new office manager.

Isaac and Esther lived in a place called Tank Lane. There were no sidewalks or indoor plumbing, and sewage ran downhill along an open trough. The only way residents could access water was from a fountain situated in the middle of the square. The sole source was a large tank buried under the fountain. The city would refill it once every week. The area lacked anything resembling colour, unless one could call dirty, dank, dismal and weather-beaten a colour.

Ruth swallowed her fear and headed into the neighbourhood – up the muddy slope, and towards the ramshackle row house where her aunt and uncle rented a small flat. There was no lighting on the stairs leading to the second floor. Ruth had to be careful where she stepped. On the landing, she knocked on the door. The sound echoed along the empty hallway. It was a lonely place.

Her aunt answered the door. Esther was a small, slender, quiet woman who appeared older than her years. She looked put-upon and had the pallid air of someone who was seldom outdoors. The fact that she had fallen short of her brother's expectations – marrying "a clod like Isaac" – weighed heavily on her. She was wearing a dark, plain dress and an apron covered in flour. She tried to be cheerful but couldn't quite manage.

Ruth handed her the insurance forms. In exchange, Esther took a still-warm matzo from the cupboard. Before she gave it to Ruth, she looked her firmly in the eye.

"I know you must be hungry. But, whatever you do, don't

tell your uncle I gave you this. That would upset him. I must not do that."

Ruth hated matzos. She took a tiny nibble of the unleavened bread, thanked her aunt and handed her the insurance papers. Then she slowly backed towards the door. As she made her way down the dark stairway, her aunt waved goodbye. Although she herself had the freedom to run about and explore whatever took her fancy, Ruth knew her uncle seldom allowed her aunt to leave their apartment. The last thing she saw her aunt do was to wipe a tear from her eye. Poor Aunt Esther, she thought.

Ruth didn't eat the rest of the unleavened bread her aunt had given her. But she didn't have the heart to throw it away. She cracked it and put it in her pocket.

Ruth's father was standing at the front door when she arrived back home. She ran to him and put her arms around his waist. He smoothed her hair and led her inside.

Joseph never shouted at Ruth when she was late for dinner, since it was usually just the two of them.

2

The Rosenbergs and the Abdullahs

Ali's parents had emigrated to St. John's from their Christian Maronite village in the mountains just north of Beirut. Their village looked down on the Kadisha River at the bottom of the rugged Wadi Quannoubine gorge – the Holy Valley of Saints – where, many years earlier, Maronite Christians had fled the persecution of the Ottoman Empire.

As a young boy, Shafeek loved to ride the roiling rapids in his homemade raft and bathe under the river's cascading falls. Majedah preferred the tranquility of her parents' kitchen and her volunteer work at the Church of St. Daniel.

The one thing they had in common, above all else, was their love of music. Shafeek tended towards the reeds – the mijwiz and minjjayrah being his instruments of choice. Majedah preferred the strings – the lute, the lower-toned buzuq, the oud and the two-stringed rebab in particular. She loved the way it perfectly accompanied her singing.

Soon after they were married, Majedah and Shafeek took over the operation of the local grocery store in the town square. They added a small café and terrace out front. In the summer, it was frequented by the many tourists from Beirut who sought to escape the oppressive heat of the city and immerse themselves in the cool mountain air and the wonderful scent of the cedars of Lebanon that covered the hills and valleys. But their tranquility was not to last long.

Like their ancestors before them, they too began to feel their Christian faith under attack from a predominately Muslim population. Local officials imposed taxes that Majedah and Shafeek saw as unreasonable. When they tried to complain, the powers-that-be threatened to take their business from them. However, when attempts were made to close the Church of St. Daniel because a neighbouring family had complained that the choir was causing a disturbance on Sunday mornings, that was the last straw. Majedah and Shafeek decided to escape to a less turbulent life in the New World.

They applied to the Lebanese government for a permit to leave the country but were denied. The reason given was their failure to show sufficient deference to the government officer. After much soul-searching, they decided to abandon all that they had worked for and to flee the confines of what they began to see as not so much their home, as their jail.

Under cover of darkness, they took all that two horses could carry – including Shafeek's mijwiz and his beautifully-decorated tablah hand-drum, and Majedah's rebab and daf tambourine. The two of them travelled by foot along the perilous back hills of their beloved country, through Syria, Jordan and finally Egypt, where they booked passage on the first ship headed to the New World.

The ticket they bought read "Cairo to St. John's, Dominion of Newfoundland, via the Straits of Gibraltar". They knew where Gibraltar was, but St. John's? All they knew was that it was in the New World and far from the tyranny they had suffered in Lebanon. To them the New World meant freedom. Besides, St. John's was the first stop in the New World and therefore the cheapest and most affordable fare. Before they boarded the ship, they gave their two weary horses to a beggar at the port. Their generosity was rewarded with a hollow smile.

Their first port of call was Tel Aviv. Majedah and Shafeek had never been to Israel and they wanted to keep it that way. Their present circumstances, however, precluded that.

Both Majedah and Shafeek had grown up with a profound mistrust of Jews. They held Jews responsible for the death of Jesus Christ. From a young age, they had been taught that Jesus had rebelled against what he had seen as corruption, and had preached Christian love of one's fellow man. The all-powerful Jewish Scribes and Pharisees had seen that as a threat and had colluded with the Romans to have Jesus crucified. Unforgivable! Majedah and Shafeek were convinced that Jews would turn on anyone if given the opportunity.

They decided their best course of action was to keep out of sight and not interact with them if at all possible. Jews were not to be trusted!

When they arrived in Beirut, they took more evasive action. They locked themselves in their cabin and prayed that the local Lebanese authorities wouldn't find them. They had, after all, escaped Lebanon illegally and had taken a dangerously circuitous route to Cairo so as not to be found out. They feared that, if discovered, they would be imprisoned. Fortunately, their luck held out.

Athens was their next stop. Then Palermo, Rome, Marseilles and Barcelona. Their final Mediterranean port of call was Gibraltar. When finally they passed through the straits and into open water, they heaved a sigh of relief and offered prayers to God Almighty. Their next stop would be in the New World.

One chilly April, after six weeks of stomach-churning sailing across the Mediterranean and then the Atlantic Ocean, Majedah and Shafeek began to sense excitement in the air.

Word quickly spread that there had been sightings of fishing boats off the port side. They headed for the railings.

Through the dense fog, they saw men in dozens of small rowing boats. Some hauled in fishing lines by hand. Others waved their arms in welcome. When their ship got closer, Majedah and Shafeek could also see a much larger ship off in the distance. They were told it was the mother ship, and the fishermen were Portuguese.

When the fog finally lifted, they got their first sight of land. As they sailed closer, the seas became rougher. Waves crashed against towering cliffs and tumbled over pebbled beaches. What they didn't see was anything resembling a harbour capable of accommodating their large ocean-going vessel.

The disappointment on their faces slowly faded when they spotted a lighthouse and a tall stone tower above a rocky cliff farther along the coast. Between the lighthouse and the tower they saw a small opening in the headlands. A large three-funneled steamer pushed its way through and towards the sea. Majedah and Shafeek looked at each other and grinned.

With its face turned firmly eastward towards the North Atlantic, St. John's was the nearest port of call for any ship headed to North America. Small in size, it more than made up for it in welcome refuge. Weary European seafarers had been seeking protection there from the turbulent Atlantic Ocean for centuries. What brought them back year after year were the teaming schools of cod on the continental shelf that surrounded the island. It was the mainstay of most of the thirty thousand people who lived there and the commercial backbone of the economy.

Once through the Narrows, a tug sped towards their ship and guided it farther into the harbour. They passed dozens of vessels of various sizes at anchor. Others were moored two or three deep at the wharves. Majedah and Shafeek hugged each other when they saw the many church towers scattered through the city. Christians!

Before they left the ship, they said goodbye to their fellow Lebanese passengers who were Halifax-bound, and joined other immigrants who, like them, were about to make St. John's their new home. They were directed towards the Customs shed farther along the dock.

The wharf on which the shed was located had as many gaps in it as did the walls. The only light came from the open windows and doors. The Customs officer they met couldn't read their identity papers because they were written in Arabic. When he asked them to say their names, the only name that sounded even remotely familiar to him was 'Abdullah'. He stamped their papers and entered their names as 'Mr. and Mrs. Abbott'. Their old name would not survive in the New World.

St. John's was a visceral shock to them. In a hansom cab, on their way to the Crosbie Hotel on Duckworth Street, they saw faceless people sealed inside heavy woolen jackets, with hoods pulled up to protect them from the furious April gale. Like lost souls, they trudged silently down snow-encrusted sidewalks, alongside two-storey-high snowbanks and manure-covered roads. Colourless, onion-crate-like wooden dwellings lined the streets. Large burned-out gaps bore witness to buildings that existed no more. Raggedly-dressed children picked the pockets of derelict men, gut-splattered fishermen slashed the heads off dead-eyed fish, and sozzled sailors led desperate women down dark alleyways into loveless embraces.

Shafeek put his arms around Majedah and pulled her to him.

During the next few months, they made every effort to get

their minds around the local dialect. It proved to be more challenging than first thought. They had learned some English at school, but it was rudimentary at best. 'Hello', 'Good-bye', 'Thank you', 'Where is', and 'How much' weren't going to get them very far.

Whenever the opportunity presented itself, they did their best to engage in conversation with any and all. They were gobsmacked, however, by phrases like 'I'm gutfounded', 'You got me drove cracked', 'I dies at you', 'You're some crooked', 'How's she hangin', 'Whaddya at', 'Stay where yer to 'til I comes where yer at', 'Long may yer big jib draw' and 'It's some mauzy out'.

To add to their challenges, they also found the customs daunting. They seemed to revolve around loud, boisterous yammering while drinking copious amounts of Screech rum. They didn't fully understand the stories or most of the lyrics to the songs. But they gamely tried to imitate the animated arm gesticulations, bounding about, stomping of feet and clanging of spoons. They tried to sing along with 'I'se the B'y that Builds the Boat', 'The Kelligrew's Soiree', 'Lukey's Boat', 'The Squid-Jiggin' Ground' and 'The Ryans and the Pittmans', but mostly they floundered in the attempt. Shafeek liked one song in particular though. The first words of 'The Ode to Newfoundland' reminded him of his beloved Lebanese 'Smiling Land'. "When sun rays crown thy pine-clad hills, and summer spreads her hand", always brought a tear to his eye.

To help them better fit in, Majedah and Shafeek decided to take a bold step. Harry Walsh, who lived across the street from the temporary rooms they were renting, had often invited them to join him and his friends at his Saturday night soirées. One night, they accepted his offer.

When they went in Harry's kitchen, everyone had their heads

in their instruments, and no one looked up. They did, however, when Shafeek started playing his mijwiz and Majedah her daf.

One by one, Harry and his friends stopped playing. Shafeek and Majedah waved their arms and invited them to join in. Suddenly 'The Kelligrew's Soiree' had become 'The Lebanese Soiree'. Harry's kitchen had never heard anything like it.

While they enjoyed the music and the camaraderie of fellow musicians, Shafeek and Majedah did not love the weather. Accustomed as they were to the sunny climes of the Levant, St. John's was consistently dreary, with rain, drizzle and fog being the order of the day. The only exception, it seemed, was the snow, which fell almost constantly during the interminable winter. In feet, not inches!

Another challenge was the food. They found it to be monotonous and dull – cod, fried in one way or the other, accompanied by mounds of potatoes either boiled or cut into strips and fried. It seemed that if Newfoundland had a delicacy, it would be cod again. But this time it would be the tongues and cheeks, fried as usual.

Fruit and vegetables were virtually non-existent. The exception was something called Jiggs' dinner which consisted of salt beef, cabbage, carrots, split green peas tied up in a cloth bag and boiled to a paste. And the ever-present potatoes. To their horror, everything was thrown into a pot of water and boiled to within an inch of its life. At least it was a break from the cod.

Having come from a country with a decidedly eastern-Mediterranean diet, they knew there were alternatives. Instead of bemoaning the local diet, they saw it as an opportunity. They would draw on their experience back home and set themselves up in the grocery business.

To that end, they set their sights on finding a permanent

place where they could live, carry on trade and start a family.

They discovered there was a sizable Jewish community that had set up businesses on Water Street. Because of the centuries-old battles in the Middle East, though, they decided it best to keep a safe distance from that part of town.

In their continuing search, they learned, much to their surprise, that several fellow Lebanese families had made New Gower Street their home and had started small businesses there. They decided to do likewise.

Before long, they had found the perfect place: a reasonably-priced building with a store fronting onto the street, and ample room upstairs for living. Ali was their firstborn, followed closely by Aiden and Sami.

They chose to specialize in providing products that other businesses in St. John's didn't carry. That meant communicating with not only wholesalers in Montreal, but also with those in Lebanon. Gradually they built up their stock of olives, bulgar, yogurt, nuts, peas, dried fruits, beans and seeds of various kinds, pickled vegetables, grains, olive oil and sumac.

When their first shipment of supplies at last arrived from Lebanon, Shafeek made his way to King's Wharf. The Customs officer called him over.

"What's all this, then?"

Shafeek named some of the various produce and spices.

"What are they used for?"

"Cooking," answered Shafeek.

"You eat them?"

"Yes."

The officer pointed to a light-brown substance.

"What's this?"

"It's for when we have parties."

"You eat that too?"

"Sometimes."

"Smells awful."

"It's an acquired taste."

The officer handed it back to him. Shafeek quickly put it into his overcoat pocket. He had a smile on his face as he left the Customs Hall. Not everyone appreciated the benefits of having blond, Lebanese hashish on hand.

Between raising their children and managing the household, Majedah also took control of how their store was to be organized. With the help of their newly-acquired in-house maid, Erin O'Shea, she placed large, round wicker baskets full of fresh fruit and vegetables, as well as imported dried fruits and grains in front of the counter and on the floor up against the opposite wall.

On the shelves attached to another wall, she arranged glass jars full of preserves and pickled vegetables. The shelves behind the counter were packed with tinned goods, cookies, bottled drinks and cigarettes – goods that were more familiar to the local residents.

Next to the stairs that led to the upstairs living quarters, she positioned an icebox in which she kept her yogurts and milk. The candies, coveted by the children, were arranged on the counter – the more expensive five-for-a-penny varieties at the front, and the less expensive ten-for-a-penny ones at the back.

Not only did they sell from their shop, but Shafeek, like his seafaring Phoenician forefathers before him, would travel by steamer up and down the coast of Newfoundland selling goods unavailable to the townsfolk of isolated communities along the way. In exchange for salt cod, seal pelts, fur and any other meagre trade goods the locals might possess, Shafeek supplied salt, sugar, flour, cooking oil, vinegar, thread, yard goods and anything else in demand.

In places like Bay de Verde, Bonavista, Musgrave Harbour and Twillingate, he sold from the wharf or on-board ship. In Fleur-de-Lys, he had his own ocean-front warehouse in which he displayed his goods, and chatted with the townsfolk.

When Ali was older, he often went along for the ride. It didn't take much to coax him into song. But a good salt beef and cabbage boil-up didn't hurt. The locals adored him. He was never happier.

Although Ali's father was the salesman, he was also a kind, gentle man who knew it was better to leave the decision-making to his wife. Majedah took her role on with feverish enthusiasm and an iron hand. Maintaining their family traditions was an obligation to be cherished and celebrated.

Prime among those traditions was a blind devotion to the teachings of Holy Mother Church. She insisted on Sunday nine o'clock mass, weekly confession, nightly family rosary, as well as bedside evening and morning prayers. They were compulsory, and not a matter for discussion.

As well as keeping constant vigilance over adherence to the religious side of life, Majedah also presided over the domestic side. She insisted they rise at seven o'clock sharp seven days a week. Beds were to be made immediately, and night-clothes were to be removed before anyone was allowed downstairs. Before breakfast was served, hands and faces were to be washed. Teeth had to be brushed directly upon leaving the breakfast table. Daily chores and weekly baths were mandatory, and malingering was not permitted under any circumstances. Attendance at all family meals was obligatory. Tardiness would not be tolerated!

So, when Ali returned late for dinner after Ruth's initiation into the mob at Scanlon's yard, it was Majedah who was ready to pounce. Shafeek did his best to calm her down. He asked her to forgive Ali one last time. Majedah fumed and didn't talk to her son or her husband for the rest of the evening.

———

Unlike most of the residents of St. John's who could trace their heritage back centuries to Catholics from Ireland or to Protestants from England, Ruth's father, Joseph Rosenberg, was a relative newcomer too. He was born near Warsaw to an Ashkenazi Jewish family. His father, Abraham, was a much sought-after tailor, and his mother, Thelma, was an accomplished violin teacher. Joseph was their first child.

From an early age, Joseph could remember his father and mother railing against Russian interference in Polish affairs. Abraham feared being swallowed up by them and sought ways to protect themselves and their son, including moving to the New World as some of their relatives had already done. Although a worthy dream, he had great difficulty making it a reality. He felt an enormous obligation to maintain their ancestors' traditions, and not to let them be crushed by barbarian Russian invaders. He could not bring himself to abandon their homeland and let those devils reap the spoils.

When it came to their son, however, Abraham and Thelma saw things differently. Although they loved him very much and would have hated to be separated from him, they also felt Poland was not a place where he could realize his full potential as a tailor, a trade he had learned from his father.

They decided to send him to America and put him in the care of Abraham's brother, Azriel, and his wife, Golda. They operated a ladies' apparel shop in Brooklyn. Joseph's parents were sure he would be in good hands. Azriel and Golda didn't have children of their own, so they were exceedingly happy to do all they could to help their nephew.

Joseph was thrilled when his parents told him the news. He was eighteen with ideas of his own. He knew America would be the place for him to become his own man.

His journey across the Atlantic was long, tedious and sometimes treacherous. The furious storms and constant threats from guileful thieves taxed his resolve.

When his ship finally docked in New York, however, he shrugged all of that off. He was the first one down the gangplank. He approached the Customs Officer with his identity papers in hand.

When the official opened the papers, he asked no questions. He simply burst out laughing and called another officer over, who began laughing too.

"Is that your real name?" he asked.

"Yes," said Joseph. "Why?"

"Oh, nothing. Just asking."

They waved him through, still laughing.

After the initial greetings and introductions, Azriel and Golda explained why the officers had reacted as they had. It was his family name. Joseph was confused. In Poland, his family name was quite common. But his aunt and uncle insisted he should seriously consider changing it.

At first, Joseph was devastated.

His aunt and uncle listed off the most common Jewish last names they could think of and encouraged him to pick one. 'Josef Rosenberg' had a nice ring to it, but apparently there were many Josef Rosenbergs around. So he took a bold move. He changed the 'f' to a 'ph'.

Goodbye, Josef Schlepper. Hello, Joseph Rosenberg. Welcome to America!

During his first few months in New York, Joseph's aunt and uncle set about teaching him the ins and outs of New York's *schemata* rag trade. Golda showed him how their clothing store operated and introduced him to fellow shopkeepers, while Azriel showed him around the garment district in midtown Manhattan, as well as the fur district farther south.

Joseph was mesmerized by the complexity of it all. It seemed to operate effortlessly – from the tailors, cutters and pressers right down to the peddlers pulling and pushing racks of clothing along the busy sidewalks.

When Azriel and Golda discovered that he was actually a very good tailor in his own right, they found him a job in the ladies' clothing shop owned by their friend, Ezra Feinstein. Ezra was a very successful tailor. It was in one of his shops that Joseph met Ezra's daughter, Sarah.

Sarah was a sharp-witted young woman. She was also sharp-tongued. And ambitious. She knew Joseph wasn't from her class, but she saw his potential. When Joseph started his courtship, she coquettishly entertained his hesitant advances.

After a socially acceptable period of time, he asked her to be his wife. She agreed, under one condition. She would not accept any lowering of the standard of living to which she was accustomed. Joseph accepted that condition and promised to live up to her expectations.

Joseph and Sarah moved into the apartment in Sarah's father's elegant house in Manhattan's upper west side. After five years of marriage, Sarah had given birth to two girls – Ruth first, then Lilly. Joseph loved his daughters dearly. He quickly became comfortable in his new life as a devoted father, husband and aspiring entrepreneur.

He was less comfortable with the loose-living and wantonly promiscuous society he saw, where satisfying one's baser instincts seemed to be the predominant order of the day. The bawdy houses, dance halls, peep shows and darkeded alleys shocked him. The shock lasted until his first game of poker.

It was fun, but dangerous fun. That was what attracted him. He learned that he liked to take chances. The rewards were tantalizing. What attracted him most about poker was the bluff.

He loved Fraunces Tavern the first time he saw it. Fraunces was located at the corner of Pearl and Broad Streets. It had existed at that location in one form or another since the middle of the seventeenth century. The tap room, with its cast iron and glass exterior, was easily accessible from street level.

When the bartender discovered that Joseph would be interested in a card game, he directed him to a table in the far corner. Four men were already involved in a game. He asked to join them.

The first hand looked promising. He was dealt three aces. As the game progressed, however, he became more uneasy. He convinced himself that the other player still in the hand was holding a full house or four of a kind. Joseph folded. As the man was raking in the money, he sniggered.

"Just got off the boat, did ya?"

He flicked his cards in Joseph's face, then stuffed Joseph's money into his pocket and strutted out of the room.

Joseph picked the cards up off the floor and turned them over. Nothing, not even a pair. That lesson hit Joseph hard. He realized poker had less to do with what you held, than with what the other guy thought you held. The lesson he didn't learn that day, however, was that bluffing could just as easily go the other way.

He made every effort to keep his dark secret from Sarah. The nights he'd return home late, he would tell his wife that he'd had a heavy workload, or meetings with prospective wholesalers or ongoing decisions regarding new clothes and future fashion trends.

Although Joseph had begun to feel more at ease with what the westside night-life had to offer, he didn't entirely give in to its enticements. He continued to toil six days a week in the incredibly competitive New York clothing business, and he earned just enough to support his young family. But he still longed for the day when he could set up his own business and explore the many ideas that filled his head.

His opportunity finally came when his boss sent him on a buying trip up the northeastern seaboard in search of pelts for fur coats. The trip took him to St. John's, the capital of the Dominion of Newfoundland. He was twenty-eight years old.

He was surprised when he discovered that St. John's didn't possess most of the amenities abundant in New York. For an *au courant,* budding entrepreneur like himself, he saw easy pickings.

On his return to New York, he couldn't wait to tell Sarah the good news.

"Sarah, put down those dishes," he declared as soon as he entered the house and found his wife in the kitchen.

"Welcome home, darling," said Sarah. "How was your trip?"

"The trip was great. What I saw was even better!"

"Whales?" she asked excitedly.

"We're moving!"

"Don't be silly. We're not moving anywhere."

"When you hear what I have to say, you'll agree with me."

"Joseph, my darling, we discuss things in this house so that you don't do anything rash. Remember?"

"We're discussing it now."

"Telling me we're discussing it now is not discussing. It's telling."

"Listen! I landed in a town called St. John's. It's in a country called Newfoundland."

"Never heard of it."

"Of course not. No one has. That's the wonderful part of it all."

"How can it be wonderful, if no one has ever heard of it?"

"No one has heard of it and no one goes there."

"Sounds delightful. I can't wait to see it."

"You won't have to wait much longer," said Joseph.

"I was joking. Why would I want to see a place that no one else wants to see?"

"Because it's all outdated and lacks any sort of variety."

"It sounds ghastly."

"No, you don't understand. We could take over the place and run it like our own little fiefdom."

"Why do you always exaggerate, Joseph? It's not one of your better qualities."

"I don't exaggerate."

"There you go exaggerating again."

"Sarah, you know I've always wanted to start my own business. But I can't here in New York. We could never afford to."

"Especially with what you bring home."

"For what we'd have to pay to rent a shop here, we could buy a whole building in St. John's. I could be my own boss, and you and the girls could live in the lifestyle we've always dreamed of."

"Where is this Newfoundland of yours?"

"It's an island north of Maine."

"I didn't think there was anything north of Maine."

"There is and it's called Newfoundland. Here's my plan."

By the end of the evening, he had worn her down. Sarah reluctantly agreed to at least take a look at this northern

Shangri-La. They made arrangements to leave five-year-old Lilly with relatives. But Ruth – now seven – would travel with them. Joseph swore that if they didn't like St. John's, they would return to New York, no questions asked.

Upon their arrival, Sarah couldn't believe her eyes. It was the first week in October and it was already snowing. The houses crammed together horrified her. Electricity was virtually non-existent. She couldn't understand a word anyone said. There was no way she would agree to live in a frozen backwater shantytown. She would have nothing whatsoever to do with "this damned place".

Joseph, however, had staked everything on moving to St. John's. He knew he was right. St. John's held the answer to his dreams. Sarah didn't share that view.

When they told Ruth that her mother would be taking her back to New York, but that her father would be staying behind, Ruth refused to leave. As much as it would break his heart to not have his daughter with him, Joseph told her it was for the best. Ruth ran to her room.

When she emerged, she was wearing his straw hat and carrying his stick. She stood in front of him, tipped her hat, twirled her stick, soft-shoed and sang, "The tots sang 'Ring-a-Rosie', 'London Bridge Is Falling Down'."

They both cried.

Over the course of the next week, Joseph pleaded with his wife to let Ruth stay with him. Otherwise, he'd be alone with no family to temper his mood. Sarah refused to budge.

He promised her that if things didn't work out as he had planned, he would bring Ruth back to New York. Sarah didn't believe him.

"I am, after all, Ruth's father," insisted Joseph.

"You'd never be able to take care of her," admonished Sarah.

"You can barely take care of yourself."

That gave Joseph the in he was looking for. He promised to hire an older, experienced woman to take care of Ruth in Sarah's absence. Sarah began to realize the inevitable: Joseph would never give up until he got what he wanted. She grudgingly relented.

Hannah Epstein answered the ad in the Daily News. In Joseph's eyes, she had the perfect qualifications: she was the daughter of a Jewish merchant in Holyrood, not far from St. John's. She had glowing references from parents who had previously put their children in her care. And she was thirty-five, several years older than Joseph. She even had her own sewing machine, which pleased Joseph greatly.

After much soul-searching, and reassurances from Hannah that Ruth would be in good hands, Sarah agreed to put her daughter into Hannah's care.

Sarah took the next boat out.

Her last words to Joseph were called out from the deck of the steamer.

"You'll know where to find me, if you ever change your mind."

He couldn't imagine ever doing so.

Joseph's first venture in St. John's was to open Rosenberg's Jewish Delicatessen with an aim to serving the Jewish population and anyone else who might want to try something different. As it turned out, the locals didn't want different. A week after he had opened, he arrived to find his windows smashed, his goods missing and red paint splattered all over the Star of David above his front door. As he was taking stock of the damage, he was approached by Simon Goldstein, who owned the jewellery shop next door.

"Quite a mess, isn't it," said Simon.

"Who would do such a thing?" asked Joseph.

"Have you had breakfast yet?"

They walked across the street to a small restaurant Simon often frequented. When they were seated, Joseph turned to him.

"Why?"

"They know the Mogen Dovid above your door is a Jewish symbol and not everyone likes Jews, as I'm sure you know."

"I thought I had left that behind."

"A Jew can never leave that behind. It will follow him no matter where he goes."

"What am I going to do, Simon?"

"If you want my advice, a Jewish delicatessen might not be the best choice for a business here in St. John's. Do you have any other interests?"

"I'm actually a tailor by trade. I make ladies' clothing."

"So what are you doing in the food business? Open a ladies' clothes shop, why don't you? There's a vacant store further along Water Street. Number 365. Go talk to the land-lord. Mention my name. He's a friend of mine."

"Thanks, Simon. I'll do that."

"One more thing, Joseph. Don't put 'Jewish' in the name. And, as much as I hate to say this, don't put the Mogen Dovid above your door. None of the other Jewish merchants here have one."

Joseph followed his advice and a month later he opened the doors on Joseph Rosenberg – The First American Ladies' Tailor.

Simon was right. Without any reference to Jewishness, the business was a success. Discerning women, seeking something other than off-the-rack clothing, flocked to his shop.

Joseph's dresses took a decided move away from the lavishly-decorated, multi-layered, narrow-waisted Gibson Girl look of the pre-war era. Gone were the highly-coveted, S-shaped body contours of the ideal ladies' hourglass figure. Gone were the constricting swan-bill corsets that emphasized low, full chests and curvy hips. Gone were the narrow waistlines, the high boned collars, the heavily-frilled blouses, and the hip-hugging, fluted skirts that flared at the bottom with trains brushing the floor. Gone too was the voluptuous, ever-so-fragile lady. The jazz-crazed Roaring Twenties had begun and flappers were all the rage.

Joseph's designs stressed a simplicity that had not previously been seen in women's fashion. His inventions embraced comfort and a lighter, more natural effect. The new woman was vivacious, sassy and emancipated. She wanted her clothes to stress the shapeless, androgynous *la garçonne*, boyish silhouette made popular by Coco Chanel and Jean Patou: dropped waist, shorter hemlines, and flattened breasts and hips that so beautifully complemented the sleek bob hairstyles and cloche hats of Louise Brooks and Clara Bow.

Joseph took pride in his skill at recognizing a customer's needs, and took full advantage of his ability to supply that need.

The shop was a success in another way, too. It gave onto the many wooden finger piers of St. John's harbour through which all forms of illegal goods from the French colony of St. Pierre would pass virtually unhindered. Soon, in the wee hours of the morning, it was not uncommon to find Joseph and his now eight-year-old daughter, Ruth, lowering strong lengths of rope out one of their back windows, while darkly-clad men on the wharf below attached boxes of St. Pierre contraband – Canadian booze, American cigarettes, French perfume and wine – to be hauled up and tucked away into Joseph's back room.

One year later, at the age of thirty-two, ever restless and drunk on success, Joseph began to look for an additional challenge. He found it by opening a cinema.

Surreptitiously located in rented rooms next to a billiard hall, on the second floor of a rather miserable building directly across the street from his ladies' tailor shop, The Wonderland Theatre charged five cents admission. Patrons could see breathtaking moving pictures and be entertained by songs and music that were unrivaled anywhere in the city.

Movie reels arrived from Halifax every two weeks. Patrons were thrilled by Lillian Gish's melodramatic near-escape adventures in 'Way Down East', by Mary Carr and her real-life children in 'Over the Hill to the Poorhouse', and by Douglas Fairbanks's dazzling swordplay in 'The Mark of Zorro'. If you failed to attend, Joseph liked to think, you would be missing the greatest show St. John's had to offer.

The mayor and councillors, church ministers and priests, fire and police chiefs, concerned parents, moral reformers and insurance adjusters, however, were outraged. They saw it to be a wicked, commercialized fire-trap. Eventually, the police raided the building and discovered that Joseph had also taken to showing rather unseemly movies after hours, not to mention selling bootleg booze and very revealing French postcards. He was hauled before the court.

When Joseph took his place in the dock, a female social worker came and sat next to Ruth. He was addressed by the Chief Justice.

"Mr. Rosenberg, you have been charged with the showing and selling of banned pornographic materials as well as the selling of illegal alcohol at The Wonderland Theatre, premises you rent." He paused. "Where is your lawyer?"

"I will represent myself, Your Honour."

"That is a very risky way to proceed. You know that, don't you?"

"Yes, Your Honour. But I feel no one else really understands my position."

"And what is your position?"

"I'm innocent, Your Honour."

The judge smiled and said, not unkindly: "You've been caught red-handed, sir. The police found and removed from premises that you rent the items I just mentioned. You have broken the law."

"With all due respect, Your Honour, the law is wrong. There is nothing untoward with what I do at The Wonderland."

"There most certainly is! And the law is not wrong," said the judge, less kindly. "You are!"

"I beg to disagree. I only make these things available to very discerning and discriminating adults. They know what they want. They don't need the law to tell them what to do. They can make up their own minds. No one was harmed."

The judge bristled.

"You don't seem to understand, Mr. Rosenberg. Private individuals don't make the laws to suit them. The laws are made by the courts and a democratically elected government."

"So, you think you know everything just because you have power to wield? You think you know what's good for me better than I know myself?"

The judge pointed his finger at him.

"Mr. Rosenberg, I hold you in contempt of court. I also order you to be evicted from the above-mentioned premises. Bailiff, seize the accused!"

The judge banged his gavel down.

"You can't do that!" Joseph exclaimed, outraged. "Are you trying to ruin my cinema business?!"

He picked up his stick, and waving it in the air, vaulted out of the dock and headed for the bench, where the judge recoiled.

He didn't get very far. The bailiff grabbed him before he could get close enough to do any harm to the Chief Justice.

Joseph was sentenced to two weeks in the local lock-up. His beloved Wonderland Theatre was ordered shut down. He had to pay a one hundred-dollar fine, and Ruth was to be assigned to the care of social services. Joseph's wings had most certainly been clipped.

When Ruth saw her father forcibly grabbed by the arms and put in handcuffs, she tried to run towards him. The social worker held her back. Ruth kicked the woman in the shins, cried out to her father and ran towards him. He bent down and she wrapped her arms around his neck.

"Daddy, take me home," she cried.

"They won't let me, sweetheart. I have to stay with them."

"I want to go with you," she begged.

"I won't be long. I promise."

Under protection of the court, Ruth was temporarily placed in a foster home. She knew her father had done something that other people didn't like, but she didn't understand why she couldn't go home with him. She refused to speak to anyone in the foster home and continually called out for her father. She resisted all food and had to be forced to eat.

The consequences of having his little girl taken from him hit Joseph hard. He decided to change tack. He knew that since the local Jewish congregation didn't have a permanent synagogue, they were having difficulty engaging the services of a full-time rabbi. So, in an effort to be seen as trying to make amends – and, in the meantime, attempting to garner favour and acceptance from other Jews – he volunteered as the stand-in rabbi.

It was a self-inflicted obligation that proved more challenging than he had thought. Although he came from a family that took its faith very seriously, Joseph had a more *dégagé* approach. He was, of course, familiar with the Torah. But it was best not to query him on the details.

He had no problem believing that the Hebrew God was one, whole and complete. On the other hand, he also had no problem believing that the Christian God – made up of the Holy Trinity of Father, Son and Holy Ghost – was also one, whole and complete. He saw them as merely different facets of the one true God.

As far as he was concerned, whether or not Jesus of Nazareth was a Divine Being and the Son of God who became human to save us from our sins, was for biblical or scholarly discussion and had no relevance in everyday life.

Moreover, whether a person believed that their faith derived only from the five written books of Moses, or the entire Bible, or also included oral traditions, rituals, prayers and ethical actions, was of no importance to Joseph. As long as the congregation believed in something and no one got hurt, he was fine. The faithful knew that about him, but looked the other way as long as he didn't expect them to adopt his liberalized approach to Jewish religious doctrine.

Joseph did, however, test their patience when, after several years without his wife, he 'took up' with Hannah. As well as taking care of Ruth – as Joseph had hired her to do – she had also taken to helping out in Joseph's workshop.

The synod elders tried to look the other way. But their wives were outraged. They knew what Joseph was up to when he was often seen sneaking into Hannah's ground-floor flat late at night. Some boycotted synagogue amid cries of "Shame on you!" Others took it out on their husbands, accusing them of encouraging Joseph in his sinful ways.

Joseph was not about to give up his dear Hannah. He knew he needed her and that she brought out the best in him. Hannah understood Joseph. Although she knew he would say all the right things to her but seldom followed through with his promises, she felt he loved her in his own way and would never hurt her.

Although Hannah and Joseph weren't married in the conventional sense, Ruth referred to her as her step-mother. But, as much as Joseph was extremely fond of Hannah, she knew she took second place when it came to his affections. There was only one true love in Joseph's life and that was unquestionably his beloved daughter, Ruth.

The two families had much in common. Both the Abbotts – as the Abdullahs came to be known – and the Rosenbergs – as the Schleppers came to be known – had newly arrived in a city where they were the outsiders. Both had to abandon their family names to accommodate their new environments. And both had escaped persecution in their native lands from age-old enemies who sought to stifle their independence and eradicate their closely-held traditions.

Yet, for all their similarities, the Abbotts and the Rosenbergs were very different.

To Majedah, Jews had been, and still were, the enemy, while Joseph had no particular animosity towards Lebanese. He had more of a live-and-let-live approach to people from different cultures – in fact, to life in general.

Although they had both set up businesses in St. John's, the Abbotts played it strictly by the book. Joseph, however, hadn't quite gotten around to reading that book.

Whereas the Abbotts were set on closely adhering to the Christian Maronite customs in which they had grown up, and which traditions they were determined to pass down to their children, Joseph quickly adapted to his new environment and understood the need for change and individual expression.

While both families loved their children dearly, Majedah was convinced that religion and tradition must be adhered to at all costs and that children should be sworn to uphold these beliefs. The old ways came first. Children came second.

Joseph hoped his children would follow his family's religion and traditions. Majedah insisted on it. It would be a crucial difference.

Part II

3

Ruth and Ali

Ruth and Ali spent much of the summer together. As a full-fledged member of Ali's Gang, she was now entitled to all the benefits of gang life. She learned their secret handshake, how to whistle using two fingers, and where and how to collect scraps of metal to sell to the iron monger.

Their preferred stomping grounds were the wharves. Portuguese fishermen taught them how to play soccer, Spanish fishermen showed them how to avoid the horns of charging bulls, and French sailors taught them how to uncork a bottle of wine using a house key. They were becoming world travellers without even leaving home.

The two friends were also becoming local singing sensations. Their voices blended so sweetly, Ruth's father encouraged them to compete as a duo in the summer talent show at Bannerman Park. They made it to the final round, and were certain their version of 'I'm Always Chasing Rainbows' would woo the audience. It did.

Then it was Vivian Summer's turn. She was four years older and called herself 'Your Summer's Sweetheart'. When the teenager walked onto the stage doing her best not to stumble – perched as she was atop her mother's red high-heeled shoes and dressed in a daringly-short pink skirt, knee-high white socks and a yellow tight-fitting blouse – Ruth and Ali knew they didn't stand a chance. They were right. The judges – all men – couldn't look away from this 'vision of loveliness'. It seemed to matter little what she sang. It was how she sang it that stole the judges' hearts, and eyes. It was unanimous. Your Summer's Sweetheart – First Prize!

Ruth and Ali were furious. Hannah calmed them down.

"Take that as a lesson," she advised. "Stick together, and let no one get over your time!"

———

When, alas, summer drew to a close, it was time to see what Grade Three had in store. Ali's first day went off without a hitch. He loved the crowds, the pushing and shoving. He took school as it came. The only thing that bothered him was the teachers. They seemed more interested in wielding the leather straps hanging from their belts to strap defenseless boys than they were in welcoming one and all back to school. He was always wary of his teachers and kept out of the way of their straps. No one beat up Ali!

Ruth, on the other hand, was more reflective. She thought back to her first day of Grade One, and the note her teacher had given her to bring home to her parents. She hadn't been sure what the note said, but she had sensed it wasn't good.

Her father and Hannah were sitting in the kitchen when she arrived home that day. Hannah was frying up fatback scrunchions for Joseph's beloved cod tongues and cheeks.

"Pop, they told me to take my Mogen Dovid necklace off," she sobbed.

"Don't you ever do such a thing!" Joseph demanded.

"They asked me if I knew my Catechism and if I had made my First Communion yet. What are Catechism and First Communion?"

"I can tell you they're not Jewish," said Hannah dismissively.

"I don't want to go back there," said Ruth. "They scare me."

"They'd scare anyone. They're nuns. Catholics, from The Presentation Sisters," said Joseph.

"I want to go to a Jewish school."

"There aren't any Jewish schools in Newfoundland," said Joseph wearily.

"Let's move then."

"We can't," said Joseph. "I'm sorry, sweetheart."

"I hate school!"

"I don't blame you," said Hannah.

"Pop, my teacher gave me a note. Here."

Joseph read it, then handed it to Hannah.

The next day, Joseph and Hannah walked Ruth to school. When they entered through the front door, they were met by the Mother Superior. The expression on her face was enough to scare the antlers off a moose.

"Follow me," was all she said.

She turned and led them into her office just off the main entranceway of the school.

"Mr. and Mrs. Rosenberg, you may sit here," she demanded more than asked. "Ruth, you stand right where you are."

"Your note said you wanted to talk to us," said Joseph.

"Is your daughter baptized?" the nun asked.

"We're Jewish," said Hannah.

"That is none of my concern," said the Mother Superior.

"Are you Jewish?" asked Joseph with an innocent tone.

"I'll have none of your insolence here," the nun replied.

Joseph winked at Hannah. "No wonder Ruth didn't like her first day at school."

"Let me make this very short," said the Mother Superior. "If your daughter doesn't get baptized, she can't attend our school. In fact, she can't attend any school in St. John's."

"We'll school her at home then," said Hannah.

"That's against the law," said the nun. "It's also against the law not to go to school."

"So you're telling us that if Ruth doesn't get baptized, she can't attend school anywhere in St. John's?" asked Hannah incredulously. "And to not attend school is against the law?"

"You should be thankful we are prepared to welcome your child into Holy Mother Church," said the Mother Superior. "Baptism is a sacred sacrament. Not every Jew gets that privilege, especially considering what they did to Our Lord Jesus Christ."

"He was asking for it," said Joseph under his breath.

The Mother Superior pushed back into her chair.

"What did you say? That's blasphemous!"

"Probably has to do with me not being baptized," said Joseph calmly.

"Obviously the sooner we baptize your child the better," said the Mother Superior. "You have an immediate decision to make. Either Ruth gets baptized, or you will be called before the courts. That's all I have to say!"

Joseph and Hannah stood and began to leave.

"And take that unholy necklace off young lady," added the Mother Superior.

Ruth turned.

"I will not! It shows I'm Jewish. I will always be Jewish no matter how much you baptize me!"

Ruth was baptized two days later. It almost broke Joseph's heart. Ruth didn't take the necklace off, though. In fact, she swore to wear it for the rest of her life.

Otherwise, the year passed uneventfully. And the next, and the next. Ruth and Ali became closer. One would not make any decision without first checking it out with the other.

Joseph loved having Ali around. Ali often teased him, pushing the limits of Joseph's endurance. But much to Ali's surprise, Joseph seemed to have unlimited patience, and even set about teaching Ali how to speak Yiddish. Ali picked it up so quickly that *chez* Rosenberg, hardly a word of English was ever heard. It was Yiddish all the way.

At Ali's house, things were not so cordial. As a child, Ali's little street friend, Ruth, had been tolerated around the Abbott household. Indeed, Ali's mother even permitted Ruth into her kitchen. Majedah was an exceptional cook, coming as she did from a Lebanese village known country-wide for its cuisine. She sometimes showed Ruth how to prepare several dishes the way it was done in her native village. Ruth picked up the tricks of Majedah's kitchen very quickly and took great pride in helping prepare Ali's favourite food.

However, as Ruth began to grow into her teens, she started to sense she was less welcome around the Abbott household. She had no idea why.

Majedah had begun to notice that Ruth's and Ali's friendship was showing signs of becoming more than chummy. She was convinced that Ruth Rosenberg had set her cap for Ali, and that her son didn't seem to be putting up much of a fight. To Majedah, that meant nothing but danger for her son and her family.

In one sense, Majedah was absolutely right. Ruth had indeed set her cap for Ali. What Majedah didn't fully realize was that Ali had also set his cap for Ruth.

One Friday, when they were both seventeen, Ruth and Ali were at McDougall's Pharmacy for their usual end-of-school-week get-together. Some of old gang were there as well, including their best friend, Zane, as well as Ali's kid brothers, Aiden and Sami.

The wall behind the counter was covered in glossy-green tiles with black and white highlights. On the tiles were hung three large rectangular mirrors wrapped in lights. Between the mirrors were two round Coca Cola signs, below which were glassed-in menus of treats and eats. The counter itself had an elaborate front of square black and white tiles intermingled with glossy-green smaller tiles which rose in a fan-like pattern throughout. In front of the counter were sixteen high-backed chairs which matched the counter design.

However, what really stood out were the soda fountains. They soared through the blue-green tiled countertop like dolphins breaching the ocean waves. The cherries on top of the fountains were the translucent high-gloss porcelain knobs. The place was a thing of beauty. There wasn't anything like it anywhere else in St. John's.

McDougall's renowned wall of mirrors and lights was made for preening and surreptitiously eyeing anyone who entered. It was in these mirrors that Ali saw Skeeter Dunn saunter through the swinging doors, followed by his own little gang, like gunslingers entering a saloon.

Ali smelled alcohol, and trouble. He'd had run-ins with Skeeter before, and although he was a few years older than Ali, they were in the same class. Skeeter had been held back at school and consequently carried a huge chip on his shoulder – one he constantly hoped someone would try to knock off.

Skeeter and his henchmen surveyed the place as though they were casing the joint for a heist. He saw Ali, smirked and moseyed up to the other end of the soda fountain counter. After a nudge or two to his gang, Skeeter turned towards Ali. The Charleston was playing on the jukebox.

"Hey, blackie!" shouted Skeeter. "Garlic breath still getting you down?"

Aiden and Sami gave him a quick glance. Ali ignored him.

Skeeter noticed Ruth.

"That your girlfriend, camel jockey? I like that young and innocent look."

"Piss off," said Aiden dismissively.

Skeeter shrugged off the comment and called to Ruth.

"Hey, sweetheart. Do you like older men?"

"Doesn't he mean stupider?" Sami chuckled to the others with a smile on his face.

"What's the matter, gorgeous? Cat got your tongue?"

Ruth silently turned her head towards Ali. Skeeter strolled up to her.

"What's a little cutie like you doin' with this pack of losers anyway?"

"Why don't you go back to your friends," said Ruth. "Looks like they miss you."

Skeeter looked towards his gang.

"O-o-o-oh. She's got a tongue after all. Wanna dance?"

Aiden turned to face him. "She wouldn't stoop so low."

Skeeeter pointed his finger at him. "You sayin' I'm not good enough for her? All I want is a dance."

"Why don't you dance with one of your boyfriends over there," said Ruth. "Might be more your style."

"Sharp little chickie, ain't ya," said Skeeter.

"Get lost," said Ruth.

"Don't say that. Come here. I'll show ya what a real man has to offer, that lover boy here don't got!"

Zane tried to intervene. Skeeter pushed him aside.

He grabbed Ruth and pulled her towards the juke box, trying to force her to dance with him. Ali walked over and put his hand on Skeeter's shoulder.

"Take your hands off her!"

That was just what Skeeter was waiting for. Without any warning, he turned around and took a broad swing at Ali.

The fight was short. Ali had been boxing for years and had no real trouble avoiding Skeeter's wild haymakers. After a couple of well-placed punches, Skeeter fell to the floor. Ali looked down at him.

"Don't you ever touch her again! Got that?"

Ali took Ruth by the arm and led her back to the counter. Behind them, Skeeter got to his feet.

"She ain't worth it anyway. I can do better than her anytime, anywhere." He jerked his head at his friends.

"Come on, guys, let's get outta here and leave that trash to themselves."

At the door, he turned.

"I'll get even with you one way or the other, you sissy boy. That's all I gotta say."

"Looking forward to it," said Ali.

—

Since Ali was the eldest son, he was Majedah's most immediate concern. She was determined to do whatever it took to avoid ending up with little, half-Jewish ragamuffins running around the house, especially ragamuffins whose grandfather would be Joseph Rosenberg. She saw Joseph as a purveyor of filth and over-priced, indecent clothes. More proof that Jews were not to be trusted.

Majedah had become disillusioned with life in general in

the country she and her husband had chosen as their new home. At first, she had seen its better side. However, as time went on, she began to focus more on what she saw as hedonistic and not in keeping with the strict moral values to which she had been brought up to adhere. This led to her becoming more rigid and embittered.

She was determined that Ali would marry a Lebanese girl – preferably one from her native village back in Lebanon, despite living halfway around the world. She was certain a suitable Christian Maronite future daughter-in-law would not be hard to find. In her quest for an eligible bride, she wrote letters to anyone in Lebanon whom she thought might be able to help. However, in her zeal, she hadn't thought to ask Ali what he thought about it.

She was elated when she received a letter from an old friend, Naseem Farouk. What he had to tell her warmed her heart.

Majedah broached the subject with Ali when his friends had gathered at their house for his eighteenth-birthday. Although Ali had invited Ruth, she didn't attend.

He knew why. Ruth hadn't felt welcome there since the day Ali's mother had taken her aside a few years before and had had an overly blunt conversation with her.

"Ruth, today is your thirteenth birthday, isn't that so?" Majedah had asked.

"Yes, Mrs. Abbott. Thanks for remembering." Ruth smiled.

"You are a teenager now."

"That's right, Mrs. Abbott."

"Have you had your period yet?"

Ruth stared at her in disbelief.

"Well, have you?"

"Mrs. Abbott, I don't think you should be asking me about such things."

"I don't care what you think. Answer me!"

"No! I won't answer you. It's none of your business!"

"I demand that you treat your elders with respect and answer the question."

"In that case, I demand that you treat me with equal respect and not ask me questions that don't concern you. You're not my mother!"

Majedah looked at her with disgust in her eyes.

"Your mother. The closest thing you have to a mother is that harlot who sleeps with your father. You know they're not married, don't you?"

"Who cares!"

"Exactly! Knowing your kind, you'd probably end up doing the same thing with my Ali if left to your ways."

"Makes no difference to me either way. Look what marriage has made of you. I'd rather Hannah be the way she is than be a spiteful person such as yourself."

She turned and ran out the door. Majedah shouted after her. "You stay away from my son, do you hear? Jews and Lebanese don't mix!"

Majedah never forgot that conversation, and felt enormously satisfied with herself. She thought it had gone well. Ruth would know her place and not try to get her claws into her son.

She had that conversation in mind as Ali and his friends were leaving the house after his party. She was sitting on the couch in their second floor living room waiting for their maid, Erin, to bring in the tea she had asked for. Majedah called to her son.

"Ali, come here for a moment."

"Can't now, Mom. I'm off out."

"It'll only take a minute."

"Okay, one minute. That's all I got."

Majedah patted the couch. "Come here. Sit next to me."

While Ali was settling in next to his mother, Erin entered the room and set the tea service on the table in front of them.

"You look beautiful as ever, Mother," Ali smiled. "The belle of New Gower Street."

"Oh, Ali, always the flatterer."

"Mr. Ali, will you be having tea?" asked Erin demurely.

"Erin, how many times have I asked you not to call me Mr. Ali? Ali will do."

He turned to his mother.

"What's up?"

"You're eighteen now and not a child anymore. Don't you think it's time for you to start making serious plans to find a wife?"

"Mother, not that again. Please stop talking about me marrying a Lebanese girl. I'm just not interested. Try to understand."

"And you should try to understand and listen to what I'm saying."

"I know exactly what you're saying. You think you have my best interests at heart. But as far as me marrying a Lebanese girl is concerned, well ... that's really your thing, not mine."

He paused a moment. "I know. I'll marry Erin instead." He winked at their maid.

"Ali, be serious," admonished Majedah. "This is no laughing matter."

"You like me, don't you, Erin?"

Erin was, in fact, only two years older than Ali. And if truth be known, had always had a crush on him. She fidgeted and blushed. Majedah cast her eyes heavenward.

"God forbid! She's only a girl from out around the bay, for heaven's sake."

"What does that matter. I think she's cute."

Ali thought back to a few years earlier, when he was fourteen years old. Erin was sixteen. On the way to his bedroom, he had passed Erin's room. Her door was ajar. What he saw frightened him as much as it roused his curiosity. She was standing in front of her mirror and in the process of undressing.

Ali's first thought was to run away. Instead, he stopped and stared. He couldn't take his eyes off her.

Erin saw him in her mirror and continued undressing. It was the first time Ali had seen a naked woman. When he saw her start to slowly turn around, he broke out in a cold sweat and ran back to his room.

He was quickly brought to reality by his mother's voice.

"Erin, leave the room!"

Erin obediently returned to the kitchen, but kept her ears open. Majedah turned to her son once again.

"Nothing is more important than keeping our family traditions alive and not letting them be swept under by what passes for morals in this country we're living in."

"Mother, the guys are waiting for me outside. I gotta go." He stood up and headed towards the door.

"Do you remember me talking about my neighbour, Naseem Farouk, back in Lebanon?" asked Majedah.

"Mother, please. I really have to go."

"Remember me telling you about his daughter, Ammita?"

Erin moved closer to the living room door.

"The spoiled-rotten one?" asked Ali.

Then he paused. "Mother, wait a minute!"

"Mr. Farouk has agreed to discuss you and Ammita getting married. Isn't that wonderful!"

In the kitchen, Erin put her hand to her mouth in shocked disbelief.

"No, Mother! That is not in the least wonderful. I'm simply not going to do that. First of all, she's fifteen years old!

"I was fourteen when I married your father. Look how happy we are. We have you!"

"Second, she has probably never been allowed out of her father's house except maybe for an ice-cream cone now and then."

"She's a lovely girl. I have pictures of her...."

"Third, she probably doesn't speak one word of English."

"Ammita started taking English classes last month...."

"Fourth, and this might come as a bit of a shock to you, Mother. I don't love her!"

"What does love have to do with it? It's simply the right thing for a young Lebanese man to do."

"What does love have to do with it? Everything!"

"It might take some time for you to...."

"Time? I'm not talking about time, Mother. I'm talking about no bloody way!"

"Ali, please, your language."

Ali stood up. Erin ran back into the kitchen.

"That's it, Mother. I've heard enough!" He stormed out of the room.

Majedah went to the door to plead with him to come back, but Ali had already fled down the stairs and out of the house. She returned to the living room and sat back down on the couch. She was convinced she had gotten her point across and that he would eventually see the truth in what she had said. Then again, as far as she was concerned, Ali really didn't have much to say about it. It was for his own good. He'd thank her someday.

4

The Continental

It was around this time that Ruth began to notice a change in her father's behaviour. He was beginning to show signs of wear and tear. The stock market crash of 1929 had started to reduce demand for Newfoundland's major export, salt cod. The reduction in income had affected every part of the local economy. Joseph's customers were becoming more circumspect in their purchases. He tried to interest them in his latest fashions, but more and more he noticed a hesitation on their part.

Moreover, his gambling had begun to take its toll. He couldn't stay away from the tables. Worse still, he had lost his touch. He was convinced that his only way out was to play even more in the hope of hitting the big jackpot, a target that was becoming more and more elusive.

Ruth and Hannah were worried. They knew gambling wasn't just harmless fun. Ruth begged him to devote more of his time to their last remaining business and his first love – original, handmade, ladies' clothes. On many occasions he swore he would do just that. But the next card game drew him in like a moth to a burning flame. Ruth was nineteen and had her hands full with the business already. She feared that one day those hands would be too full and all their hard work would be for nothing.

Joseph was aware of Ruth's concerns. Although he realized that, as a father, he was duty bound to provide for his daughter's future well-being, he also knew his demons had the upper hand. Ruth would need a suitable husband with good prospects who could take care of her. He was pretty sure Ruth had Ali in mind. He also thought it wouldn't do any harm to have a backup plan. He knew just the man. Jacob Arenberg!

Jacob was another expat living in St. John's. He had left his home in Southampton, England, in an effort to see the world. Ruth liked Jacob. She trusted him. He was a few years older than she was, so she would sometimes go to him for advice. Unlike most of the men she knew, he was always well turned out, dapper and debonair.

Ruth first met Jacob when she was sixteen. She was walking along Job's Wharf doing research on a high school project when she noticed him. He looked like he was about to board a ship. He was tall with wavy blond hair and dressed in a well-pressed, dark-blue uniform with shiny brass buttons. He had a white lanyard around his left shoulder. She walked up.

"Is that your ship?"

He smiled. "Not exactly my ship. But I do work on it."

"What do you do?"

"I'm an officer in the Merchant Marine."

"Hmmm.... My name's Ruth Rosenberg."

"Hi, Ruth. Mine is Jacob Arenberg."

Ruth was surprised to hear a name so similar to hers.

"Are you Jewish?" she asked.

"Kinda."

"How wonderful!"

"How about you?" asked Jacob.

"I'm Jewish too."

"That's also wonderful."

"I like your accent," said Ruth. "What is it?"

"I'm from England. How about yours?"

"Good-old, east-end townie drawl."

He laughed. "Nothing wrong with that."

"Can you help me with something?" she asked hesitantly.

"I'd be glad to. What is it?"

"I'm working on a high-school history project about ships that visit the harbour, and the countries they come from. Can I ask you some questions?"

"Sure."

Ruth reached into her school bag and took out her scribbler and pencil. She put on her work face.

"What brought you to St. John's?" she queried.

"I have relatives out around the bay that I wanted to visit."

"Are they Jewish too?"

"Yes."

"Do you live in St. John's?"

"When I'm not aboard ship."

The ship's whistle blew, signaling all hands on deck.

"Sorry, Ruth, I have to go. Wanna see me off?"

"Sure!"

Ruth closed her scribbler. They joined the other men at the gangplank. While there, Jacob introduced her to one of his fellow merchant marines.

"Ruth, I'd like you to meet a shipmate of mine. His name is Antonio."

Antonio was roughly the same age as Jacob. But unlike him, he had a stocky, muscular build. He greeted Ruth, bowing and tipping his hat.

"*Buon giorno, signorina.*"

"Huh?" asked Ruth, confused.

"Antonio is from Montreal, Ruth," interjected Jacob.

"Yes," said Antonio. "Half Italian, half French-Canadian."

"I know some French," boasted Ruth. "I learned it in class. I can say *bonjour,* and *au revoir,* and stuff like that."

"Very impressive," said Antonio. "Are you Jacob's girlfriend?" he teased.

"Don't be silly," blushed Ruth.

Jacob punched him in the arm.

"We just met here on the wharf," said Jacob. "Ruth is doing a school project on merchant marines like us."

"Can I interview you too?" asked Ruth hopefully.

Antonio bowed. "I would be honoured."

Ruth opened her scribbler again.

"How come you're not in uniform like Jacob?"

"Uniforms aren't for engine room grunts like me," answered Antonio.

The ship's whistle blew again.

"Sorry, Ruth," said Antonio. "The ship's a-callin'."

Jacob turned to Ruth.

"Maybe I'll see you when we're in port again?"

"I'd like that."

The two men climbed the gangplank, turned and waved to her. Ruth yelled up.

"My father owns a shop on Water Street. We're at number 365."

"Maybe I'll drop by when I get back," yelled Jacob.

"Don't forget!"

Indeed, Jacob did drop by when he was next in port. In fact, he dropped by whenever he could. Joseph liked having Jacob around, especially when he discovered Jacob had a Jewish grandmother back in England and relatives in Brigus, not far from St. John's.

He and Joseph became good friends. They would often

laugh and joke over a beer or two. Joseph knew Jacob wasn't really a practitioner of the faith, but that didn't matter much to him. Whether or not he attended synagogue was neither here nor there to Joseph. What was more important was that Jacob had Jewish blood flowing in him from his mother's side. He had a lot of time for Jacob and Jacob had a lot of time for Joseph.

Jacob liked Ruth. He liked her passion, her drive and her devotion to her father. There was something exceptional about her. However, he could never quite put his feelings towards her into words. Words and reason were never Jacob's strong points.

For Jacob, the world turned in mysterious ways. His role was not to fight it, but to let it lead him wherever that might be.

Over time, Jacob also got to know Ali. He saw that Ruth and Ali were very close. He knew Ali could take care of himself and quickly realized it would be best not to get in his way. However, he would never stand by and let Ali, or anyone else, cause Ruth any harm. Chivalry to Jacob was more than a romantic fairy tale from a distant past. It was everyday life.

For her part, Ruth liked Jacob well enough. But she wouldn't hear anything of her father's gentle hints that any Jewish woman would be blessed to have him for a husband. There was no room for speculation. She already knew who she wanted to marry – the boy who'd stuck up for her since she was a little girl.

Moreover, her father's gambling and their failing business were what concerned her the most. Ruth decided that drastic measures were needed. Instead of trying to stop him, she decided to join him. Not in the actual card gambling, but at his favourite place to gamble, The Continental.

The Continental was tucked away in an alley close to the

harbour, remote enough to give the nightclub cover from unwelcome, prying eyes. The area was not for the shy or timid, and the uninitiated would find it daunting to say the least. Few of those from the well-heeled upper echelons of St. John's society – firmly situated in the leafy streets of uptown – dared spent much time there.

On any given day, one could hear Spanish, French, Russian, Norwegian and Portuguese spoken on the streets and in the shops surrounding the harbour. As is the case for most people who visit abroad, these men, although of limited resources, were expected to bring back souvenirs and gifts to their loved ones who hoped for their safe return.

Since those men spent most of their time among the muck, guts and constant dangers of the North Atlantic fishery, they were unaccustomed to the finer things of life. Consequently, it was common to hear these cash-strapped fishermen try, in broken English, to bargain for some delicate item of feminine lingerie or other for their wives or girlfriends back home.

In contrast, the elite among them – the captains and the first mates – had a more privileged way of life. They had resources available to them that the ordinary working-class fishermen and sailors didn't have. But no matter what their rank or standing, what brought them all together was The Continental, where the motto was, "Ask no questions, and no questions would be asked of you."

Ruth believed that if she could be at the nightclub when her father was there, she could keep an eye on him and stop him from going too far on any given night. Her only problem was how to do so without compromising her reputation. She knew exactly whom to ask.

Ruth and Ali had made plans to go see a double bill at the Nickel Theatre: Al Jolson in 'The Jazz Singer' and Ramon Novarro in 'The Pagan'. The Nickel was on the top floor of the Benevolent Irish Society's St. Patrick's Hall in the heart of the city. It was an imposing stone building and was the centre of all things Irish in St. John's. For five cents, the audience was treated to cartoons, Pathé Newsreels plus two full-length movies. In contrast to Joseph's ill-fated Wonderland, the Nickel was a haven of civility. Consequently, it had not been shuttered. Ruth resented that. She missed the excitement of her father's old cinema.

Ali, however, was thrilled, at the prospect of actually being able to hear Jolson speak and sing 'My Mammy', Ali's own signature tune. Ramon Novarro singing 'Pagan Love Song' was more along Ruth's line. They met in the line-up outside the theatre.

"Do you know a club called The Continental?" asked Ruth.

"Does a mother know her baby?"

"Don't tell me you've been there?"

"Not only have I been there, I know the owner, Rosie Maaloof. She's my first cousin."

"Really?"

"On my mother's side. But Mom would never admit it. She won't even admit Rosie exists. Apparently, she's the black sheep of the family."

"How come you never told me that?"

"It never came up, I guess."

"Pop spends almost all our money gambling there. I'm looking for a way to stop him. Or at least to slow him down."

"Good luck! Joseph is a tough guy to corral."

"I'd love to be able to be around when he's there so I can keep an eye on him. But from what I hear, I don't think it's the kind of place where I should be hanging out."

"Nah, there's nothing wrong with The Continental. I've been there lots of times. I almost grew up there, although I'd never want Mom to know."

"You're full of surprises, aren't you."

"You'd love Rosie. Well, maybe love might be too strong a word. She's not everyone's cup of tea."

"What should I do? Any suggestions?"

As Ruth expected, Ali, indeed, had many ideas. Only one of which didn't make her blush.

"What say we get the old duo back together?"

"What duo?"

"You and me, of course. Singing! Remember Bannerman Park? Vivian Summers?"

Ruth cast her mind back.

"Your Summer's Sweetheart," Ruth said, nodding her head. "Short skirt and all."

"How could I forget."

"We were the best, and those bloody judges knew it."

Ali suggested that he and Ruth form a musical act and give Rosie first dibs at booking them for what he was sure would be a sold-out, rave-review, money-making, very long engagement at The Continental.

As he saw it, Ruth had the looks and a dream of a voice. And he was "The Boy Wonder", suave as all get-out and in firm possession of a voice uniquely equipped to belt out a tune. He was convinced that Rosie would have no other choice but to hire them on the spot. He even had a stage name picked out, The Jazz Singers.

"So, what do you think?" he asked excitedly. Ruth just stared at him. Ali carried on.

"Gotta take chances in life or you won't get anywhere."

"Are you serious about this?"

"You love to sing, don't you? We were great whenever we sang together."

"Yes, but in a nightclub in front of strangers?"

"They won't be strangers for long."

"And you'd be singing too?"

"The Boy Wonder shuts up for no man!"

"And Rosie would actually give us money for performing there?"

"Absolutely!"

"Pop and me could definitely use the cash."

"And you could keep an eye on him in the bargain."

"Two birds with one stone."

"That's my girl."

As Ruth was climbing the stairs towards her bedroom that evening after her night out with Ali, Hannah called out to her.

"A letter came for you today."

"Are you sure? I never get letters."

"Well, you have one now."

Ruth read the return address. Her eyes widened and a smile came to her face.

In her room, she sat at her desk in front of the window and ever-so-gently unsealed the envelope, taking great care not to damage it. When she opened the neatly folded pages inside, a pressed red rose fell out. She picked it up and inhaled its scent.

My Dearest Ruth,

Do you remember me? I hope you do. I'm your sister,

Lilly, from New York City. That kind of rhymes, doesn't it.

The last time I saw you, you were boarding a ship with mother and father and leaving New York on your way to Newfoundland. I was standing next to Auntie Sadie. I was to stay with her on the upper west side while you were away. I was very sad to see you go and even sadder when I found out that you and father were not to return.

I was only a little girl then but I remember you very well. Even though you were two years older, you were always kind to me. I fondly recall us walking with our parents in Central Park and getting ices from the vendor by the lake. You liked raspberry and I liked strawberry. It seemed the sun always shone in those days.

It has been very hard not seeing you all these years. I never did get the whole story from mother. All I really know is that you live in St. John's. That doesn't mean we can't be friends though, does it.

You might be wondering why I got in touch with you after all these years. One of the reasons is that father finally wrote to mother. Sadly, I don't remember him much. Mother never really told me a lot about him, only that he was a ladies' tailor and had set up business in St. John's. She also said he was pig-headed, stubborn and a tad reckless. I'm not sure if that's true. But if it is, I think I might have more than a little of him in me. I hope you won't hold that against me though (ha-ha).

In his letter, he told mother how much you help him. That is so good to hear. You must be very proud of him. Please give him a big hug and kiss from me. I'm still his daughter, after all! I hope this awful stock market crash hasn't affected him too badly.

I miss you so much. It seems like I miss you more and more as I get older. Please, please write me back. I'll be checking the mail every day. I love you very much.

Your little sister,

Lilly

P.S. Are you still writing poetry? If so, maybe you could send me one. I would love that! I have cherished the one you wrote me just before you left. Do you remember? It's about a little girl who lost her sister. It was so sad. Hopefully you and I can find each other again one day.

Lilly's letter affected Ruth deeply and brought back fond memories of her early years in New York. She hadn't realized how much she had missed not having a sister to grow up with, and in whom to confide. She took a sheet of paper from her desk drawer and dipped her pen into the inkwell.

My sweet, sweet Lilly,

Oh, what a lovely surprise to get your letter. My heart swelled. I too have missed you terribly over the years. We were so young when we last saw each other. I was seven, and you were five. Mere children. I hope mother is fine and that she still remembers me. It has been hard living so far away from her and you for so long. I think of you often.

Yes, father has a shop here and is doing famously. He dresses all the finest ladies in the latest fashion. I help him as much as I can, but he is the one with the flair.

He'll be so happy to hear that you and I are finally in communication with each other. I'll read your letter to him. He'll hang on every word and will undoubtedly ask me to read it several times.

I would love to hear back from you with all your news. We have much to catch up on. I too will check the mail regularly. I love you very much too.

Your big sister,

Ruth

P.S. Yes, I still write poetry, although I don't tell many people. However, you're different. I'll share one with you someday. I'll try not to make it so sad this time.

Ruth reached inside her desk drawer again and took out an envelope. She folded the letter and put it inside. Then she placed Lilly's letter, along with the red rose, back inside its envelope. She went downstairs and got a stamp from the kitchen drawer. She then left the house and mailed the letter.

She had a sister again.

During the next few days, Ruth and Ali took turns going over the nightclub-appropriate songs they knew. It was not impressive. When Ruth suggested 'The Sidewalks of New York', Ali simply laughed.

He asked his two kid brothers, Aiden and Sami, to suggest material for him and Ruth to perform.

Eventually, the four of them came up with a variety of songs they thought would fit the bill. They broke them into three categories. Ali's solos, which were on the jazzy side. Ruth's solos, which were heavy on the blues side. And the duets, which were up-tempo and fun. They ticked off all the basics: Fats Waller, Louis Armstrong, Eddie Cantor, Bessie Smith, Fannie Brice, Irving Berlin. And, of course, a few Al Jolson and Ramon Novarro tunes.

But what to wear? Fortunately for Ruth, Joseph had recently made her a gorgeous cocktail dress. She had tried it on several times but hadn't as yet worn it. She thought it a little too revealing. However, if her father thought it appropriate for his daughter to wear, who was she to argue? The dress had a tight-fitting, low-cut, dark-red bodice covered in black sequins. It flowed in curved lines from the neckline to the waist, and stopped mid-thigh. From there, her father had suspended a black-beaded fringe, which was v-shaped at the front and stopped mid-calf at the back. Topped off with an oriental-styled shawl, low heels to accommodate Ali, and a cloche hat, she was ready for their debut at The Continental.

Ali didn't have much of a wardrobe to speak of, so he asked Ruth if she could help out. Unfortunately, she was busy with her own outfit and didn't have time. He sat on the edge of his bed and racked his brain thinking of someone who could come to his assistance. That was when Erin walked down the hall and past his room.

"Erin! Can you help me with something?"

She stopped and stood in the doorway.

"I always have time for you, Mr. Ali."

"It's Ali, for God's sake."

Erin repeated his name slowly.

"Ali."

"I was wondering if you could give me some advice."

"What kind of advice?"

"I need something special to wear."

"Are you going on a date? I haven't been on a date in ages," she sighed.

"I'm singing at my cousin's nightclub tonight. I want to look my best."

She smiled. "That shouldn't be too hard for you."

"Nice of you to say. I was hoping for a woman's touch."

"I'm certainly a woman."

"Would you help me pick out something?"

"I'm not sure I'm allowed to do that. Your mother always told me I wasn't ever to be in your bedroom when you're there. Even to clean it."

"Come in, for heaven's sake."

Erin entered his room.

"What exactly do you want me to do?" she asked.

"Come here."

Erin walked over to Ali's open clothes closet and stood as close to him as she dared.

"Tell me something," she said wistfully. "You once told your mother that I was cute. Did you really mean that?"

"You're more than cute, Erin. If Ruth wasn't my girlfriend, who knows...."

Erin glared at him, her eyelids lowered. Ali turned his eyes back to his clothes closet.

"How about this shirt with this tie and these pants?" he asked in an effort to collect himself.

"I don't think so", said Erin, crestfallen. "The shirt is yellow, the tie is green and the pants are ... orange? I'd go with something less complicated, if I were you."

"You pick something out."

Erin squeezed past him, rubbing his shoulder with hers as she came closer to his closet.

"How about this suit back here? Why don't you try it on?"

Ali turned his back to her and quickly undressed. Erin made a passing effort to avert her eyes.

"How does it look?" he asked.

Although the pinstripe suit with the wide lapels was a little tight here and a little tight there, and in Erin's opinion made him look like a gangster, she bit her tongue and agreed that it would do nicely. His choice was made.

All dressed up, with somewhere to go, Ali made his way to Ruth's house. He was anxious to get back to singing on stage again and to make a big impact at The Continental. Ruth, however, was a little more cautious. She knew the reputation The Continental had, so she decided to proceed carefully.

Joseph met him at the door.

"You look like you just got out of jail," he mocked.

"Very funny," retorted Ali.

"Just like your suit."

"Is Ruth ready?"

Joseph shouted up the stairs.

"Ruth, John Dillinger is here!"

Ruth appeared at the top of the stairs and began to make her way down.

The first thing Ali saw was her shoes, then her legs, her dress and finally her face – smiling and radiant – as she sashayed towards him. He was speechless.

"Don't just stand there doing your best guppy impersonation," she teased. "Take a lady's arm and lead on."

Ali did as he was told.

"Where are you two off to?" asked Joseph.

"For a stroll along the harbour," answered Ruth.

"We might also have dinner somewhere," added Ali.

As they were leaving, Ruth turned towards her father.

"What are you going to do tonight while I'm not here?"

"Not quite sure yet."

"Harry Lauder will be on the radio doing a special broadcast from England. You might want to listen."

"Thanks. Have a good time."

As soon as Ruth and Ali were out of sight, Joseph grabbed his hat and stick and bolted out the back door.

———

The Continental was not for everyone. But if you wanted to gamble, drink cheap booze or spend an hour or two in the company of women who'd seen it all, it was the place to be. You just had to get past Tommy Chan, the club's doorman and bouncer.

Tommy Chan was a Chinese Newfoundlander whose family had emigrated from China much as Ali's parents had come from Lebanon and Ruth's father had come from Poland. His parents ran a hand laundry and always had a smile and a quick hello for any and all customers. Unfortunately, none of that had rubbed off on their one and only child.

Tommy hated his parents, and everything they stood for. He hated them for having to slave away night and day in the steam and filth of other people's clothes, barely managing to eke out a meagre existence. He hated them for having chosen to live in a place like Newfoundland. In fact, he hated them for having moved from China in the first place. He hated them for forcing him to tend the counter and suffer the abuse and ridicule heaped on him by heartless customers. "Chan, Chan, the Chinaman", they called him. "No tickee, no shirtee", "Shittee on shirt-tail, five cents extra", they mocked. Whenever he walked down the street, someone invariably shouted to him: "Chinkee, Chinkee Chinaman, sitting on a fence. Tryin' to make a dollar out of fifty-five cents." He hated being the son of mere launderers and vowed to one day take his revenge out on all those who enjoyed the happiness that he was deprived of.

As he grew older, he could not put aside the pain he had endured as a child and be a productive member of the complex, multi-racial society that was developing in St. John's. Instead, he made a vow never to come out on the losing end in what he saw as an unfair world. To him, people were to be used merely to further his own ends, and to be forcibly taught a lesson whenever they got in his way.

In some ways, he had a lot in common with Ruth and Ali. Their parents had emigrated to St. John's from distant shores, they had set up businesses and had suffered abuse at the hands of bigots. However, whereas Ruth and Ali chose to love those around them, Tommy saw fairness in his cruelty. People usually get what they deserve, he often said.

———

Joseph got to The Continental in record time that night. He knocked on the door. Tommy slid the peep hole open and peered outside.

"About time. Get in here!"

Joseph entered. Before he even got past the door, Tommy shoved him up against the wall.

"Okay, Rabbi, where's my money?"

"I know, Tommy. I'll pay. Don't worry. I got some coming to me right here tonight, later on."

That was a stretch, for Joseph knew full well that the money he was talking about was now in the pocket of some guy at the poker table whom he was hoping to relieve of it.

Tommy pushed his finger hard against Joseph's forehead.

"You and those friggin' excuses of yours."

"I promise, Tommy. For real!"

"I'll be waitin', Rosenberg. Don't mess it up. This is your last chance!"

Before he could regain his composure, Joseph was almost knocked tail over teakettle by an onrushing Skeeter Dunn.

"Hey, Rabbi. Didn't see you there. Be more careful next time. By the way, how's that cute daughter of yours?"

Joseph ignored him and headed to the poker tables.

<hr/>

Ruth had to adjust her eyes to the lighting, or what passed for lighting, as she entered The Continental. As she did, the lay of the land began to come more clearly into focus. She saw a large unadorned room with a long bar on the left and a stage beyond that. There were tables and chairs spread in a semicircle around a dance floor in front of the stage. Poker tables were lined up against the wall on the right. Standing at the bar were a bunch of men, mostly with their arms flung over scantily-dressed women. At the tables and throughout the hall, other women chatted with the men they passed.

The exception to these women was sitting on a throne-like chair in the middle of the dance floor. There Ruth saw a young woman dressed to kill in the fashion of an Iberian courtesan. She was resplendent, with a wonderfully-exotic red rose in her deep-black hair. By her side within easy reach was a uniquely Newfoundland touch – a Screech and Coke. A line of men stretched halfway across the room, each meticulously outfitted in various officer's uniforms of their respective countries. All were awaiting their dutiful turn.

Ruth watched carefully as each supplicant, one after the other, approached the woman, had a brief word in her ear, lovingly kissed her hand and laid his offering at her feet. Ruth could clearly see an array of gifts King Solomon would have envied. Ali whispered in Ruth's ear.

"Voilà! Madame Rosie Maaloof!"

———

If one imagined the area around St. John's as being the side-view of a face that looked up towards the sky, then the city would be the cheek. The harbour, the eye. The face of the Southside Hills, the eyelid. And the top of the hills would be the Brow – or "the furrowed brow," as some called it. It was full of crevasses, nooks, crannies and closely held secrets. It was a place where anyone could hide and no one would dare come looking for them if they valued their lives. Rosie Maaloof was a child of the Brow.

Situated as it was atop the Southside Hills, the Brow looked down on spectacular and unobstructed views of the harbour, the city and the surrounding area. The sun and moon rose behind the hills and set directly in front, making for breathtaking sunsets and moonsets.

However, what would be the most sought after and coveted real estate in most other cities, in St. John's, the Brow was to be avoided at all costs. Although close to St. John's as the crow flies, it was in some ways as remote as any outlying parts of the Kentucky Appalachian Mountains. During the snow and ice of winter, the treacherously-winding road that twisted and turned its way up the side of the Southside Hills was virtually unconquerable. That meant that for a considerable part of the year, the Brow was inaccessible and therefore cut off from the rest of St. John's. It was a world unto itself.

Rosie's father, Amir, was Majedah's brother. In Lebanese, his name meant 'a successful and flourishing man'. Amir was anything but. Majedah had originally brought him and his wife, Adeline, over from Lebanon to help with the Abbott family business. Amir had other plans.

Once he had arrived, he avoided his sister and her family at all costs and went his own way, which in Amir's case was highly illegal. His specialty was fencing stolen goods from anyone who needed to make a quick buck. He was a valued ally among thieves, and adept at what he did. Unfortunately, he wasn't quite as good at avoiding the law. He spent most of Rosie's life in and out of prison. That left Rosie's mother to provide for their needs as best she could.

When Rosie was eight years old, her mother moved in with Joe Furlong, a man who lived in what would generously be called a simple home. It was, in fact, so simple, it didn't have electricity or running water. There were no bathroom facilities, except for a crumbling outhouse out back. The only source of heat was a wood stove in the kitchen that rendered the rest of the house – exposed as it was on top of a prominence on the Brow – almost unlivable.

Since the new man, Joe, was even more unreliable than Rosie's father, her mother was forced into a lifestyle decidedly unmentionable in genteel society. Not only did she have to worry about how they were going to survive, but how to keep Rosie safe from Joe when she wasn't around. Rosie learned a lot from her mother, not least of which was how to take care of herself in a world dominated by men.

For all of that, despite having to live a life unthinkably hard to most people, Rosie Maaloof never wanted to be anything other than what she was. From an early age, she learned to expect nothing to be handed to her. She knew she would have to work hard, and found the idea inspiring.

On some of her forays into St. John's, Rosie's mother would

take her to see the sights. Rosie loved to jostle with the crowds in the shops along Water Street and marvel at the toys and dolls that packed the shelves. She insisted on trying on the dresses and hats in the girls' department even though she knew they couldn't afford them. She loved it anyway.

A ride onboard the electric street trolley, as it trundled its way along the crowded streets and past the shop windows full of wondrous things, was a true joy.

Her treat at the end of the day would be a plate of French fries, a slice of lemon meringue pie and a chocolate ice cream soda float at The Sweet Shop. It was a new world to Rosie. She loved everything about it.

As much as she relished the town's hustle and bustle, the one thing Rosie demanded above anything else was to visit her first cousin, Ali. He was her favourite. And nothing but fun.

Although Ali's mother permitted Rosie and her mother into the house, she would never leave either of them alone with her son. As far as Majedah was concerned, she was familiar enough with their backgrounds to know she didn't want any of that for her boy.

———

Ruth knew nothing of Rosie's past. When she saw the men lined up in front of her at The Continental, Ruth had many questions. Why were they giving her those presents? What could they be? Did she have some magical hold on them, or was it simply generosity on their part? Or was it something more nefarious.

After what seemed like forever, the crowd in front of Rosie finally dispersed and she surveyed her domain. When her eyes finally rested on Ali, she quickly put down her drink and sashayed across the floor toward him.

"Cousin Ali!" she shouted for all to hear.

"Rosie, long time no see," Ali called back as she approached. "You're looking as sexy as ever."

To show her appreciation, Rosie twirled herself around, ran her hands sensually down her body, then flung her arms around him. What Ruth didn't expect to see was the big kiss Rosie planted on his lips. What surprised her even more was that Ali didn't seem to resist.

He nodded toward the stack of gifts piled up in the middle of the room.

"That's quite a haul you got there."

Rosie winked at him.

"Those guys get what they pay for!"

She nodded sideways towards Ruth. "Who's the filly?"

"Rosie Maaloof, may I present Ruth Rosenberg."

"Any relation to that rabbi guy who hangs out around here?" asked Rosie.

"That 'rabbi guy' as you call him is my father," said Ruth indignantly.

"No harm intended," shrugged Rosie.

She turned to Ali. "She your girlfriend?"

He demurred. "Well...."

Ruth interrupted him. "We've known each other for ages."

"Done the dirty deed yet?"

Ruth made to leave but Ali held her back.

"Got a bit of an attitude, don't she," said Rosie.

She looked at Ruth and sized her up and down.

"Nice dress, though."

Rosie grabbed each of them by the arm and led them to the nearest table, shouting to the bartender for three rum and Cokes. When seated, Rosie exchanged stories with Ali about when they were kids, about how they would play 'House' and 'Doctor and Nurse'. She giggled and causally flicked her hair back off her shoulder.

"Remember how you would show me yours and I would show you mine?"

She gave Ali a kiss on the cheek.

Ruth twisted uncomfortably. Rosie turned towards her.

"Ali's mom and dad would throw a conniption whenever they caught me hanging around. Bad influence and all."

"Bad in a good way," added Ali.

Tommy Chan and Skeeter approached their table. Tommy whispered in Rosie's ear.

"In a minute!" said Rosie impatiently. "Family comes first."

"You're not gonna like it," said Tommy.

"In a minute I said! Say hello to Ali."

Tommy looked past him and leered at Ruth.

"She one of the new girls?"

"I wish," said Skeeter with a smirk on his face.

"She's the rabbi's daughter," said Rosie.

"Rosenberg", scoffed Tommy. "What a loser."

Ruth rose from her chair, the blood rushing to her face. "How dare you!"

Rosie parked herself between Ruth and Tommy, nudging him towards the back of the hall.

"Sorry kids, gotta go. Some trouble with a couple of sailors out back. Even *my* girls have their limits!"

From his chair, Ali grabbed her hand as she made to leave.

"I'm calling in a favour."

"Anything illegal?" asked Rosie.

She took the rose from her hair, bent down and gave Ali another kiss on the lips.

"Ever lovin' kissin' cousins," said Rosie. "Us Lebanese gotta stick together, don't we." She handed the rose to Ali.

Ruth was relieved as she watched Rosie and Tommy disappear through a door next to the stage. She wasn't quite sure what to make of it all. Tommy she could figure out. Rosie was a different matter.

It was then that she noticed her father. He was seated with a bunch of men – including Jacob Arenberg – at one of the tables. She went over, Ali trailing behind. Joseph looked up from his cards. His face dropped.

"Ruth, what are you doing here?" he asked, making a fruitless attempt to hide the cards in his hand.

"So, Harry Lauder...?" asked Ruth, with her hands on her hips.

"That was your idea, not mine," said Joseph. "Besides, Harry Lauder gives me the willies. 'Roamin' in the gloamin' with me wee doech-an-doris'. I'd like to doech-an-doris him."

The other men at the table chuckled. Joseph tried to change the subject.

"Aren't you going to say hello to Jacob?"

Jacob wasn't actually playing; he was there more as an observer. He knew Joseph's business wasn't doing particularly well and he didn't want to see Joseph get into even more debt. Above all else, he didn't want Ruth to have to deal with her father causing any more harm to them because of his reckless behaviour. Especially since Jacob was well aware of what Joseph had put up as collateral at a poker game several years earlier, and lost. He had to keep that secret from Ruth no matter what. Joseph was like a father to him, and Jacob was very protective of Ruth. He would never let anything harm her.

"Hi, Ruth," said Jacob.

"I didn't know that you came to this kind of place," she answered.

"I like to hang out here with Joseph once in a while."

"And I didn't know you were into cards," Ruth added.

"I'm not. I just like to watch how things unfold."

"Well, at least Pop has a friend around."

Rosie reappeared and approached Ali.

"You and your girlfriend wanted to talk to me about something? Follow me."

At the bar, Rosie spoke directly to Ali.

"So, what's on your mind?"

"We have a proposition for you," he replied.

"A threesome?"

"Is that all you ever think about?" asked Ruth.

"Must be boring being such a prude," said Rosie.

Ali interrupted.

"We've put together an act that we thought you might like to feature at The Continental. We're going to call ourselves The Jazz Singers."

Rosie pointed at Ruth.

"Is old iron pants in the act?"

"Just in case you haven't noticed, I'm actually standing right here in front of you," said Ruth indignantly. "If you have any questions about me, address them to me. Not Ali!"

"Well, excuse me!" exclaimed Rosie.

"I'm not here to beg," said Ruth defiantly. "And I don't expect to be treated like you might treat the rest of the women here!"

"Well, la-di-dah! Listen to you! Think you're better than everyone else, do you? That kind of attitude won't get you anywhere in my place. Why don't you just lift up those petticoats of yours and hightail it right out of here!"

Ali interrupted and took Ruth's arm.

"Ruth, why don't you and me step outside for a minute?"

Ruth's reply to Rosie was curt.

"I could use the fresh air!"

Joseph, meanwhile, was having troubles of his own. Tommy had pulled him from the poker table and sat him down in a chair in the back room. Skeeter was standing menacingly behind him. Whenever he tried to stand up, Tommy pushed him back into the chair.

"You got the money you owe me, Rabbi?" barked Tommy.

"Not exactly," said Joseph. "The cards aren't falling my way."

"Speaking of falling, have you ever wondered what it would feel like if you were to accidentally fall off the roof?" Tommy threatened.

Skeeter chipped in.

"Want me to take the rabbi up there and show him the view? On a clear day you can see Cabot Tower."

"Wait a minute, you guys," said Joseph. "I got a proposition for you."

Rosie entered. That made Joseph even more nervous. She looked at Tommy.

"Did you get your money yet?"

Tommy took hold of Joseph's head and turned it to face Rosie.

"Ask *him!*"

"Listen," Joseph stammered. "I got a big shipment of ladies' sealskin coats packed up and ready for shipment tomorrow. They're headed to Canada and the US. How about I give them to you instead? They're worth a lot of cash."

"What am I going to do with women's sealskin coats?" asked Tommy. "Do I look like that kind of guy to you?"

Skeeter let out a high-pitched giggle.

"Wait a minute, Tommy," said Rosie. "The rabbi might be on to something there. Whitecoat seals?"

"Yes, best quality," answered Joseph. "For export only."

Rosie turned to Tommy.

"Gotta be worth a pretty penny, I bet."

"Take them," Joseph said. "You can sell them. That should cover at least half my debt. I'll say they were stolen and collect the insurance money. Then I can also give you what I get from the insurance and that should clear my debt. How's that sound?"

"I'd look like a real lady in one of those coats, wouldn't I, Tommy," said Rosie.

"You get in deeper all the time, don't ya, Rabbi," smirked Tommy.

"May God help me," Joseph sighed, casting his eyes towards heaven.

"Skeeter, take the truck to the rabbi's shop tomorrow," said Tommy.

When Ruth had cooled down, she and Ali went back inside the club. He sat her down at one of the tables and went to find Rosie.

"Sorry about that, Rosie. Ruth has a mind of her own. That's why I like her, in fact. Can we show you our act?"

"That girlfriend of yours is lucky she's with you. I can't say no to my favourite cousin, can I. I wouldn't get my hopes up, though. Trying to get the attention of this crowd ain't gonna be easy. They're not really here to be serenaded, if you get my drift."

"Thanks. Where's the band?"

"Talk to Chuck. He's the guy at the bar with the salt and pepper hat."

Ali waved to Ruth. She joined him at the bar.

"Ali, this place is awful."

"Cool down, Ruth. It's gonna work out fine. You'll see."

After much cajoling, Ali convinced Chuck to lead them backstage. What they saw was not encouraging. One guy was asleep on a cot. Another had his head in his hands and was moaning like a hurt dog. A third was shouting at a girl in an effort to made her do something she obviously didn't want to do.

"Please don't tell me this is the band," said Ali.

"Afraid so," Chuck grunted.

"They're in no shape to play," said Ruth.

"Sure they are," said Chuck. "All it takes is a nudge or two."

Ali handed a sheet of paper to Chuck.

"These are the songs we'd like to sing. Do you know any of them?"

Chuck handed it right back without even taking a look.

"Just start singing. We'll follow you. Nobody cares what we do up here anyway. Come on, Larry, snap out of it!"

Ali walked onto the stage to warm up the audience. He tried a couple of jokes. As Chuck had warned, no one paid him the slightest attention.

He waved to Ruth and Chuck. They, and the band, joined him on stage, taking up their positions. Ali tried again.

"Hello, out there. We're gonna sing you a song from Al Jolson's latest movie, "The Jazz Singer". It's called 'Toot Toot Tootsie'. Give me a 'D', Chuck."

Ali and Ruth started in, but they quickly turned back to face the band. The drummer was playing a waltz, the fiddle player thought it was a jig. On the piano, Chuck was playing a ballad. Eventually, unable to follow what Ali and Ruth were singing, the band stopped playing all together – all except the drummer, who soldiered on with his solid, three-four waltz.

The rest of evening went on like that. The only reaction

– if one could call it that – from the audience was when Ali finally pushed Ruth into singing 'The St. Louis Blues'. Calls of "Take it off!" were heard scattered throughout the room.

After a handful of songs, Ruth and Ali retreated backstage. He was surprised and elated to see that Ruth was upbeat. She had an idea in mind that, although daring, she was sure would get the audience's attention the next time they played The Continental.

5

Sealskin Coats

The next day, Joseph didn't get to the shop until late morning. The run-in with Tommy had taken its toll on him. But he was sure that the sale of the sealskin coats would generate enough money to get Tommy off his back. At least for the time being.

He was in the warehouse waiting for Skeeter and going over some details with his bookkeeper, Isaac, when he heard the front doorbell. He walked into the shop and was stopped cold.

In the doorway stood Majedah Abbott with a big smile on her face. What was she doing in his shop of all places? He was convinced she wasn't there to buy fabric.

"Are you still open, Rabbi Rosenberg?"

"Well, I don't believe my eyes."

"May I come in?"

"If you wish."

"I hope I'm not disturbing you," she said, entering the shop and brushing some fabric off a cluttered chair with a look of undisguised distaste.

"What brings you to my door today?"

"To be quite frank, Rabbi, it's my son, Ali."

"He's a good boy, that Ali."

"He's about to get married, you know."

"Excuse me?"

"Yes. In a couple of months."

"That can't be."

"It is."

"Is this some kind of joke?"

"Not at all."

"To whom?"

"Ammita Farouk. She's the daughter of a friend of ours back in Lebanon. She's a Maronite Christian just like me and my husband."

"And Ali knows about this?"

"Of course. He's really looking forward to it. He has even helped with the wedding list."

"I'm sorry, Mrs. Abbott, but that's hard to believe."

"It's true. We're all very excited!"

"Well, I'll be."

"You might be wondering why I would tell you this now."

"Why, indeed?"

"I hate to say this, but I'm afraid Ali might be taking advantage of Ruth – making her promises he has no intention of keeping, just to have his way with her."

Joseph stiffened. "I can't imagine Ali doing such a thing."

"It would be awful if things were to get out of hand. You have thought of grandchildren, have you not?"

"Of course. What father doesn't think of having grandchildren someday?"

"Well – and this is very important – would you and your family rather have a Jewish man for Ruth, or a Lebanese one like my son? Someone who'd protect her. Isn't your main concern that your daughter not get hurt?"

"Of course it is!"

"Well then, the best way to keep Ali away from any trouble he might cause Ruth is for him to marry his Maronite bride-to-be. And for Ruth to marry a Jewish man. I'm sure there is a suitable husband somewhere out there for Ruth. She's young and beautiful and deserves nothing but the best."

"Ruth can make her own choices."

"All I'm asking, Mr. Rosenberg, is that if the subject ever comes up, I would appreciate it if you could discourage any further romantic dealings between Ruth and Ali. That's all."

She stood up and went to leave, then turned back towards Joseph.

"Of course, you and Ruth will be invited to the wedding. We hope to see you there. We have a lot to celebrate."

Joseph flopped down into his chair. If what Majedah Abbott had just told him were true, Ruth would be devastated. Heartbroken. He couldn't simply stand by and see his daughter destroyed.

His thoughts went to Jacob. Although Joseph knew Ruth didn't love him, he was a good man. He had a well-paying job and was very fond of her. He was also Jewish and could be trusted.

As he was thinking, there was a heavy knock on the back door of his workshop. He left the shop, walked wearily past Isaac and the dozen or so seamstresses he employed, and opened the door.

Skeeter Dunn was standing there with a nasty grin on his face. Joseph's heart sank. Not only was Ruth going to have to deal with the fact that Ali was getting married, but she was also going to have to deal with the loss of their shipment of coats.

Suddenly he was ashamed of how low he had sunk. It was entirely his own fault. Giving the coats to Tommy Chan would go a long way towards paying off his debt. But everyone who had worked feverishly on finishing the coats and getting them packed and ready for export, was counting on the income from the sales to steady the ship that was his tailoring business. He had let everyone down.

He watched Skeeter back up the truck and get out. Wordlessly, Joseph led him to the far corner of the workshop, where the boxes of coats were waiting to be shipped.

But where were they? Just the day before, he and Ruth had put them here. Now, he couldn't see them anywhere. Trying to stay calm, Joseph asked Isaac if he knew anything about the coats.

"Sure," replied Isaac. "Ruth came in earlier. I think she took them to the Customs Office on King's Wharf to be shipped."

Joseph went pale.

He and Skeeter jumped in the truck and headed straight there. Ruth was standing on the wharf. There were no boxes to be seen.

Ruth had expected Joseph to be elated.

"Pop, what's wrong? You look like you just lost your best friend."

"Ruth, where are the coats?"

"They just shipped on the *SS Sylvia*. In a couple of months, we'll get paid. We'll be back on solid ground and get this debt-monkey off our backs."

Skeeter didn't bother waiting for details. Without saying anything, he got in the truck and drove off.

"Ruth, you have no idea what you've done!" said Joseph enraged.

"Pop, I know exactly what I've done. I thought you'd be thrilled."

"If you want to know the truth, Ruth, I promised I'd give those coats to Tommy Chan."

"That doesn't make any sense, Pop. Why in God's name would you do such a thing?"

"To pay for my sins. I got into debt at The Continental. I borrowed money from Tommy."

"And you were going to give the coats to that horrible man as payment for your debt?"

Joseph clasped his hands together and looked heavenward. "God is punishing me. I don't blame him in the least."

"I can't believe what you're saying. Oh, Pop, how many times have I told you to stop gambling!"

The truck pulled up again. Skeeter rolled down the window.

"Rabbi, Tommy wants to see you at Rosie's tonight. Don't be surprised if he wants to take you up on the roof to show you the sights."

He chuckled and drove off, waving his arm out the window.

"Bye-e-e-e-e."

Ruth turned to her father.

"What's that about the roof?"

"I'm lost, Ruth. I'm done for."

"What was that about the roof? Tell me!"

"Tommy threatened that if I don't give him the coats to pay down the debt, I might accidentally fall off the roof of The Continental."

"Pop, that's crazy talk."

Then she brightened.

"You know, I really don't see a problem here at all. The coats have been shipped. In a couple of months we'll get paid and then we can give that thief something to shut him up."

"You don't know Tommy. He told me he wanted the coats or the money today. When Tommy says today, he doesn't mean two months from now."

"We should go to the Constabulary."

"They can't help. I don't have any proof. Besides, the cops have had their own problems with me over the years. I'm not exactly in their good books, you know."

Ruth thought for a moment.

"Listen, Pop. I'll take care of it. I'll go see that lowlife tonight and try to straighten it out. I'll make him listen to reason. You go home. And stay there!"

Ruth and Ali had decided to get together that afternoon to go over what had happened at Rosie's the night before. He had told her he'd meet her at the back of an old warehouse in the west end of town. She hadn't been in the mood to argue.

The building had seen better days. The weather-beaten Royal Newfoundland Regiment insignia over the front door paid mute tribute to its having been used as a training facility during the First World War. Now, more than a decade later, most of the windows were smashed to bits, and bullet holes riddled the facade. A man wearing a sou'wester backwards was picking a cigarette butt out of horse manure over by the fence. A woman and another man were sitting on the ground next to the front door. The man had an old button accordion between his legs. The woman had her hand in an East End Baking Company bag. Next to them was an empty bottle of Old Niagara sherry.

"Hey, missus, got a shillin' on ya?" asked the man.

"I'll dance ya a jig," grinned the woman, as she stuffed her mouth with bread.

Ruth could hear what sounded like a band practising inside. She shouted Ali's name. Much to her delight, she heard him shout back.

She found him at the back of the hall. Ali, Sami and Zane were there as well.

Although his brothers showed no interest in taking to the

ring as Ali had, they most decidedly did take an interest in music. Many a night they would gather in their living room and bang out song after song – Aiden on the piano or whatever took his fancy, Sami on the saxophone or clarinet, and Ali on the trumpet or piano belting out melodies at the top of his lungs.

Aiden was easy-going and looked up to his older brother. He would often follow his lead. Sami, on the other hand, was a bit of a comedian. It was impossible to get a serious word out of him. Zane was a solid drummer and the son of Joe Murphy – Chief of the Constabulary. He waved his drumsticks at Ruth.

"Ali, what's going on?" asked Ruth.

"After that mess last night, I decided to forget Chuck and his merry band of knuckleheads and go with the best. You're looking at our very own band!"

Zane gave a smashing drum roll, and Aiden ran his fingers up and down the piano keys.

"I bet you didn't expect to find a piano here, did you," said Aiden. "And some of the keys actually work."

"Don't pay any attention to that guy looking out the window," said Sami. "His name is Woody. He's an American off one of the boats. He wants to join the band, but I told him, who needs a trombone player?"

"You guys do," Woody shouted.

"Gotta love his spunk," Ali acknowledged.

"You're full of wonders, aren't you, Ali," said Ruth.

"They don't call me the Boy Wonder for nothing," said Ali with a broad smile.

"So, what you're telling me is that you plan on having your brothers and Zane play with us at Rosie's?" said Ruth. "They're great musicians I know, but they're underage. Rosie would never let them play in her place."

"I dropped by to see her this morning and she told me she could care less," said Ali. "She knows all the cops on the beat and does them lots of favours. They won't be any trouble if she gives them what they want. And Rosie's got plenty of that.

"What are we going to do about Woody over there?" asked Zane.

"Hey, Yank," shouted Ali. "Come over here and show us what ya got."

"Thought you'd never ask," answered Woody.

"It's time to jazz it up!" howled Ali.

For the next two hours, they played their hearts out and barely took a breath. At the end, they all agreed they needed a trombone player after all.

While the boys were packing up their instruments, Ruth pulled Ali aside and told him about her father's predicament. Ali didn't seem at all perplexed. He told her not to worry. He'd have a word with Rosie and she'd straighten it out. They'd get the party into full gear that night at The Continental and have some fun.

Ruth's mind was put at rest, at least for the time being. It allowed her to think a little past what her father had done, and focus on the idea she had cooked up to get the attention of the audience.

She couldn't wait to see how everyone would react to her daring plan.

—

Ali ran home after band practice, stormed through the store past his father and up the stairs to where the family lived.

"Hey, Mother of mine."

"I have some very good news," said his mother excitedly.

"If it's about me marrying Ammita Farouk..."

"How did you guess?"

"Mother, I..."

"Our two families have exchanged gifts, and the dowry has been set. She arrives in a few weeks. She will stay with your Aunty Shada until the wedding."

"What?! Are you stark raving mad?"

"We have also arranged for a Maronite priest to be brought in from Canada to conduct the ceremony."

"Mother, stop talking!"

"I'm so relieved that we have finally worked it out."

"Call this whole thing off. Now!"

"Mr. Farouk is looking forward to meeting you."

"I'm warning you, Mother...."

"They're a wonderful family. You will see. You should be happy."

"If you push me, I swear you'll regret it."

"Ali...."

"Mark my words. You're going to be sorry!"

"Please don't say those kinds of things."

He stormed out of the room. Majedah yelled after him.

"She's arriving in a few weeks!"

Ali ran to his room and paced up and down. He was furious. He was still fuming when Erin peeked in.

"I heard some of what your mother said to you."

"It's a load of bullshit!"

"Not to her it isn't."

"She's delusional."

"It's her reality."

"I'll show her who's in charge of my life!"

"Can I help?"

"What did you have in mind?"

It hadn't been Erin's intention to take advantage of the

situation. She just wanted to tell Ali that everything would be okay. However, his proximity caused her real feelings for him to surge. She wrapped her arms around him and kissed him.

Ali hadn't expected anything like that to happen. However, his desire for revenge and anger towards his mother blinded him from all caution.

They fell on the bed together.

Years later, when he thought back, Ali would often trace everything to that moment. But when it happened, he wasn't thinking at all.

On her way to The Continental that night, Ruth stopped by the shop and picked up a few things she'd need to pull off her stunt. She had almost finished loading them into the van when Jacob walked by.

"Can I help you with that?" he asked.

"Nah, I got it."

Ruth slammed the door of the van shut.

"Where are you off to?" asked Jacob.

"The Continental."

"Mind if I tag along?"

"Hop in."

During the drive, Jacob noticed that Ruth was unusually quiet. He tried to lighten the mood.

"Rough crowd last night."

"Tonight will be better."

"Never say die, huh?"

"Jacob, do me a favour, will ya?'

"What's up?"

"Stay close to Pop tonight. Please try to keep him away from Tommy."

"Money problems?"

Ruth didn't answer.

"I know Joseph can be reckless sometimes," said Jacob. "You know you can count on me if you need anything, don't you."

Ruth pulled the van to a screeching halt at the back of the club. She jumped out. Jacob followed.

"Need a hand unloading?" he asked.

"Thanks, but it's a surprise."

Inside The Continental, everything was humming along as usual. Rosie was doing her usual gift-grabbing in receipt for her being more than willing to give her mostly-male customers exactly what they wanted.

Ali had arrived early. He was filled with guilt for what he and Erin had done. He felt his life spinning out of control and couldn't see any way of stopping it.

Ruth found him backstage.

"Where are the guys?"

Ali didn't answer.

"Hey, Ali. Did you hear me?"

"What?"

"I asked you where the guys are."

"Oh yeah."

"What's wrong?"

"I just got a lot on my mind."

They heard a banging on the back door and Ali went to answer it. The rest of the band members were standing there. Since they were underage, they had decided to take precautionary measures by wearing disguises. Aiden was wearing a mustache that drooped down over his chin. Zane was wearing a long black beard that almost covered his entire face. Sami was doing his best clown imitation by wearing a fake nose with large round red circles painted on his cheeks. Even

Woody, although not underage, had decided to go along with the gag. He was wearing dark sunglasses and sporting a pair of moose antlers on his head.

Ruth walked over.

"Got anything for the mummers?" they all shouted.

With their backs to the audience, they dragged their gear through the door and onto the stage. Then, still with their backs to the audience, they returned backstage.

Ruth lowered the house lights. She had found a jerry-rigged spotlight that she hoped would function in a pinch and spotted it centre stage. She walked out to face the audience. There was a tall object draped in a sheet beside her.

As Ruth had expected, no one noticed. The men were busy chatting up the girls. The card tables were full. Tommy was roughing up some drunk at the door. Business as usual.

Ruth took out her compact and started powdering her nose. Still, no one paid any attention. Finally, a guy sitting at a table directly in front of the stage spoke up.

"What's under that sheet?" he heckled.

"What sheet?" Ruth responded, re-applying her lipstick.

"That sheet right next to you."

"This sheet?"

"Stop yer foolishness!"

Ruth bent down and lifted the sheet ever so slightly.

"Do you like open-toed, high-heeled shoes?" she asked suggestively.

"What the hell's going on up there?" shouted the man.

Ruth lifted the sheet a bit more.

"How about mid-thigh, sheer-silk stockings? Oh, and look. A white garter belt."

The guy nudged the girl sitting next to him. When she saw what was happening, she nudged him right back. So Ruth lifted the sheet a little further.

"Are those satin tap panties she's wearing?" she swooned.

By this time, most patrons in the hall had noticed what Ruth was doing. One guy at the back shouted out.

"Is that your girlfriend?"

"Isn't she wicked," giggled Ruth.

Someone in the audience whistled.

"What else you got under there?" yelled a guy at the bar.

Ruth lifted the sheet even further.

"A matching bra," she mewed. "Looks like a D-cup to me." Some in the crowd applauded.

"My kinda' girl!" shouted a man at the back of the room. Ruth removed the sheet entirely. More applause broke out.

"Red lips and blond hair," gushed another man at one of the poker tables. "I think I'm in love!"

"Are her seams straight?" joked a woman in front.

"Let me see."

"Slap her on the ass while you're at it," shouted the bartender.

That's when the cry went out. It quickly spread throughout the room.

"Take it off! Take it off!"

Ruth had heard that cry the night before. But this time it wasn't aimed at her. Ruth cupped her hand to her ear.

"I can't hear you!" she goaded.

As the shouts got louder, Ruth started to remove one of the gloves. She dropped it to the floor. She then slowly removed the other glove.

"Don't stop!" shouted someone in the middle of the room.

Ruth slowly removed the negligee. She let it fall to the floor. The crowd cheered wildly.

"Show us her tits! Show us her tits!"

Ruth undid the bra strap, but didn't remove the bra entirely.

"Before I give you that naughty little thrill, wouldn't you like to know her name first?"

"Who cares!" shouted one of the patrons.

"Ladies and Gentlemen – or whatever you are – may I present, straight from the display window at Bowring's Department Store – Mademoiselle Mannequin!"

The place went wild. Ruth struggled to make herself heard above the din.

"And ... after a sold-out performance at the local lock-up, please welcome Newfoundland's very own tribe of reprobates, The Jazz Singers!" Ruth slapped the mannequin hard on the ass.

With that, and wearing their disguises, Aiden, Sami, Zane and Woody came running onto the stage. They flailed their arms in the air, jumped as high as they could and bumped into each other. The audience loved it.

"Have another drink and sing along if you want," Ruth shouted. "It's called 'The Alcoholic Blues'!"

Backstage, Ali was still trying to deal with what he had done. He had never deliberately kept anything from Ruth before. But this was different. It would break her heart.

He pulled himself together and finally joined the others onstage. The audience joined in on the chorus.

"I've got the blues. I've got the blues. I've got the alcoholic blues."

Ali followed that song up by bravely singing a jazzed-up 'Ain't Misbehavin'. Ruth, who had changed into shabby street clothes and was standing under something resembling a lamppost, slowed it down with a stunning full-out blues version of 'My Man'. She and Ali then joined together and did a humourous take on 'Makin' Whoopee', complete with suggestive heavy eye-rolling *à la* Eddie Cantor. 'Blue Skies' and

'West End Blues' filled out the first set.

Their second set started with the entire band doing an improvised comedy sketch *à la* 'Perils of Pauline' in which Woody, the villain, tied Ruth – the damsel in distress – to imagined railroad tracks. She, of course, escaped imminent death and was rescued by our hero, handsome Harold, played by Ali. The melodrama was an instant success. There were cries of "More. More. More."

As she was leaving the stage after the second set, Ruth saw her father enter the front door of the club. She wasn't pleased to see him there, especially after all that had happened earlier that day.

"I told you to stay home. Can't you listen to me for once!"

"Tommy told me he wanted to see me here tonight, and here I am. He wouldn't take it lightly if I didn't show up."

"Ali said he would have a word with his cousin, Rosie, and straighten it all out."

"Ali is Rosie's cousin? Well, that can't hurt. Has he talked with her yet?"

"No. He doesn't seem quite himself tonight. Something's happened, but he won't tell me what it is."

"Knowing him, he might never get around to it. How are you?"

"Why do you ask?"

"Oh, I don't know. Just asking."

"Now you're sounding like Ali."

"I suppose I should go in and face the music."

"Don't you dare! Go over there and have a drink with Jacob. I'll sort this out."

—

The back room at The Continental was not what one would

call a congenial place. Aside from a long rectangular table and a few chairs in the middle of the room, all Ruth could see were boxes of booze scattered here and there.

Tommy was seated at the table. Skeeter was hanging about not doing much of anything. Rosie was also there. In front of her, she had a tin box into which she was counting money. They barely looked up when Ruth walked in.

"Can I speak with Tommy alone?"

"We got no secrets here, eh Tommy?" answered Rosie.

"I want to talk about the money my father owes him."

"He'd owe me a lot less if you hadn't shipped those bloody coats off to God-knows-where," said Tommy.

"You just need to be patient, that's all," answered Ruth.

"In my line of work, patience isn't a virtue," said Tommy. "It shows weakness. And I'm not a weak kinda guy."

"Anyway, when your old man gets his hands on that money, who knows what he'll do with it," said Skeeter. "He's not the most reliable person in the world."

"You don't know my father at all," said Ruth.

"Hey, listen," said Tommy. "Come over here. You and me can have a little chat."

Ruth hesitantly made her way to the table and sat down.

"I bet you've never been this close to a guy like me before, have ya," said Tommy.

"What kind of guy is that?" asked Ruth sarcastically.

Tommy leaned over the table.

"Turns ya on, does it?"

"Be careful, dearie," cautioned Rosie. "A can of worms, with you-know-who being the biggest worm of 'em all."

"You know what?" said Tommy. "I'm thinkin' there just might be something a pretty young thing like yourself could do to satisfy me."

He put one hand on Ruth's leg and cupped one of her breasts with the other. Ruth slapped him in the face. She got up off the chair and made her way towards the door. Tommy rushed after her, grabbed her from behind and pushed her up against the wall. As he pressed himself against her and ran his hands down her body, Ruth froze.

"What's the matter, sweetheart?" asked Tommy. "Maybe you want me to slap ya around a little. Would you like that?"

"Maybe she should join the convent and get it over with," said Rosie.

Tommy laughed and made his way back to the table.

"I want our money tonight one way or another," he said. "And I don't care how you get it!"

Ruth left the room shaken. She leaned against the wall for support. Aiden called to her from the stage. It was time for their third set. She tried to collect herself.

She and Ali had rehearsed a routine doing a lighthearted take on what they thought Fred Astaire and his sister, Adele, would look like as they twirled to 'Dancing in the Dark'. The idea was that they would turn the lights off on the stage, and Ruth and Ali would stumble-dance around in the dark while banging into everything, especially the drums.

When Ali took her into his arms, she was ramrod-stiff. He felt shame and longed to make things right. How he was going to do that, he hadn't quite figured out yet.

They started their dance well enough. But increasingly, Ruth slowed down. Finally, she stopped dancing altogether and ran offstage. Ali and the band soldiered on in a valiant effort to save the night.

They ended the show with a tribute to Al Jolson. Ali brought the house down with his winning version of 'My Mammy', replete with him falling on one knee while pouring his heart out as he sang "I'd walk a million miles for one of your smiles, my mammy".

While the band was packing up, Ali went looking for Ruth. He saw her sitting at a table with Jacob. Ali and Jacob both wanted to know what was wrong. Ruth started to tell them the whole story. When she got to the part about Tommy trying to have his way with her, Ali quickly turned and headed towards the back room. Jacob followed and caught up with him.

"Ali, wait a minute!"

"Get out of my way! I can't stand by and let that son-of-a-bitch treat Ruth like that!"

"I know. Neither can I. And I plan to do something about it."

"What could you do that I can't do?"

"Pay off Joseph's debt. Or enough of it, anyway, to shut Tommy up."

That hit Ali hard. Until that moment he hadn't realized that Jacob was so concerned with what happened to Ruth and her father. He wondered whether Jacob had romantic feelings for Ruth, or if it was merely out of concern for Joseph.

"That's a lot of money you're talking about, Jacob."

"I have some savings. I'm prepared to help Ruth and Joseph. This is way too much for her to have to deal with."

Ali hesitated.

"You have feelings for Ruth, don't you."

"That's a good way of putting it, I suppose. But you probably suspected as much all along. Don't tell Ruth I'm going to do this, will you. I'd rather not have her know anything about it."

"I have to tell her something. She's going to wonder why Tommy backed off."

"Tell her you had a chat with Rosie and called in some

favours. She said she would calm Tommy down. Tell her Tommy has agreed to wait until the payment for those coats comes in. Then Ruth can pay off the rest of the debt."

"Will Ruth believe that?"

"It all depends on how you tell her."

Jacob walked past Ali and into the back room.

———

On their way back home, Ruth and Ali took the long route. Instead of heading straight to Ruth's house, they walked along the harbourfront.

The moon was beginning to rise over the Southside Hills, illuminating the harbour with a soft glow. Ruth took Ali's arm and rested her head on his shoulder. She could feel his body move with hers, and was comforted by the familiarity of it.

Eventually they stopped by the wharf behind Joseph's shop, sat on the edge and let their legs dangle over the side. She and Ali had never really put into words how they felt about each other and what their futures might have in store. She thought that then would be as good a time as any. She took his hand, turned his head towards hers and leaned in to kiss him. Ali moved his head away and abruptly stood up.

"Did I do something wrong?" asked Ruth.

He bent down and took her face in his hands.

"Don't even think that," he said. "If there's anyone to blame, it's me. I got myself into it and I'm the only one who can get myself out of it."

"Got yourself into what?"

Ali looked out at the harbour, but didn't answer.

"I hate to see you like this," said Ruth.

"And I hate to be like this."

"You know I love you, don't you."

"I do. And I love you too. Please be patient with me."

"I will always be here for you. No matter what."

A weary sadness overcame Ali. He wished with all his heart that what Ruth had just said could be true. But would she ever be able to forgive him for what he and Erin had done? Would it even be fair to expect her to?

Ali took Ruth into his arms and kissed her like he had never kissed her before.

6

Erin O'Shea

"Erin, what are you doing here?"

One night, a couple of months later, Ali was shaken awake. At first, he couldn't see anything. But, as his eyes adjusted to the darkness, he was surprised to see Erin standing over him.

"Ali, wake up!"

"Is that you, Erin?"

"Get out of bed!"

"You shouldn't be here."

"I'm pregnant!"

Erin had been born in Witless Bay on the southern shore. Her father, Seamus, was a fisherman. He had been a fisherman since he was ten years old. He didn't have much of a formal education. But as far as he was concerned, he had as much education as he would ever need.

Erin's grandfather had been a fisherman, and so had his father. In fact, according to the stories that the family would often tell while gathered around the wood stove in the kitchen at the back of their modest two-storey home tucked away in the harbour, the O'Sheas had been fishermen since they first came from Ireland almost 200 years before.

In order to earn enough money to support his family of

seven, Seamus and his sons would load up his little boat with all the tackle they would need and enough provisions to do them for the day. They would head out of Witless Bay towards the open sea off the east coast of the Avalon Peninsula – six days a week, at five o'clock in the morning. Any money he earned, he gave to his wife, Irene, who would then climb the stairs to their second floor and tuck the cash beneath a floorboard under the canvas in their bedroom. It was a meagre but sufficient existence.

On Sundays, Seamus and his family, along with almost everyone else in their tiny village, would walk to the local church and sing the praises of their creator. For Seamus the Holy Trinity was church, family and hard work. He had no time for anyone who didn't feel the same way.

Erin, like her father, was tough and hard working. However, unlike her father, she loved school. She was a good student, and was happy to learn new things. Her favourite pastime was to explore the hills at the back of their home.

When Erin was thirteen, her parents sat her down and told her something she thought she would never hear. Things weren't going well with the inshore fishery and times were hard. School was a luxury they couldn't afford. Since there weren't many, if any, job prospects where they lived, Seamus and Irene told her they were going to put her in service with a good family in St. John's.

Erin was devastated. Although she didn't know exactly what being in service really entailed, it meant she would have to leave school and Witless Bay – where all her friends and family lived – and move to St. John's, a place where she had never been and where she knew absolutely no one. The prospect of leaving all she loved scared her to her core. So much so, that she took it upon herself to hide where no one could find her. If they couldn't find her, they couldn't make her go to St. John's.

She was certain she could survive in the woods. She packed some clothes and food, and, when everyone was sleeping, she snuck out the back door of their house. She had planned everything, right down to bringing a book to read on her favourite bolder over by Murphy's farm. What she hadn't planned on was Newfoundland's notoriously unpredictable weather.

The rain came down in buckets and drenched her to the bone. Then the rain turned to snow. Then the wind came up and turned the snow from a gentle flutter into an almost horizontal, full-out blizzard. Fortunately, she hadn't strayed too far from home. When morning came, she was happy to hear her father call out to her. He took her home, wrapped her in a warm blanket and comforted her. Her ordeal was over.

Several days later, her parents packed her bags and walked her to the main road where the bus to St. John's stopped. As she boarded, she could see her father standing next to her mother. Seamus was bolt upright and straight as an arrow. Irene was leaning heavily against her husband, and in tears. She watched them get smaller until she couldn't see them or Witless Bay anymore.

The final thing her mother had done before Erin boarded the bus was to attach a hand-written note to her jacket. The note read: Mrs. Abbott, I'm Erin O'Shea.

Eight years later, Erin was still living in St. John's and still working for Mrs. Abbott as her in-house help.

—

Ali jumped out of bed.
"What did you just say?"
"I said I'm pregnant!"

"Erin, I...."

"What am I going to do?"

Ali's mind went blank. Then slowly the implications of what Erin had just told him began to sink in.

"Oh, my God. But it was only once!"

"Once is enough."

"We should never have done that."

"But we did! What am I going to do?"

Ali hesitated.

Erin shook him. "Say something!"

"Oh, Erin. I'm so sorry."

"Sorry? Is that all you have to say? Sorry?"

"Are you sure it's mine?"

"How dare you!"

She walked over and sat on the bed.

"I'm lost. Nobody will ever have me now."

"Don't talk like that."

Erin looked up at him with hopeful despair in her eyes.

"Would *you* have me?"

"Erin, I ... well...."

"God help me!"

—

Ali didn't sleep for the rest of the night. He lay awake in bed trying to work out what he was going to do.

He was happy to see morning come. He went to the window and looked out. The sun was slowing rising and spreading its light over the ocean and through the Narrows. He felt some comfort in that. He got dressed and headed straight for the harbour. There was a reassuring snap in the air. He raised the hood of his jacket and braced against the wind.

Jacob's ship was moored at the dock. He was engaged

in deep conversation with his shipmate, Antonio, when Ali approached. Jacob was about to leave on a training mission in preparation for new marine standards that were long overdue. Ali had said that he would see him off that morning.

Jacob knew there was something wrong as soon as he laid eyes on him. Ali dodged every question Jacob asked him, but eventually he wore Ali down.

Jacob couldn't believe what he was hearing. He gave Ali an extra key to his house and told him that if he ever needed to get away from all that was going on in his life, it would be a good place to find refuge. No one would think of looking for him there. Then he was gone.

As his ship made for the Narrows, Jacob watched Ali standing alone on the wharf. He wished he didn't have to leave when his friend needed him the most. But duty was duty.

Ali slowly headed home.

His father was opening the shop as he saw Ali come down the street. From Ali's gait, Shafeek knew something was troubling him.

His suspicions were confirmed when Ali entered the shop. He looked haggard. Shafeek wanted to talk to him before he went upstairs, but couldn't bring himself to do so. He was well aware that Ali and his mother didn't exactly see eye to eye. He knew they were both strong-willed people. He was never surprised when they would clash over what should or shouldn't be done, and he never took sides.

But he knew there was trouble – big trouble – on the way. He would have liked to warn his son, but didn't know how.

As Shafeek watched Ali walk through the shop and up the stairs, he knew what Ali was in for, but he remained silent. He was torn between loyalty to his wife and loyalty to his son.

As Ali was making his way past their living room, he heard

his mother call out to him. He ignored her, went straight to his room and lay down on his bed.

He thought things couldn't get any worse for him. Then his mother walked into his room.

"Ali, where have you been all morning?"

Ali continued to lay on his bed with his back to the door.

"I insist you get up and come downstairs with me. I want to introduce you to some people."

Ali didn't respond.

Majedah left the room. Finally, he could get some rest and try to think things through. That was, until his mother came back. Ali closed his eyes.

"Ali, may I introduce you to some very lovely people who want to say hello," said Majedah. "They arrived late last night when you were in bed. I didn't want to wake you."

Ali opened his eyes to see his mother and father. A man and a young girl were standing next to them.

"Ali, I would like you to meet Mr. Naseem Farouk and his beautiful daughter, Ammita – your future bride!"

Ali jumped up from his bed and pushed each of them in turn out of his room. He slammed the door behind them.

Things had gotten much, much worse.

———

After a few minutes, Ali heard his door slowly creak open.

"Ali, it's us – me and Sami," whispered Aiden.

"I'm done for," said Ali. "You have no idea."

Ali then proceeded to tell his brothers what he had told Jacob earlier that morning. Their jaws dropped in disbelief.

Ali stood up and made for the door.

"Come on. Let's get out of here!"

Mr. Farouk and his daughter were standing at the top of

the stairs blocking anyone who might try to get past them. Shafeek stood by his wife's side.

Mr. Farouk had expected a warm welcome from his future son-in-law. Instead, he faced an embarrassment beyond anything he could have ever imagined.

With an anger in her voice that Ali had never heard before, his mother spoke.

"What kind of son does this to his mother?"

"Mother, please move aside."

"You have shamed me. You have shamed your father and all our family. You have shamed Mr. Farouk, his daughter and all *their* family. How could you be so selfish? You think only of yourself!"

"I told you many times that I didn't want any part of this marriage of yours."

"What you want doesn't matter in this family. You have to accept your responsibility. You must take Ammita as your wife and be a good husband to her."

"Mother, you don't understand. I wouldn't make a good husband for any woman."

"Shame on you!"

"Mother, get out of my way!"

"What has gotten into you? Why are you like this?"

"Mother, don't make me tell you. You'll regret it."

"My God! What have you done?"

Tears came to Ali's eyes.

"I've cheated on Ruth, the only woman I actually love. I'm not fit to marry anyone, let alone this young girl."

"All men do things like that. It's expected."

Ali hesitated.

"Is it expected that I sleep with Erin? She's pregnant with my child! Is that expected?"

He pushed his way through and ran down the stairs.

Majedah, Shafeek, Mr. Farouk and his daughter stood in stunned silence. None of them did know what to say. No one wanted to make eye contact. Ammita couldn't understand English very well, but she knew something terrible had happened.

Mr. Farouk slowly took her hand and led her down the stairs and into their room. Her father quickly told her what had transpired, and she broke into tears. He hugged her and told her they were going to pack their bags. Majedah rushed through the open door of their room. Shafeek stood in the doorway.

"Please, don't act rashly," said Majedah. "Ali often exaggerates things to get his way and that's probably why he said what he did."

"It didn't sound that way to me," said Mr. Farouk.

"You've come so far," said Majedah. "Don't leave now. Ammita and Ali would be so good together."

"You need to learn from this, Majedah. Your son isn't to blame. You are!"

With that, Mr. Farouk and his daughter picked up their bags and left the house. Majedah collapsed onto the bed. Shafeek sat down next to his wife and put his arms around her.

"Majedah, you can't control what Ali does. We are not in Lebanon anymore."

"It's all her fault," said Majedah. "She put Ali up to this."

"You don't know that, Majedah."

"I always worried she would do something like this."

"I'll go see what she has to say."

He stood up. Majedah grabbed his arm.

"Don't you dare. I'll deal with her myself!"

"Majedah, please don't."

She ignored him and rushed out.

She quickly climbed the stairs to Erin's room on the third floor and banged on the door. Erin opened it. The two women stood facing each other.

"I heard that whole conversation," said Erin.

"After all we've done for you and you treat us like this!"

"Ali only slept with me to get back at you."

"How dare you put the blame back on me."

"If you had just listened to what Ali was telling you, none of this would have happened."

"None of this would have happened if you hadn't taken advantage of my son and used him to rise above your station."

"Ali is a grown man. He knew what he was doing."

"You're not even married. That child can't be blessed by Holy Mother Church!"

"Is what your church thinks more important than your own flesh and blood?"

"You have brought shame on this family."

"If there's any shame here, it's on you."

"I suppose you're happy now that you've ruined my son's future and turned him against me."

"The way I see it, you've done that all by yourself!"

It had been more than a week since Ali had revealed that Erin was pregnant with his child. During that time, he had stayed as far away from home as possible. On one hand, he was relieved that his so-called bride-to-be had been sent packing. But, on the other, he was more confused than he had ever been in his life. He had no idea what to do. The thought of having a baby with Erin was more than he could come to terms with. All he thought about was what Ruth and her father would say.

There was no way he could explain what had happened that would not make him look like a total heel.

While all that hung over him, his most immediate concern was the band practice. He had been relieved to see that Ruth hadn't shown up yet. It gave him time to settle himself down.

He was putting the finishing touches on a new song when Ruth and Woody walked in.

"Where have you two been?" asked Ali.

"I was at the harbour welcoming a navy buddy of mine from the States," said Woody. "He just arrived on a ship from North Carolina. The sailors on board will be spending a few weeks here in St. John's."

"The girls at Rosie's will be happy to hear that," said Zane.

"He knew I was living here and playing with a band. He put up a notice asking who would like to play with some local musicians. A bunch of guys signed up."

"Tell them the best part," Ruth interjected.

"A few of them played with some very famous bands back in the States," said Woody. "Louis Armstrong, Red Hot Peppers, Duke Ellington, Bix Beiderbecke. One guy was actually an arranger with Glenn Miller!"

"And they want to play with us?" asked Ali incredulously.

"You guys aren't afraid, are you?" asked Woody.

Ali looked around the room to see the boys' reaction.

"How about tomorrow?" asked Ali.

"Can't see why not," said Woody.

Ruth was getting ready for the big night at Rosie's. She couldn't imagine what it would be like to actually sing with a professional band. She came down the stairs dressed to kill.

"I'm off, Pop."

"The Continental?"

"Yup! We're expecting some American musicians to play with us tonight. Ali spent the day whipping us all into shape."

"How are things with you and Ali?"

"Fine. Why?"

"Ruth, come here. Sit down next to me for a moment."

"I'm already late, Pop."

"What I'm about to tell you, you are going to find very hard...."

"Don't be so melodramatic."

He took her hand and looked her in the eye.

"Ali is engaged to be married to a girl from Lebanon. She might be here already."

"Are you making this up?"

"I wish I were."

"That's impossible. Where did you hear that?"

"His mother came into the shop and told me."

"Does Ali know about this so-called marriage?"

"According to his mother, he's very excited about it. He even worked on the wedding list with her."

"There must be some mistake."

"Ruth, who knows, it might be for the better."

"How could Ali marrying another woman be for the better?"

"It would mean that you'd be free to marry a Jewish man and give me Jewish grandchildren."

"I can't listen to this anymore!"

Ruth jumped up, almost knocking the table over in the process, and stormed out as her father went on:

"Now, I'm not saying that Jacob Arenberg would be a good match necessarily, but he comes from a Jewish family. He would make a wonderful husband."

While Ruth was angrily making her way to The Continental, Ali was with the band setting up their gear. Needing some advice, he sought out Rosie. She'd never let him down before.

"Rosie, there's something I want to ask you. It's kind of a touchy subject...."

"Who've you gotten pregnant?" Rosie asked with a laugh.

"Exactly."

"What? I was only kidding."

"I'm not. I don't know what to do."

"I suppose it's that girlfriend of yours, Ruth."

Ali shook his head.

"Erin, our live-in help."

"Knock me over with a feather!"

"What am I going to do?"

"Do your parents and girlfriend know about Erin?"

"My parents do. Not Ruth."

"Do you want the baby?"

"To be honest, I just wish this would all go away."

"You're still a naïve little boy, aren't you, Ali."

"Erin thinks so."

Rosie thought for a moment. Then she looked around the room. She turned back to Ali and continued very slowly and deliberately.

"There's a guy I know who used to be a doctor. Doc Harrison. He lost his licence to practise after he got in a bit of trouble with the law up in Halifax. He's helped a lot of girls who've gotten themselves into this kind of predicament. If they've got the cash, that is. You know what I'm talkin' about, don't you?"

"Isn't that illegal?"

"Only if you get caught."

"I couldn't ask Erin to do a thing like that."

"Would you rather have a baby with Erin and deal with the

116

fallout from your family and your girlfriend?"

Ali thought deep and hard.

"See the guy wearing a brown trilby hat over there at the bar? That's Doc Harrison. Come with me."

Ali and Rosie made their way to the bar. She made the introductions and then she left them to it.

Doc was a tall, nicely-dressed man who spoke slowly, but well. He was obviously educated and projected an air of confidence. He put Ali at ease, and they talked freely. Doc was very open about his having lost his medical licence and, surprisingly, held no grudges.

He asked questions about Erin's health, family background and how far along she was. Ali was not of much help. Doc didn't seem to expect otherwise. He could get that information when he talked directly to her. There was only one question that Doc Harrison insisted had to be answered. Did Ali have the money?

Ali hesitated.

"Look me up again when you got cash in hand," said Doc. "But don't leave it too long. It could be too late."

As Ali was making his way towards the stage, he noticed a group of men dressed in sailor's uniforms walk into the club. His heart jumped when he saw that they were carrying instrument cases. He walked up to them.

"Americans, right?"

"Guilty as charged!" one of them said.

"You guys here to play?"

"Sure are, chief."

"My name's Ali. Which one of you is Woody's friend?"

"That'd be me. Buzz is the name."

They all had names like that: Flash, Stud, Cheese, Beefcake, Romeo, Rhino and Slick.

"Follow me," said Ali.

They made their way to the stage. On the way, each of them grabbed a chair. After some quick hellos and pats on the back, they got down to business.

They arranged the chairs in a semi-circle around the stage and organized themselves in groups. The trombone player placed himself at the far left-hand side. Woody sat next to him. Two trumpets completed the brass section. A pair of saxes came next, with Sami being the third. To their right, was the rhythm guitar and bass. The piano player was on the far right. Aiden slid in next to him. On a riser at the back, sat Zane surrounded by his drum kit. In the centre, stood Ali, with trumpet in hand. Ruth hadn't shown up yet. That meant that Ali would have to double on vocals as well.

He turned around and faced the band. He saw twelve sets of expectant eyes – all focused on him.

"Where do you want to start?" asked Ali.

"What's the use of prohibition?" shouted Buzz.

"You produce the same condition," rhymed Woody.

"'Crazy Rhythm' it is then," said Ali. He gave a four count and they started in.

Rosie turned around to get a good look at what she heard coming from the stage.

'Crazy Rhythm' was followed by 'Black Bottom', and the dance floor filled with customers. Rosie smiled.

As the band were laying down their instruments after the first set, Ruth burst onto the stage.

"Where have you been?" asked Ali. "You missed...."

"Are you getting married?" she blurted out.

"Is that a proposal?" asked Ali.

"Don't be flippant with me! Are you getting married?"

"Where did you get that idea?"

"Your mother told Pop. The girl from Lebanon. Is that true?"

"Let's sit down for a minute."

"I don't want to sit down. Answer me!"

"Let me explain...."

Ruth didn't wait for an explanation. She slapped him hard in the face and rushed off the stage. The band sat in stunned silence.

Ali wanted to run after her. Instead, he sat on the edge of the stage. He realized the mess he'd gotten himself into. Aiden came and sat down next to him.

"Aiden, do me a favour, will ya? When you see Erin at the house, ask her if she can meet me at McDougall's tomorrow night around eight o'clock."

"Why don't you ask her yourself?"

"Just ask her, will ya?"

"Okay! I'll ask her."

"Give my apologies to the guys. I'm done for the night."

On his way out to the club, Doc Harrison called out to him.

"Was that the girl you told me about?"

"No, that was my girlfriend."

"You really are in trouble, aren't you."

"Can I see you at your place tomorrow night around nine o'clock?" asked Ali.

"Bring the lucky lady with you. The one that's not your girlfriend."

Ali fingered the key in his pocket that Jacob had given him.

The next morning, Ruth knocked on Jacob's door, looking for a friend. Ali opened it. She turned and ran. He gave chase and caught up to her.

119

"Let me go! I hate you!"

"I'm not getting married. My mother made it all up."

"Why would she tell Pop if it's not true?"

"She arranged the whole thing without me agreeing to it, but I refused."

"I don't believe you."

"How can I convince you?"

"Get your mother to tell me."

"I'm the last one she wants to see right now."

"Why? What have you done?"

"That's another story."

"More secrets?"

Ruth pushed him aside. Ali ran after her again.

"How about my father? He'll explain it to you. Ask him who's telling the truth, me or my mother."

Ali's father was in the store when Ali knocked on the window. Shafeek looked up. Ali waved and motioned for him to come outside.

Ruth had many questions. Ali was relieved his father was more than able to assuage her concerns. However, while Shafeek didn't express it explicitly, his eyes pleaded with his son to tell Ruth the whole truth.

"Now do you believe me?" asked Ali expectantly.

"I can't understand how your mother could simply assume you would marry that girl."

"That's Mom for ya."

"I'm sorry I didn't trust you, Ali. Will you forgive me?"

"*You* have nothing to apologize for."

"No more secrets. Okay?"

On her way home, Ruth had a spring in her step. Hannah

met her at the door with an annoucement.

"Another letter came for you. It's from your sister, Lilly."

Ruth grabbed it from Hannah's hand and ran up the stairs to her bedroom. She jumped onto her bed and opened the envelope. A photo fell out. She took a quick glance.

Darling Ruth,

Hi-de-hi! I can't believe we're writing each other. I'm so excited! Your words are music to my ears. My big sister still loves me.

My news? I don't know where to begin. I just finished high school and would like to take some time off before I start college. Mother doesn't seem to mind. She thinks I'll only get into trouble there. I told her, "Isn't that what college is for?" (ha-ha). She blew her top!

I know a lot of boys, but I don't have a steady boyfriend. They all seem so immature. Do you have a beau or anything? If you do, I bet he's gallant and loves you and treats you like a true lady. I hope to have the same thing someday.

Wouldn't it be great if one day we could see each other again. That would be so amazing! In the meantime, here's a picture of me and mother. I'm the one with the big smile on my face. That smile is for you – and father, of course. Hug him for me again. I can't wait to hear back from you. Hi-de-ho!

Your kid sister,

Lilly

Ruth picked up the photo and looked at it again – this time more closely. The two women weren't exactly the same as in her memory any more, but she loved them all the same. She went to her desk and starting writing.

Lovely Lilly,

What a beautiful picture you sent. It warmed my heart. You both look very happy. You are so beautiful. I love the way you have your hair down like that. Very daring. Make sure to tell mother that I think she's also very beautiful. Tell her I said, "Like mother, like daughter." I'll make sure to show it to father. He loved the first letter you sent. I'm sure he'll love the picture equally as much.

Yes, I have a boyfriend. I think you'd like him if you ever met him. I've known him since I was a little girl. I'll tell you all about him someday. There's a lot to tell.

And here's a secret for you. Father has a girlfriend. Her name is Hannah. I call her my stepmother. Don't tell mother though. It might upset her.

Here's a picture of me, father and Hannah. It was taken not that long ago. Doesn't he look handsome! And Hannah, is such a lovely lady. I'm the one resting my head on father's shoulder.

By the way, have you made any plans as to what to do during your time off before beginning college? If so, tell me all about it! I can't wait to hear back from you again. My cup runneth over.

Ruth

Ali arrived at McDougall's just before eight o'clock. He took the corner booth. When he saw Erin enter, he smiled and waved to her. She sat down opposite him. There was a lot riding on this conversation.

"How are you feeling?" asked Ali.

"Terrible. I called my mother in Witless Bay and asked her if I could come home. When I told her what happened, I could hear her telling Dad. He came to the phone."

"What did he say?"

"He asked me if I had gotten married without telling them. When I said no, he almost came through the phone at me. He told me I had broken God's commandment and God will have His vengeance. He said I was no longer his daughter. I could hear Mom crying and pleading with him."

Ali reached his hand out to her in an effort to comfort her.

"Ali, what will I do? I can't go home. And I'm sure your mother won't let me continue to stay at your house."

"Pay no attention to what Mom says. I'll take care of her. You just continue doing your job as usual."

Ali rose from his seat and sat down next to Erin.

"About the baby...."

"*Our* baby."

"You're going through with the pregnancy?"

"That's what usually happens when you're pregnant."

"If you do, things won't ever be the same."

"I know that."

"It's not easy having a baby out of wedlock in St. John's."

"Things would be easier if you felt different about me."

"Erin, now hear me out. I've heard of a guy in town. He used to be a doctor. He has helped a lot of women in situations like this."

"You can't be serious."

"We can talk with him and see what he has to say. You don't have to commit to anything. But he might be able to help."

Erin turned and looked him directly in the eye.

"I wish I'd never fallen in love with you."

―――

As they made their way to Doc Harrison's, they hardly spoke a word. Under different circumstances, the moonlight that softly illuminated the harbour would have served as inspiration for a couple walking side by side towards a common destination.

Doc answered the door.

"Doc, this is Erin."

"Are you the young lady Ali told me about?"

Doc started off slowly. He asked general questions about where she was from, where she worked, her age and her medical history. Eventually, he got to the point.

"Do you know what an abortion is?"

Erin's body drooped. She turned to Ali.

"You don't love me. You never will."

"Erin...."

"This baby is all I'll ever have of you. It's as close to you as I'll ever get. It's part of you. And it's part of me. No one can take that from me. Never!"

She ran out of the house in tears.

Ali stared at the closed door. How could he have encouraged Erin to have the child dragged from her body against her will and cast aside as so much trash? That was so heartless. Surely, he was better than that.

7

Consequences

"You're back already?

Although Jacob had planned on being at sea for several weeks, his ship was forced to return to St. John's much earlier. He hadn't seen Ali since the day he had left port. Although it was a lot to wish for, he hoped he and Ruth had worked things out. He decided to visit her and her father, but vowed not to mention Ali. Ruth answered the door.

"What happened?" she asked.

"Can I come in?"

"Of course."

Hannah rose from her chair. Joseph came down the stairs.

"Hey, Jacob! Boring trip as usual, I bet," said Joseph.

"Just the opposite," he replied. "We had to rescue the crew from a ship headed to Halifax from St. John's. It sank about twenty miles off Port aux Basques."

"All hands safe?" asked Ruth.

"Miraculously," answered Jacob.

"Those are treacherous waters off the Cabot Strait," said Hannah.

"We had to bring them back to St. John's for medical attention. It was the SS *Sylvia.*"

Ruth gasped.

"Oh no! That's the ship we sent the coats on."

"Oh, my God!" said Joseph, putting his hand to his mouth in shock.

"They were insured, right?" asked Jacob.

"Of course," said Hannah.

"Don't worry," said Jacob. "They'll take care of it for you."

Joseph collected himself.

"My customers will be disappointed," he said.

"They'll get over it," said Hannah.

"I'll drop by the insurance office tomorrow," said Joseph.

"It would be nice to get something out of all that insurance we pay every year," said Ruth. "And we can finally pay off Tommy and a bunch of bills."

When Joseph arrived at the insurance office the next morning, he walked to the desk and told the clerk what had happened. Joseph answered all his questions and was told to wait while the clerk retrieved his file. The clerk came back and told Joseph he couldn't find an insurance policy in his name. Joseph asked him to look again. The clerk left. After a few minutes, his supervisor came out to speak to Joseph.

"I'm sorry, Mr. Rosenberg. There is no insurance policy in your name with this firm."

"You must be mistaken. I've had insurance here for over ten years. My bookkeeper renews it every year."

"Not this year, he didn't."

There had to be an explanation. Maybe Isaac had changed insurance companies and didn't tell him. Of course, that had to be it!

When Joseph reached his shop, he went immediately to the office and opened the filing cabinet. He couldn't find a current insurance policy or any receipts. He thought maybe

Isaac had filed them away with the end-of-year documents. He practically tore open the boxes. He couldn't find anything. He felt himself start to panic. He picked up the phone and called Isaac.

When he finally arrived, Joseph ran up to him.

"Isaac, I'm so glad you're here. I've been looking for our insurance papers but can't find them anywhere. Dig them out for me, will you?"

"The insurance?"

"Yes, where is it?"

"It's here on my desk."

"You've paid it, right?"

Isaac hesitated for a moment.

"Me and Esther had some money problems...."

"What does that have to do with my insurance?"

"I only borrowed the money. I didn't steal it."

"You took the money that was supposed to pay for the insurance?!"

"Don't worry. I'll pay it back."

"You bloody idiot!"

Joseph grabbed him by the lapels and punched him with all his might. Isaac ran out of the office with blood streaming from his nose.

Joseph paced up and down the room. He felt like his whole world was beginning to close in on him. He wondered how he was ever going to explain it to Ruth, let alone to Tommy. The very thought chilled him to the bone. There was a knock on the door. Joseph looked up and saw Tommy peering through the glass. He tried to hide.

"Rabbi, I know you're in there. Open the door!"

Joseph did as Tommy demanded. He nervously tried to put a good face on things.

Tommy's voice was menacing. "Say, did you hear about the *SS Sylvia?*"

Joseph hummed and hawed.

"Yeah ... musta been, ah...."

"Skeeter tells me that was the ship your daughter shipped those coats on."

"Is that so?"

"You got insurance, right?"

"Well, that's the thing...."

"I've had enough of you, Rabbi. We're finished. You just dug your own grave!"

As Joseph was trying to come to terms with Tommy's threat, Ali was making his way home. He ignored the cold damp fog that had gripped the city and walked with determination in his step. He hadn't been home since the disastrous scene with Mr. Farouk and his daughter. That mattered little to him now.

When he entered the store, his father was restocking the shelves, while Sami tended the counter. His father was happy to see him.

"Dad, where's Mom?" asked Ali.

"In the kitchen, I think."

"I want to talk to her. I'd like it if you could be there as well."

"Sami, can you mind the store for a few minutes?" asked Shafeek.

"Sure, Dad."

When Ali and Shafeek reached the top of the stairs, they could see Majedah in the kitchen. She was bent over the stove and taking bread out of the oven. When she saw Ali standing there, she turned back to what she was doing.

"Mom, we have to talk," said Ali.

Majedah fidgeted uncomfortably..

"My bread...."

"Can wait," said Ali. "I'll meet you and Dad in the living room."

Ali made his way to the third floor and went straight to Aiden's room.

"Mom and Dad are in the living room," said Ali. "I need to talk to them. It would be good if you were there too."

"I was wondering when you'd come home," said Aiden.

"Living room in two minutes!" said Ali.

Erin was in her room taking a break from work. Her hair was tied up with a large, wide black band. She was wearing her work clothes. When she saw Ali's reflection in her mirror, she walked to her bed and lay down.

"Erin, I want to set things right with you."

"I'm not killing our baby!"

"I wouldn't have it any other way."

"It didn't seem that way last night."

"I've treated you horribly. I'm not asking forgiveness, just that you hear what I have to say."

"And what is that?"

"Mom and Dad and Aiden are in the living room waiting for me. I told them I want to talk to them. I would like you to be there, too."

She didn't move. He reached his hand down to her.

"Please?"

She hesitated, then took his hand. They made their way downstairs. Ali was still holding Erin's hand when they entered the living room.

"Mom and Dad, please sit here on the sofa. Aiden, take a seat in the armchair. Erin, you can stand here next to me."

"But I have flour all over myself," said Majedah.

"I want to talk about Erin," said Ali.

"Yes, I think that would be wise," said Shafeek.

"As much as everyone might like to think otherwise, Erin is pregnant and I'm the father," said Ali.

Majedah squirmed and looked down at the floor.

"I have treated her badly," said Ali.

"May she burn in hell for the shame she has brought on our family," said Majedah.

"Mother, you have to stop this!"

Shafeek spoke up.

"Majedah, ask yourself what Our Lord Jesus Christ would have done. Would he have turned his back on a young woman who needed his infinite wisdom and love? Would he have cast aside a magnificent creation of nature simply because its mother was not married?"

"I want that trollop out of my house!"

Erin made a run at Majedah. Ali held her back.

"You're a heartless, self-centred, vindictive woman, Mrs. Abbott," said Erin angrily. "I've given you my best during the years I've worked for you. All I get back from you is hate and venom. You're the one who should be ashamed!"

"We have to get control here and stop hurting each other," said Shafeek.

"Mom and Dad, this could tear our family apart," said Aiden. "Are we not better than this? Can we not open our hearts and minds and welcome the child?"

Ali walked over to his mother. She was seething.

"Mother, no matter what you say, I'm standing by Erin."

He sat down beside her.

"Please listen to what I'm about to tell you. If you kick Erin out, I'm leaving too. Is that what you want?"

Majedah stood and walked towards Erin.

"This is all your fault. Mark my words. You're going to rue the day you ever met me!"

She pushed Erin aside and walked out.

———

Jacob felt he had waited long enough. It was time for Ali to step up and tell Ruth about Erin. He found Ali in the store.

"Nice to see you working for once," Jacob said with a smile.

"Don't let it get out. It might ruin my reputation."

"Speaking of your reputation, has Erin made a decision about the baby?"

"She's keeping it and staying here with us. I told Mom that if Erin goes, I go."

"Ali, it's time you told Ruth."

"I figured that was why you were here."

Ali had been thinking hard and long. There were pros and cons. If he were to tell Ruth about Erin, at least it would be out in the open. On the other hand, he could quite possibly lose the only person in the world he loved more than himself.

"She'll find out anyway, you know," said Jacob.

"I couldn't stand to see the look on her face, Jacob."

"You love her, don't you?"

"Of course I do."

"The true lover does not treat his loved one in this way."

"Maybe I'm not a true lover."

"It's time for you to find out."

Ali paused for a few seconds.

"Jacob? Why don't you tell her? I can trust you. You wouldn't exaggerate or dramatize it."

"She could take it the wrong way."

"She knows you'd never hurt her. If anyone has hurt her, it's me."

"You shouldn't be putting this on me, Ali."

"It's 'cause you're a better man than me, Jacob."

"You just haven't found your real self yet. You will."

———

Although Ruth hadn't yet heard from her father exactly how much insurance money they would be getting as compensation for the lost sealskin coats, it didn't stop her from attempting to figure out how it would be allocated. If her calculations were correct, Tommy would get his money back and many of their bills could be paid. Unfortunately, that didn't leave much left over for the business. But at least it would ease the pressure and give them time to get back on their feet.

Ruth heard a long banging on the front door. She descended the stairs and peered through the front room window. She ran to the door. Jacob was out of breath.

"Ruth, thank God you're home!"

"Jacob, what's wrong?"

"The shop's on fire!"

———

Joseph cast a mournful shadow as he stood in front of his beloved shop engulfed in flames. Hannah had her arm around his shoulder. As a youth, he had relished the fires he and his friends would build by the lake behind his father's house. The warmth helped tame the chill in the Polish summer's late-night air. This fire was different. He felt no warmth. He felt no sense of wonder.

The Fire Chief walked up to him.

"Are you Mr. Rosenberg?"

"My God," whispered Joseph to himself as he looked at his burning building.

"Are you Mr. Rosenberg?" the Chief repeated.

"My sins are washing over me."

"Please answer me, sir. Are you Joseph Rosenberg?"

"Not the Joseph Rosenberg I once was."

"Can you shed any light on what might have caused your building to be ablaze?"

"I'm ruined."

Ruth and Jacob ran up to where Joseph and Hannah were standing. Joseph stood ramrod-still. Ruth threw her arms around him and wouldn't let go. Hannah hugged them both. The Fire Chief spoke softly to them.

"It would be best if all of you were to return to your homes and let us deal with this. I'll drop by later tonight or tomorrow morning and tell you what we found."

Jacob approached Ruth, Joseph and Hannah. He turned them from the fire and headed to Joseph's house. They failed to notice Tommy and Skeeter standing in front of Callahan's Bar.

"Where's that boyfriend of yours?" yelled Skeeter. "Don't got the stomach for fires?"

They kept walking. Tommy shouted out to them.

"Home screwing that maid of theirs, I bet!"

They stopped in their tracks and turned around.

"What did you just say?" Ruth demanded.

"At least he can't get her pregnant this time," said Tommy with a look of faked shock on his face. "He already knocked her up."

"Randy bastard," added Skeeter.

Ruth turned back to Jacob, her father and Hannah. Jacob couldn't bring himself to break the silence. Joseph and Hannah looked at each other in shocked disbelief.

"What? He didn't tell you?" snickered Tommy.

Ruth turned to Jacob. "Is it true?"

Jacob tried to speak, but he found himself lost for words. You could hear the gloating in Tommy's voice.

"Go ask him yourself, if you got da guts."

Ruth didn't remember what happened next. She didn't remember walking along the street, past darkened shop windows and late-night revellers immersed in song. She didn't even remember Jacob, Joseph and Hannah insisting they accompany her to make sure she'd get home safely.

She did, however, remember approaching Ali's house and not seeing a single light illuminate its interior. It looked cheerless. Sinister even. She also remembered standing under the window where she knew Ali's bedroom to be.

A scream arose from the depths of her soul and almost burst her lungs as it filled the night air. It was an agonizing wail.

"Ali! No! Tell me it isn't true! You and Erin! And a baby! Come out and face me!"

Inside the house, everyone came to their bedroom windows that were shuttered against the cold evening wind. Shafeek stood behind Majedah. Aiden and Sami watched with sorrow in their hearts. Erin held her abdomen and tears streamed down her cheeks. The neighbours, sensing something momentous was happening, went to their windows too.

Ali didn't move. He lay huddled on his bed with his hands covering his ears.

Ruth ran to the door and pounded on it with both fists.

"You told me you loved me!"

The house remained darkened. There was still no response.

"I loved you with all my heart. You are a coward and I never want to see you again for as long as I live!"

The neighbours slowly moved back from their windows.

Hannah approached Ruth and took her arm. Ruth turned, laid her head on Hannah's shoulder and wept uncontrollably. They led her away.

During the next couple of days, Ruth barely left her room. When she did, she ignored all who tried to get through to her. When a knock came, it was ignored. When a note was pushed under the door, it remained unopened. Ali had been at the centre of her life for almost as long as she could remember. He had never let her down, and had stood by her through thick and thin. That was no longer the case.

One morning, Joseph left the house for an appointment with the Fire Chief to assess the damage. Hannah had suggested he take Jacob with him for moral support. Joseph promised to be back just after lunch.

As dinner approached, Hannah began to worry. He still hadn't returned. By eight o'clock, she was beside herself. The fire, and all that had gone before, had unnerved her. Joseph not being home as he had promised simply added to her anxiety.

She went to Ruth's room and knocked. As usual, there was no reply. She didn't bother to knock a second time. She opened the door and walked in. Ruth was sitting at her desk, deep in thought, a half-eaten sandwich beside her. Hannah spoke with determination in her voice.

"I'm worried about Joseph."

Ruth didn't look up.

"He promised he'd return after lunch. He's not back yet. That's unlike him."

Ruth didn't move.

"I know you've been hurt terribly," said Hannah. "But it's time to leave what Ali did behind you. You're bigger than that."

Ruth still remained silent. Hannah grabbed her by the shoulders and shook her.

"Look at me!"

Ruth finally turned her head towards her.

"There's something suspicious going on, Ruth," said Hannah. "One day, we find out the coats were lost at sea. Yesterday, our shop burnt down. Afterwards, the Fire Chief told us they couldn't find any of our sewing machines and inventory in the shop after the fire. Joseph still hasn't paid Tommy the money he owes him. And now, Joseph is not home hours after he promised he would be."

Ruth finally spoke.

"You think Tommy set the fire?"

"I don't know what to think," cried Hannah.

"Let's go face him!"

They headed to The Continental.

—

Skeeter heard the knock and slid open the peephole.

"Open the door before I kick it in!" shouted Hannah.

She and Ruth found Tommy and Rosie seated at a table by the bar. They could hardly hear themselves above the din.

"That was some fire," said Tommy with an innocent look on his face. "I like fires."

"And is that why you burned down our business?" yelled Hannah.

"They arrested the guy who did that this morning," said Tommy.

"Bullshit!" said Ruth.

"You don't know about that?" interjected Rosie.

"About what?" asked Ruth.

"The rabbi got arrested this morning," said Rosie.

"Yeah, for arson," added Tommy, a look of glee on his face.

"Don't be ridiculous," said Hannah.

"Go to the lockup if you think we're lying and see for yourself," said Rosie.

Ruth and Hannah headed towards the door. Tommy yelled after them.

"Now you know who really burned down that stupid shop of yours!"

The local lock-up was a grim place – dark and dreary – with a soulless feel that distressed the heart. The constable on duty that night tried to stop Ruth and Hannah. But when he approached, Ruth pushed him aside. With the constable following after them, the two women ran down the cold wet floors of the hallway containing the cells. Much to their surprise, Jacob was standing in front of the farthest cell. His hands were clasping the bars.

The cell was cramped and gloomy. The only adornment was a small wooden cot pushed up against the far wall. On top of the cot was a mattress, soiled and torn from years of neglect.

Joseph's head was bowed. He didn't look up even when Hannah called his name.

"Has he spoken to you yet?" Ruth asked Jacob.

"No. He's been like this since I got here."

Ruth turned to the constable behind her.

"I want to talk to my father. Can you open the cell?"

"I'm sorry, Miss."

"Please, open the cell," said Hannah. "There's no one else here to see us."

"I'm sorry...."

Ruth became irritated.

"What if he was *your* father? Wouldn't you want to sit next to him and comfort him?"

The constable relented. Ruth was allowed to entered the cell. She approached her father.

"Pop, you know I love you no matter what."

"We're ruined, Ruth."

"Don't talk like that, Pop."

"They said the fire was deliberately set. They accused me of doing it."

"Nonsense."

"They think I did it for the insurance."

"That's so silly."

"Especially since I don't have any insurance."

"Of course you do."

Joseph's voice fell.

"The business and coats are on the same insurance that Isaac didn't pay."

"Good God! But not the house, right?"

For the first time since Ruth entered his cell, Joseph lifted his head and looked directly at her. His face was the face of a broken man.

"Tell her, Joseph," said Jacob.

"Please don't hate me, Ruth," Joseph sobbed. "I've lost everything. But I couldn't stand to lose you too."

"Tell her," said Jacob.

Joseph took a deep breath.

"I gambled the deed to the house in a poker game five years ago. I lost. We've been paying rent on it ever since."

He started to cry. "We don't even own the house we live in."

Ruth felt her whole world crumbling around her. She stood

up and looked down at her father.

"What have you done!"

"I have destroyed all we have worked for. I have no one else to blame."

"How are we ever going to survive this!"

"You're going to need someone to provide for you, Ruth. To take care of you. Someone you can rely on. Someone who will put you first in his life and not be a victim of his vices. Someone not like me."

He looked towards Jacob.

"Jacob, come over here, will you?"

Joseph reached up and took his daughter's hands in his. "You need a husband, Ruth. One who can be trusted to always tell you the truth. And that man isn't Ali Abbott."

Part III

8

Lilly

The ship finally docked. Ruth reached down, picked up the piece of cardboard propped against her leg and examined what she had painted on it. She held it over her head and scanned the deck.

Then she noticed someone waving frantically and screaming something she couldn't hear. Ruth moved closer to the ship and watched as the young woman ran along the deck, down the gangplank and directly into her arms. They hugged and wouldn't let go of each other. Tears of joy ran down both their faces. When they finally relinquished their grip, Ruth took the girl's face in her hands.

"My God, Lilly, is this really you?" she sobbed.

"Sure as shootin'!" hollered Lilly with a big smile.

"I can't believe you're actually here."

"Believe it!" said Lilly gleefully.

"You're so beautiful."

"You're no dog yourself."

"Turn around. Let me look at you."

Lilly spun around.

"Your turn now," she said.

Ruth did likewise. They hugged again.

"Come over here," said Ruth. She led Lilly to a bench at the edge of the wharf. They sat down.

"Tell me, how is Mother?" asked Ruth excitedly.

"She's fine. She's very glad I'm visiting you. She couldn't bring herself to come with me, though. Too much water under the bridge, I suppose."

"I can barely remember her."

"And I can barely remember Father."

"That's sad, isn't it."

"When am I going to see him?"

"I didn't tell him you were coming."

"Why not?"

"I wanted it to be a surprise."

"I can't wait to see him."

"Soon."

While they were reminiscing, a hansom cab pulled up. A man jumped down and headed straight for them. He bent over and kissed Ruth on the cheek.

"Lilly Rosenberg, I'd like to introduce my husband, Jacob Arenberg."

Ali was in his room and in a deep funk. He'd been that way for more than a month. He knew that the way he had treated Ruth was cowardly. What haunted him most was the fact that he had cowered in his room the night Ruth had screamed for him to come down. He had found out that she had married Jacob soon after that. He had no illusions as to why. Not only had he messed up his own life, he had messed up Ruth's life by forcing her into a marriage that she might regret.

He missed being part of Ruth's life. The thought of the woman he loved being married to one of his best friends broke his heart. But he didn't blame her. That was all on him. Nor could he blame Jacob. He had stepped up when Ruth needed someone to lean on – something Ali himself had failed to do. How he would live without Ruth's love tormented him.

He also worried about Erin. She had called her parents again, but her father was adamant. He wouldn't allow her to return home. Consequently, she had to do her best to walk the path between fulfilling her duties as a maid and keeping out of sight of the contemptuous eye of Majedah. What would happen when the baby actually came into their lives, Ali had no idea.

He made his way downstairs. It was his turn to tend the shop. When the door opened, Mrs. Kelly walked in. She was the wife of the head of the Irish Benevolent Society.

"Is Mrs. Abbott in?" she asked stiffly.

"Mom's out shopping," answered Ali.

"I'll talk to you, then," she said with a stern look on her face.

"How can I help?"

"You should be ashamed of yourself!"

"Excuse me?"

"Living under your parents' roof with that bay girl, Erin. You're the father, aren't you."

"I think you should leave, Mrs. Kelly."

Erin walked in with a mop in her hands. Mrs. Kelly pointed her finger at her.

"There she is. Bold as brass! You shamed Ireland."

Erin turned and headed back upstairs.

"Yes, run away. But you can't run away from the shame, can you!"

Ali came from behind the counter. He guided Mrs. Kelly towards the door.

"Take your hands off me!"

He pushed her outside, where she came face to face with Majedah.

"Our ladies will never shop here again until you get rid of that sinner."

Majedah took her aside. "Don't worry, Maude. I will."

—

While Ali was doing his best to console Erin and reassure her that she needed to stiffen her resolve and push on through the condemnation of his mother and people like Mrs. Kelly, Ruth, Jacob and Lilly were making their way to Jacob's house on Bond Street. The coal man had dumped a half ton in front of the hatch leading to Jacob's basement. They had to step gingerly.

It wasn't a large house, but it was well cared for and neatly furnished. Ruth felt comfortable there and had made it her home since marrying Jacob. In particular, she liked the sitting room at the front of the house. It reminded her of the house in New York where her father would read poetry to her, play his violin and she would sing. There was a large couch up against one wall, with two armchairs facing it on either side. In front of the sitting area, there was a small, but efficient, fireplace. Along the other wall was an upright Heintzman piano.

Jacob took Lilly's luggage up to the spare bedroom. When he came back downstairs, he found Lilly playing the piano. Ruth was standing behind her. She had her hands on her sister's shoulders.

"Ruth, I love your house," said Lilly.

"It was Jacob's first," said Ruth.

"We both live here now," said Jacob.

"I hope so," said Lilly. "Wouldn't be kosher for a newly-wed couple to live separately. Where's the fun in that!"

"We're very happy to have you here with us," said Jacob. "I hope you'll like St. John's."

"But I do wish you had told me in your letters about you getting married," said Lilly turning to Ruth. "It was such a surprise."

"It was very sudden," said Jacob.

"Well, as long as you're in love," said Lilly. "That's what really matters."

Ruth wiped a streak of dust off the piano. "When you get yourself settled in, I'll take you out and show you around."

"Are the local boys cute?" asked Lilly with a twinkle in her eyes.

"I'll let you decide that for yourself," said Ruth.

Lilly reached into her bag and brought out a book. She handed it to Ruth.

"Do you remember this?"

Ruth took it and read the spine.

"It's the book of poetry father used to read to us from when we were kids," said Lilly. "Mother wanted you to have it."

Ruth flipped through the pages and stopped at one page in particular. She started reading.

It is an ancient Mariner,
And he stoppeth one of three.
'By thy long grey beard and glittering eye,
Now wherefore stopp'st thou me?
The Bridegroom's doors are opened wide,
And I am next of kin;
The guests are met, the feast is set:
May'st hear the merry din.'
He holds him with his skinny hand,
'There was a ship,' quoth he.
'Hold off! unhand me, grey-beard loon!'
Eftsoons his hand dropt he.

He holds him with his glittering eye –
The Wedding-Guest stood still,
And listens like a three years' child:
The Mariner hath his will.
The Wedding-Guest sat on a stone:
He cannot choose but hear;
And thus spake on that ancient man,
The bright-eyed Mariner.

"Father loved that poem," said Lilly.

"I loved hearing him read it."

"When am I going to meet him?"

"In a few days."

"Why so long?"

"He's going through a rough bit right now," said Jacob.

"What's happened?"

"Don't worry," said Ruth. "Nothing serious."

"Whatever you think."

"We have to keep it hush-hush, though. I don't want to ruin the surprise."

"It might be a bit traumatic for him," said Jacob.

"I hope it doesn't give him a heart attack or anything," said Lilly.

"No need to worry about that," said Jacob. "He's a tough old bird."

"I'll be on pins and needles," said Lilly. "I hope he'll remember this book."

"I'm sure he will," said Ruth.

She leaned over and kissed Lilly on the cheek. Lilly reached into her bag once again. This time she took out a bottle. She handed it to Jacob. He read the label.

"French champagne?"

"This ancient mariner wedding-guest might be too late for your wedding, but that won't stop us from celebrating, will it," smiled Lilly.

"Are you old enough to drink?" asked Ruth.

"Who cares," said Lilly. "I'm in a new country now with no parent around to tell me what to do. I've found the sister who I thought I'd lost forever. I'm sitting in her home right next to her husband. And I'm in the mood to celebrate!"

"Shall I get some glasses?" asked Jacob.

"Or we can drink it straight out of the bottle," said Lilly.

"We're obviously going to have to keep our eye on you," chuckled Ruth.

—

Later that night, after Jacob had shown Lilly to her room, he slid into bed next to Ruth.

"Lilly is the best thing that's happened to you in a long time."

"I'm so lucky," said Ruth.

"How long is she going to stay?"

"For as long as she wants."

He moved his hand under the covers and caressed her leg. Ruth gently pushed it away.

"You're still in love with Ali, aren't you."

Ruth rolled over and turned her back towards him.

"You know I would never rush you into anything...."

"I know that, Jacob."

"Either you'll learn to love me or you won't. No matter who you love, I will always love you. I have since the day I first met you."

Ruth reached out and took Jacob's hand in hers.

"Love has a mind of its own, Ruth," said Jacob. "It can't be controlled just because you want to control it. It will follow its own path. Love will out."

Ruth closed her eyes. She knew Jacob deserved better. But she couldn't help herself. She hadn't yet come to terms with what she had done. She hoped she hadn't married in haste, only to repent later.

—

At The Continental, Tommy was restocking the bar. Rosie was in her office counting cash. Skeeter entered.

"Hey, Rosie. I just ran into Rosenberg on the street. He don't look so good."

"At least he's not in the lockup anymore," said Rosie.

"Well, he shouldn't have pissed off Tommy like that."

Rosie looked up from her cash box.

"What do you mean?"

"Never mind."

"I do mind! What do you mean he shouldn't have pissed Tommy off?"

"Forget about it, Rosie."

She walked up to him and stood face to face.

"If you ever want to set foot in this place again, let alone keep that head of yours on your shoulders, out with it!"

Skeeter told her how furious Tommy had been when Joseph had promised the coats, but didn't deliver.

"So Tommy burned down his business? Is that what you're telling me?"

Skeeter shifted nervously.

"And you probably helped him, right?"

"Rosie, don't tell Tommy. He'll kill me."

"I might kill you myself. Save Tommy the trouble."

Rosie went to the door and called out to Tommy. He came

into the office. Skeeter cowered in the corner. Rosie started off slowly.

"Tommy, I want to talk to you about the fire at the rabbi's place."

"Ancient history," shrugged Tommy.

"Did you set it deliberately?" she asked.

"Come on, Rosie...."

"Did you or didn't you?"

"Where did you get that idea from?"

She didn't answer. Tommy turned towards Skeeter.

"Skeeter, can I speak with you outside for a minute?"

"No!" insisted Rosie. "He stays right where he is!"

Tommy became indignant.

"That son-of-a-bitch rabbi's lucky I didn't break his legs."

"You've taken this thing too far."

"That's your opinion."

"It's my opinion that counts around here."

"You better drop this thing, Rosie, or you might regret it."

"You threatening me, Tommy?"

"Don't push me, that's all."

"Or, you'll do what?"

Tommy approached Rosie.

"Ask yourself this. Do you want the Constabulary to know what really goes on around here or don't you?"

"And you ask yourself this. Do you want them to know you burned down the rabbi's business just to satisfy your own ego?"

"It's been swell knowin' ya, sweetheart," said Tommy as he turned and make for the door.

"Wish I could say the same about you!" Rosie yelled after him.

Skeeter started to follow Tommy.

"Don't you even think of it, Skeeter," said Rosie. "I'm not finished with you yet."

The next morning, Lilly was in the kitchen making herself at home. The radio was reporting on the progress of the Alphabet Fleet of coastal boats carrying passengers and freight around the island and north to Labrador: *The Argyle, Bruce, Clyde, Dundee, Ethie, Fife, Glencoe, Home, Inverness, Kyle, Lintrose* and *The Meigle*. Even though the names and places didn't mean much to her, she liked the way they rolled off the announcer's tongue.

She leaned out the back window and smiled at the next-door neighbour. He had a scythe in his hands and was valiantly hacking away at the grass in his backyard. She could almost taste the smell of it.

She couldn't wait to see her father again. For the occasion, she had brought her finest frock with her from New York. She wanted to look her best when she and her father finally did come face to face. She knew he would be impeccably dressed to the nines, as was his fashion. Like father, like daughter.

She heard a knock on the door. When she opened it, she saw a man standing there with two very large lobsters in his hands.

"Yes, may I help you?" she asked.

"Are Ruth or Jacob home?" he asked.

"I'll go get them."

"Thank you, young lady."

"Nice lobsters," said Lilly.

She closed the door and left the man standing on the steps. She called out to Ruth and Jacob. They came downstairs.

"There's a man outside who wants to talk to you," said Lilly.

"Did he say who he is?" asked Jacob.

"Nope. But he looks kind of in rough shape," answered Lilly.

"I wasn't expecting anyone," said Ruth.

"He's carrying two huge lobsters, if that helps any," said Lilly.

"I'll go see who it is," said Ruth.

"Watch out," said Lilly. "Those lobsters are alive and look hungry!"

Ruth walked to the door and opened it. She went outside and closed the door behind her. After a few minutes, she and the man came back into the house. Ruth was carrying the lobsters. She pointed at Lilly.

"Do you have any idea who this young lady could be?" Ruth asked the man.

"I'm afraid I don't," he answered.

He put out his hand and walked towards Lilly.

"This is Lilly," said Ruth.

Joseph stopped in his tracks.

It's not often that a simple event can cause a man to re-think his entire life, but that was exactly what happened to Joseph. Someone whom he had only vague recollections of as a little girl with long black curly hair and a tender smile was now standing in front of him – a vibrant, beautiful young woman. Instead of his heart bursting with joy at finally meeting his daughter again, it burst with guilt for having abandoned her to live a dream. But what pained his heart most was the look of disappointment on her face. His body sagged. Jacob led him to a chair.

Lilly grabbed Ruth by the arm and walked her into the kitchen. Jacob stayed behind with Joseph and began to explain the situation to him. Lilly laid into Ruth.

"Ruth, what were you thinking? You should've prepared me for this."

Ruth put the lobsters in the sink.

"I didn't know he was coming by today," said Ruth.

"You should have warned me. I've been waiting most of my life to see my father again."

"I'm sorry, Lilly."

"What happened to him? He looks awful."

"He's had a very difficult time here in St. John's."

"Obviously!"

"His businesses failed. The shop burned down. The police arrested him. They suspected he deliberately set the fire to get the insurance. They finally let him go when they found out he didn't actually have insurance."

"I can't believe that man is my father."

They turned around and saw Joseph in the doorway.

"I'm so sorry, Pop," said Ruth. "I should have told you Lilly was coming."

Joseph walked up to Lilly. He started to reach out to her, but pulled back.

"I thought I'd never see you again. Will you ever forgive me, Lilly?"

"For what?" asked Lilly delicately.

"For abandoning you. For leaving you without a father."

Lilly threw her arms around him.

"Oh, Father...."

"My little Lilly," wept Joseph. "After all these years."

—

Ali walked into his local pub, sat at the bar and ordered a beer. He had a lot on his mind. His most immediate concern was how Erin was going to co-exist in the same house as his mother. Especially when the baby came.

What really struck at his very soul, however, was the fact that he had lost Ruth's love and trust. He had taken her for granted, and it had cost him dearly.

The bar door swung open and Ali saw the opportunity he'd been waiting for approach.

"You wanted to see me?" asked Jacob.

"Have a seat," said Ali.

Jacob sat down and ordered a beer. Ali slowly turned and faced the man who had married the girl he loved.

"This has been a long time coming," said Ali.

"There's no need for us to be enemies, you know," said Jacob.

"Easy for you to say."

"I didn't plan it."

"But you sure followed through, didn't you."

"What would you have expected me to do?"

"Anything but what you did."

"Ruth was insistent...."

"You could have said 'no' or 'why don't we wait' or 'let me talk to Ali first'. You could have done so many things instead of taking advantage of the situation like you did."

"You brought this on yourself, Ali. It was you who got Erin pregnant, not me."

"We were friends. I confided in you. I never thought for a moment you would betray me."

"If there's any betrayal here, it's you who betrayed Ruth."

Ali turned back to the bar. He knew deep down that Jacob was right.

"You left her broken," continued Jacob. "And she couldn't believe you would have humiliated her like that."

Ali folded his arms and slumped in his chair.

"She needed someone she could trust," said Jacob. "Someone who wouldn't let her down. She turned to me."

Ali faced Jacob.

"I should have come down to talk to her that night. I should have faced up to it."

"Yes, you should have. If you had, there's a good chance we wouldn't be here talking like this."

Jacob got up and left the bar. Ali sat for a long while lost in his thoughts. He yearned to talk to Ruth, but couldn't find the courage to seek her out. Since he couldn't bring himself to meet her face to face, he chose to do the next best thing. He decided to write her a letter.

—

One bright morning, Ruth asked Lilly if she would like to accompany her on a nice long stroll around the city. Lilly jumped at the chance.

"Where should we go?" asked Lilly excitedly.

"Plans are for losers," winked Ruth.

They grabbed their parasols and sashayed out into the warm, fresh air. Lilly couldn't remember seeing such a crystal-clear, blue sky before. In New York, the buildings clothed the sky. In St. John's, the sky clothed the buildings.

They made their way eastwards along Duckworth Street, past the white-cuffed policeman directing traffic with one hand, while holding a sandwich that his wife had just given him with the other.

They visited the Great War Commemoration Memorial and watched mischievous kids firing cap guns at jiggle-bellied cops chasing them around the monument in a futile effort to prevent them from desecrating the bronze soldier, sailor, lumberman and fishermen statues fixed there in time.

Further on, Ruth introduced Lilly to the tinsmith and ironmonger. They gleefully traded old stories of the skullduggery Ruth used to get into when scavenging through the streets of

St. John's when she was a child.

"What's the going price for scrap metal these days?" inquired Ruth.

"A shilling a pound," answered the ironmonger.

"I should get back in the business of stripping lead off roofs," Ruth quipped. "Sounds like it pays better than making clothes."

Ruth and Lilly strolled through the front entrance of the Newfoundland Hotel and poked their heads into whatever took their fancy. The two tennis courts attached to the building held their attention for longer than they had expected. The lure of men in newly-pressed whites, beating back blistering serves with every sinew of their bodies while wiping beads of sweat off their foreheads, had an undeniable appeal.

Lilly struggled with the steep incline up Signal Hill. She had to stop several times along the way to give her aching legs a rest. When finally they reached the top, however, the view took her breath away. Brilliant-blue ocean as far as she could see. Several humpback whales broke through the waves and blew their spray full-force into the wind. A late-spring iceberg almost blocked the entrance to the harbour, forcing ships to line up in single file before cautiously navigating their way past the huge chunk of ice, then through the narrow passage and out into the open ocean.

It was the first time that Lilly had had a full view of the city stretched out before her. Despite the smokey haze from countless unseen fireplaces, she could see the helter-skelter magic in it. She paid close attention as Ruth pointed out the part of town where their father's shop was located, as well as where she and Jacob lived.

Lilly didn't have much interest in Cabot Tower or the cannons lined up to protect the city from intruders, though.

That was not the case, however, when it came to Ladies' Lookout. She hung on every word as Ruth told her stories of women who for centuries had used the vantage point to search the horizon for the long-awaited return of their loved ones. She felt the women's joy when the ships returned. And their grief when they did not.

As they made their way down the hill towards the city, Lilly didn't say much. But there was a lot going on inside.

Ruth, Jacob and Lilly were sitting around the dinner table. Lilly told Jacob of the walk she and Ruth had taken earlier that day. He was pleased to see that Lilly was fitting in so nicely. She was the tonic Ruth needed.

"Is there anything else you'd like to see while you're here?" he asked.

"Nightlife," answered Lilly.

"What did you have in mind?" asked Ruth.

"The wilder, the better."

Much to Ruth's surprise, Jacob suggested that she take Lilly to The Continental. He saw it as an opportunity for Ruth to show that she would not be intimidated.

"I never want to see that place again," declared Ruth.

However, the more Jacob talked, the more she thought he might be right. She couldn't hide away forever. She would not be cowed.

The next night, after much insistence from Lilly and encouragement from Jacob, Ruth and Lilly made their way to Rosie's. No sooner had they taken a table than Aiden walked over.

"Ruth, you're a sight for sore eyes!"

"What are you doing here?" asked Ruth.

"We're playing here," answered Aiden.

Ruth grabbed Lilly's hand.

"Come on, Lilly. We're getting out of here!"

Lilly resisted.

"You're worried about seeing him again, aren't you," said Aiden.

"Him who?" interjected Lilly.

"I'm not worried about it," said Ruth. "I'm not going to, that's all."

"We miss you in the band," said Aiden.

"You're in a band?" asked Lilly incredulously.

"I'm not here to talk about that," said Ruth. "I'm only here because my sister wanted to see some of the nightlife of St. John's. I was talked into it."

"I didn't know you had a sister," said Aiden, looking admiringly at Lilly.

"My name's Lilly. I'm Ruth's sister from New York."

"I'm Aiden Abbott. Ali's brother."

"Who's Ali?" asked Lilly.

Aiden looked over Ruth's shoulder and saw Ali nervously looking at them. He was standing at the bar next to Rosie. Ruth noticed Aiden staring over her shoulder and turned around. Her eyes met Ali's. She rose from her chair.

"Lilly, I can't stay here any longer. Are you coming?"

Lilly was confused.

"What the hell's going on here?"

"Don't worry, Ruth," said Aiden. "I'll keep an eye on her."

Ruth grabbed her coat and left the club.

At the bar, Rosie saw what was transpiring and decided to address the situation.

"Ruth's still mad at you, isn't she."

"Would you blame her?" said Ali.

"It's tough being married to a man she may not love."

159

"I don't even want to think about it."

"And what Tommy did didn't make things easier for her either."

"What did Tommy do?"

"I thought you would have figured that out by now."

"Figured what out?"

"That fire wasn't set by the rabbi. And it wasn't an accident either."

When Lilly finally reached home, tired but happy after a few drinks and a dance with Aiden, she found Ruth sitting alone in the kitchen. She couldn't see her at first since the curtains were drawn, and the lights were off. Only a single candle in the middle of the kitchen table illuminated Ruth's face. Her head was bent and both hands were in her lap. She looked up when Lilly walked in.

"Aiden told you about Ali, didn't he," said Ruth.

"That's quite a story," said Lilly.

"That's all behind me now."

"Do you really believe that?"

"I'm a married woman, Lilly. That's not going to change."

"But he loved you and...."

"If he loved me, he wouldn't have done what he did."

"Aiden thinks that because he loved you, he kept it from you 'cause he didn't want to hurt you."

"That's a strange way to show you love someone."

"Maybe so, but he wouldn't be the first one to make a mistake like that."

"Are you saying you think I should forgive him?"

"I'm just saying that maybe you shouldn't have acted so rashly and married the first man who came along."

"That's a hurtful thing to say, Lilly."

"The truth can do that sometimes."

"Jacob is my husband. I love him very much."

"Do you, Ruth?"

———

With that rebuke ringing in her ear, Ruth made her way upstairs to the bedroom. Jacob was already asleep. She quietly undressed. As she pulled back the covers, she noticed an envelope on her pillow. She sat on the edge of the bed, opened it and read the contents.

Ruth,

I hope you will read this note through to the end and not tear it up when you realize it's from me. I wanted to apologize for what I did, but realized that my apology would ring hollow. However, there are no other options open to me, so I have chosen to apologize and not even attempt an explanation.

You know me better than anyone and hopefully know that at heart, I am not a secretive or dishonest person. However, you will also know that I have in fact been nothing but secretive and dishonest with you. I abandoned my core principles. I hurt the woman I love. And although your feelings towards me have undoubtedly changed, in my eyes you will always be that woman.

I'm not seeking forgiveness. I'm not seeking understanding. I wouldn't be that presumptuous.

What I am seeking, Ruth, is that you not loathe me. I

fear that more than anything.

I once overheard two men discuss the question: What is worse? Betraying one's friend or betraying one's ideals? I now realize there is a third choice: betraying one's friend as well as betraying one's ideals. I, unfortunately, made that third choice.

My punishment will be loss and heartache that will stay with me for the rest of my life.

Ali

Ruth put the letter down. Her eyes reddened.

9

New Beginnings

"Just what are you doing here?" asked Chief Constable Joe Murphy.

"The officer at the front desk said that I should talk to you," answered Ali. "Do you have a minute?"

"What's it about?"

"That fire at Joseph Rosenberg's shop."

"Come into my office."

CC Murphy was a short, rotund man with red cheeks, a welcoming countenance and a sunny disposition. But get him riled up, and that sunny disposition and warm countenance could turn to ice.

His office was well lit, with windows that looked out onto Water Street and the steps leading up to Duckworth. The desk was dark-stained oak, well used, but not well loved. It was stacked high with official-looking papers. There was a single chair in front of the desk. Ali sat down.

"How's that son of mine?" asked CC Murphy.

"Zane's as good as ever," answered Ali. "Why do you ask?"

"I never see him. All he does is hide himself away in the basement and play those bloody drums of his."

"We're lucky to have him in the band," said Ali.

"So, what brings you here?"

"I'd like to report a possible case of arson."

"That's serious business."

"I think I know who set the fire at Joseph Rosenberg's shop a while back."

"We know Rosenberg didn't."

"It was Tommy Chan, the bouncer at The Continental."

"Where did you get that information?"

"Rosie, the owner."

"Did she say she was certain Tommy set the fire?"

"Well, she definitely led me in that direction. Joseph owed Tommy gambling money. He wasn't able to pay it back. To get revenge, Tommy burned down his business. Also, the Fire Chief said they couldn't find any sewing machines or inventory in the shop after the fire."

"Do you think Rosie put him up to it?"

"I don't think so, or she wouldn't have mentioned it to me."

CC Murphy rose from his desk and went to the window. He could see a tall, double-masted schooner slowly making its way through the Narrows.

"Who else would know anything about this?" asked CC Murphy.

"Skeeter Dunn. I'm pretty sure he helped Tommy."

"I'll get a couple of my guys to go have a word with Skeeter."

"I'm sure he'd love that."

"Don't count on it."

McDougall's Soda Shop was quiet, even for a Monday afternoon. That was just how Jacob had hoped it would be. He had a lot on his mind and needed someone to talk to – someone who he was hoping would understand the situation he was in.

The front door opened, breaking the silence. She walked over.

"You got your arms full," said Jacob.

"I've been shopping," responded Erin.

"Can I help you with those?"

"That's okay. I can manage."

They made their way to one of the tables in front of the window looking out onto Water Street. Erin took off her coat and put it on the back of a chair. She propped her packages up against the wall.

"Thanks for coming," said Jacob.

"I can't stay long."

Jacob fumbled with the menu in front of him as he rearranged the condiments.

"You want to talk about your wife and Ali, don't you," said Erin.

"You're very perceptive."

"Ali still loves her, you know."

"Yes, I know."

"Does she still love him?"

"From what I can tell."

"And I love him too."

"And I love Ruth."

"We're both in love with people who don't love us."

"And all four of us are unhappy. The question is: where do we go from here?"

"Are you going to leave her?"

"I would never do that."

"So, you're going to stay married to a woman who loves another man?"

"I will do whatever makes Ruth happy."

"Except leave her."

"Do you think Ali would ever marry you?"

"In my dreams. But I have no such delusions."

"Like I said before, you're a very perceptive woman."

"I have to go."

When Erin rose from the table, Jacob noticed that she was showing.

"Pregnancy becomes you, Erin."

Erin put on her coat and retrieved her shopping. She bent down and kissed him on the cheek.

"If this were a movie, you and I would both step aside and let the two young lovers ride off into the sunset."

"Real life isn't quite that simple."

Lilly was sitting on the frontroom couch and warming herself in front of the coal fire. Through the window, she could see a group of children playing hopscotch on the sidewalk. She was alone in the house, and that gave her time to think.

The idyllic life she had imagined her sister to be leading, she now saw as nothing more than the fantastical creation of a young girl's imagination. She was also convinced that Ruth's attitude towards her husband, although loving, was not love.

She hadn't written her mother since arriving in St. John's. She went to her room hoping to find a note pad. The only paper she found was a single sheet in the bottom drawer. There was something written on it. She picked it up. It looked like a poem written in a small hand. There was a title at the top. It read, 'Where Am I Going?' She started to read:

Could this be my lucky day?
Could love come from so far away?
Or another regret,
A broken duet,
A lonely heart on display?

I've sure had my fill of regretting.
On future love I'm betting.

Where am I going?
Will my road lead me to happiness?
Lost in a world full of heartache;
How to make sense of it all,
And avoid loneliness.

Headstrong and lifelong,
I will take what this world has to give.
Searching for life's little answers,
Learning to cope with it all,
And how to live.
Eyes open,
Arms wide,
Unbroken,
I'll not be cast aside.

I once had a dream
I was swimming upstream.
Everyone that I knew
Was swimming there too.
The current was strong,
But something was wrong;
I couldn't keep up
'Cause I didn't belong.

I've been different from the start,
A troubled work of art.
The blood in my veins
Has kept me oh so far apart.

But through it all I hold my head up high,
Face t'wards the sky.

Where am I going?
Only time knows the answer for sure.
Which winding road will I follow?
Which jagged fork in my path
Will hold the cure?
I want someone to hold me,
Enfold me.
Where am I going?
I'm going where love's in the air,
In the air,
Love in the air.

The signature at the bottom read 'Ruth Rosenberg'.

Lilly heard the front door open. She ran downstairs. Before Ruth had taken off her coat and boots, Lilly was in front of her. She had a big smile on her face.

"You look like a cat that just caught a juicy mouse," said Ruth as she laid the groceries she was carrying down on the hall bench.

"More like a juicy poem," said Lilly. "What does that mean?" Lilly held up the sheet of paper.

"I was looking in my desk for paper to write a letter to mother. I found this in the bottom drawer."

Ruth took a quick glance, then turned away. She hung up her coat and took off her boots. She picked her packages up off the bench and made her way into the kitchen. Lilly followed.

"Ruth, it's so beautiful."

"I wish you hadn't read it."

"I love the part that says, 'I've been different from the start, a troubled work of art.' It would make a great song, Ruth."

Ruth opened the icebox and put her groceries inside.

"Do you know anyone who could put it to music?" asked Lilly.

Ruth made her way to the sink. She filled the kettle with water and put it on the stove. Lilly persisted.

"How about Ali?"

Lilly had finally met Ali at a band practice that Aiden had taken her to.

"Stop, Lilly!"

"Aiden told me you used to sing with their band. Ruth, I think you should bury all that happened between you and Ali and get back to performing with The Jazz Singers."

"That's never going to happen."

"Never say never, Ruth."

Rosie didn't have any animosity towards the Newfoundland Constabulary when they were off duty and spending money in her club. It was a different story, however, when they showed up one afternoon unannounced and in uniform. The two cops standing in front of her were all business.

"We were led to believe you might have information relating to who set the fire at Joseph Rosenberg's shop. Do you?" asked Constable Hickey.

"Where did you get that information?"

"That's our business," answered the other cop.

"If you want to know that kind of stuff, ask Skeeter over there," said Rosie indignantly.

Skeeter was behind the bar cleaning glasses. He had his back to the cops as they approached. Constable Hickey stayed in front of the bar. The other cop walked behind it and took his place menacingly at Skeeter's side.

"So, Skeeter. Shame about that fire at Rosenberg's shop," said Constable Hickey.

Skeeter didn't turn around. Instead, he pretended he hadn't heard what the cop had said.

"Some folks are saying you had something to do with it. You wouldn't want to take the entire blame for something someone else put you up to, would you, Skeeter? That wouldn't be fair."

Skeeter kept polishing the glasses.

"Can we assume from your silence that it was actually you who was the mastermind behind the whole thing? That it was you who put Tommy Chan up to it?"

"I don't have a clue what you're talking about," said Skeeter.

He made to leave, but the cop standing next to him stood in his way.

"You have something to hide? The best way to deal with that is for us to handcuff you, throw you in the paddy wagon and drag you to our not-so-cozy interrogation room."

"On what grounds?" asked Skeeter.

"Put the cuffs on him, Constable."

"Hold on a minute!"

"I'm going to ask you one very simple question," said Constable Hickey. "If you give us a straight answer, we'll make sure things go easy on you. If not, you're going to be in more trouble than the Titanic. Listen closely: What do you know about that fire at Rosenberg's place?"

Since the day the Constabulary had released him from the lockup, Joseph had been staying at Hannah's. He could no longer stand the thought of paying rent on the house he once owned.

Hannah, for her part, liked having him around. In the past, she had taken a backseat in Joseph's life. But, when called upon, she had happily acted as Ruth's stepmother.

Hannah hadn't yet met Lilly, so she was delighted when she and Ruth came to visit one Sunday afternoon. Lilly had started to warm to her father. Joseph, meanwhile, was pleased to have his other daughter so close by. Lilly did, however, wondered why he hadn't made more of an effort to restart his business. She had discussed it with Ruth. And, while open to the idea, Ruth was reluctant to broach the subject with her father.

On this particular Sunday evening, there was no talk of business. Tea, cakes and idle chatter were the order of the day. There was a knock at the door. Hannah went to answer it. Aiden was standing there. His forehead was glistening and he was out of breath. Hannah invited him in.

"You're not going to believe this," said Aiden.

"Try me," said Lilly.

"Tommy Chan has been arrested!"

"That's the best news I've heard in months," said Ruth.

"What for?" asked Joseph.

"For burning down your business," said Aiden.

Joseph couldn't bring himself to celebrate. Ruth, on the other hand, threw her hands in the air and shouted for joy.

"About time! He's caused our family nothing but misery."

"Are you sure?" Joseph asked Aiden.

"Absolutely! Skeeter Dunn is telling the Constabulary all he knows."

"What does Skeeter Dunn have to do with it?" asked Joseph.

"From what I can figure out, Skeeter helped Tommy," said Aiden.

"Who informed the Constabulary?" asked Ruth.

"Ali did," said Aiden. "Rosie pointed him to Tommy and Skeeter, and Ali went to see Chief Constable Murphy."

Lilly snapped her fingers in joy.

"That-a-boy, Ali!"

Jacob sensed Ruth was having difficulty adjusting to the fact that her father was no longer able to provide for himself, and that she was a married woman. He had done all he could to make her happy, but that didn't seem to be enough. He felt he needed to do more.

Late one Saturday morning, he found Ruth and Lilly in the front room seated at the piano. He looked over their shoulders. They were playing Bach's Two-Part Inventions, Number Eight. Ruth was gleefully tinkling out the right hand while Lilly pounded away at the left. Since they seemed to be enjoying the battle, he didn't dare interrupt. Besides, it pleased him to see the two sisters having so much fun. After they finished, Ruth flipped through the book looking for other pieces to play. He saw his chance.

"Excuse me, but would you happen to know two beautiful young piano-playing ladies who would like to be taken to lunch by a gallant gentleman who would undoubtedly relish their company?" He grinned.

"Are you referring to us, by any chance?" asked Ruth.

"I most certainly am."

"Is the gallant gentleman paying?" asked Lilly.

"He most certainly is."

"I don't know, we're kinda busy right now," teased Lilly.

"I'll ask around though and get back to you," chided Ruth.

"You leave me no other choice but to kidnap you both!"

said Jacob, as he dived playfully at them.

Ruth and Lilly pushed back from the piano and rushed to get their hats and coats. But not before solemnly vowing to get back to Bach as soon as possible. Along the way, Jacob suggested they drop by to see if Joseph and Hannah wanted to join them. They were home and gratefully accepted the invitation.

"Where are we going?" asked Hannah.

"It's a surprise," answered Jacob.

They all locked arms and bounded sideways out the door. As they walked eastward along Duckworth Street, Ruth turned to Lilly and whispered in her ear.

"I bet he's taking us to the Newfoundland Hotel."

"Wanna check out the hunks on the tennis courts again?" asked Lilly. Ruth looked at her and smiled.

Joseph slowed down as they passed Silverman's Jewellers. Two boys were peering into the display window. A man rushed out and frantically wagged his finger at them.

"If you want to buy a watch, buy a watch. If you don't want to buy a watch, get your snotty noses away from my window!"

The boys trudged off.

Joseph called out to Mr. Silverman.

"Hey, Levi! How's the world treatin' ya?"

"Don't get me started!"

Business was brisk at The East End Store. Customers exited carrying large bags of groceries or whatever items of hardware struck their fancy.

A flatbed wagon was stopped in front, and two boys were wrestling on the back while shouting obscenities. As their mother attached gunny feedbags to the horses' heads, she shouted at the boys to quit it. The owner was standing in front of his store, speaking to the husband.

"How's the weight?" he shouted to two men weighing dried cod.

"Spot on, Skipper. A full quintal."

The owner turned to the man.

"I'll give you five dollars."

"Last year it was nine."

"Don't blame me for the friggin' depression."

Shortly thereafter, Jacob stopped abruptly in front of what looked like an abandoned building. Lilly turned to Ruth and whispered in her ear.

"I think I just lost my appetite," she said.

"Why are we stopping here?" asked Ruth.

Jacob didn't say a word. Instead, he approached the building and pulled the boards away from the entrance. He reached into his pocket, took out a ring of keys, quickly unlocked the door and stepped inside.

"Don't be scaredy cats. Come on in!"

He opened the windows and set about pushing the scattered boxes away from the centre of the floor. One by one Ruth, Lilly, Joseph and Hannah made their way cautiously through the front door and into the shop. Joseph flipped the light switch. Nothing happened.

It took a while for their eyes to adjust from the bright sunlight outside to the dark atmosphere inside. When they did, they found themselves in a surprisingly large room. There were counters along both walls, and shelves behind them. There were also two smaller rooms at the back. At first, they didn't notice those things. All they saw was a grimy, cluttered and oppressive space not fit for human habitation.

"Come back here and take a look," yelled Jacob.

"Jacob, what are we doing here?" asked Ruth.

Jacob walked from the back and stepped behind one of the

counters. He took out his handkerchief and hurriedly wiped dust off the top.

"Look, solid oak!" he said excitedly. "They're in good shape, once the dirt and grime are cleaned off ... and under-counter shelves ... and drawers with solid brass handles."

"Not my idea of a nice place to have lunch," said Lilly.

Jacob walked from behind the counter and approached Joseph. He then put his hand on Joseph's shoulder. With his arms outstretched, he shouted to all in earshot.

"Joseph Rosenberg, welcome to your new shop!"

Ruth, Lilly, Joseph and Hannah looked questioningly at each other. Jacob sensed their misgivings.

"When you fall off a horse, the best thing to do is get right back on again."

Joseph looked squarely at Jacob, who was grinning from ear to ear.

"Jacob, I want you to be serious for a minute," said Joseph. "Have you lost your mind?"

"Not at all," he answered. "I know you've been hit hard. It has taken its toll on you. Not only on you, but on Ruth and Hannah as well."

"Whatever you were hoping for, Jacob, is not going to happen. I...."

"Don't think that way," said Jacob. "You should get back to work. Restart your business. I signed a lease for this place yesterday. It's only for one year. The rent was so cheap, I paid for the year in advance. If it doesn't work out, as far as I'm concerned, no harm done."

Hannah walked up to Joseph and took his hand.

"Joseph, we can do this, you and I. You still have your talents as a tailor. I still have my sewing machine at home."

"Hannah! Joseph!" shouted Jacob. "Come back here."

He led them to one of the back rooms.

"Hannah, you can set up your machine here," said Jacob. "And, Joseph, here in the other room you can set up your office."

As everyone was looking around curiously, Joseph sidled up to Ruth.

"What do you think about all this, my daughter?" he asked, uncharacteristically subdued. "I'm not the man I used to be, you know."

Ruth paused for a minute. She moved slowly around the room.

"It would require a lot of fixing up, that's for sure. But if we're all up for it, it could work."

"I'll help," said Lilly.

"So will I," said Jacob.

"Maybe Jacob is right," said Ruth. "If we keep our expectations low, then...."

"Will you be my manager, Ruth?" asked Joseph. "I can't do this without you."

Ruth walked over to her father and locked her arm in his.

"Try to stop me."

⁓

Dear Mother,

Guess who? Sorry I haven't written in so long. Although I came to St. John's only to visit Ruth, I've been busy with so many other things as well since I got here. I've met Ruth's husband, Jacob. He's from England. He seems very nice and is very generous.

I've also met Father. He has been through a lot

since he left New York and settled here. He lost all his businesses, which has hit him hard. The good news though is that Ruth's husband has rented Father a new space where he can set up his tailor shop again. We're all busy cleaning it up and getting it ready for the public to visit. The grand opening is in a couple of weeks. We're all on pins and needles.

Finally, I'll get to the point. I want to stay here longer. I've become very close to Ruth and I really think she needs me around. She's going through a lot too. But that's a long story for another time.

They have a small college here and I'm thinking of signing up for some of their classes. Don't worry, the tuition is very cheap. The government pays a lot of it. I don't know what I would study yet, but I'm sure they'll have something that would interest me and keep me off the streets. Just kidding about the streets part. Also, Ruth has told me I can work in the shop as a sales lady if I want. That would give me a bit of pocket money, which would come in handy and hopefully help with the cost of tuition.

Also ... now just relax! I have a beau. His name is Aiden. He's very nice and treats me like a lady. I like that. I think you would like him.

You'll see that I've included a photo of us all, which I'm sure you would like to see. That's Ruth standing on Father's right. Jacob and Aiden are squat down in front and I'm standing next to Ruth. Aiden reminds me of Rudolph Valentino in "The Sheik".

I hope you and our friends and relatives are well. I miss you all, but you can rest assured I'm not wasting *my time here. To the contrary.*

Please write back. I would love to hear all the news. I must go now. We're painting the walls of Father's new shop today and stocking the shelves. I'll take a picture for you when it's finished and full of customers. I love you very much and miss you so.

Your loving daughter,

Lilly

P.S. Ruth says hello and said to tell you she hopes you'll come to visit one day. They have a spare bedroom where you could stay. It would make a great nursery, but they would have to have a baby first. That hasn't happened yet. Fingers crossed!

Lilly folded the letter and addressed the envelope. She dropped it in the mailbox on her way to the shop.

Since Ali had written his letter to Ruth, his mind had been put at rest somewhat. He no longer now wallowed in self-pity, though he couldn't bring himself to simply forget her. Instead, he threw himself into the family band and his song writing.

He was at band practice one day when Aiden and Lilly walked in.

"Hey, Ali," said Aiden. "I hear the Constabulary have been out asking questions about Tommy and the night of the fire."

Ali shrugged.

"Let's hope they can pin it on him," continued Aiden.

"I have never met this Tommy fellow and as far as I am concerned I'd like to keep it that way," said Lilly.

"You'll see him at the trial, though," said Aiden.

"I'll hold my nose," quipped Lilly.

"I hear Joseph is opening shop again," said Ali.

"The grand opening is in a couple of weeks," said Aiden. "Are you coming?"

"I don't think that would be a good idea."

"Well, do the next best thing then," said Lilly.

She handed him a sheet of paper.

"What's this?" asked Ali.

"Read it."

As Ali read it, he gently nodded his head in approval.

"Where's it from?" he asked.

"Ruth wrote it," said Lilly.

"Why are you showing me this?"

"I think you should put it to music. And make it sweet!"

———

"Is the old man in?"

Joseph and Hannah had just finished dinner and were making their way into their front room when they heard a knock on the door. Hannah went to open it and found Ruth and Lilly standing there. They had big smiles on their faces. Lilly was holding a notebook and a pen.

"Yes, he's in the front room," said Hannah. "Come on in."

Ruth and Lilly came in, made themselves comfortable in the front room chairs, and then addressed Joseph.

"We're here to interview you," said Lilly.

"What are you two girls up to now?" he asked.

"Just pretend we're from The Daily News," said Ruth.

"I don't know if I'm that good a pretender," smiled Joseph.

"Just speak the truth," said Lilly. She opened her notebook.

"So, Mr. Rosenberg, what's this new business venture of yours?" asked Ruth.

Ruth and Lilly began to pepper him with questions. He slowly started to get the hang of things. What emerged was a list of firm principles on which he hoped to build his business.

Joseph Rosenberg & Family –
The First American Ladies' Tailor

• *Business is built on confidence. Consider the needs of the buyer and make his interests your own.*
• *To sell a person something he does not want or to sell a person something at a price above its actual value is a calamity – for the seller.*
• *In the law, the buyer and seller are supposed to be people with equal opportunity to judge of an article and pass on its value. This is not so, for the seller is a specialist and understands his product. And so the buyer must depend on the honesty and good will of the seller.*
• *We make our money from our friends. Our enemies will not trade with us.*
• *Style, Finish and Satisfaction are the principles we work on.*

The next morning, Lilly made a trip to the printers and ordered five hundred flyers.

"Hi, my name is Lilly Rosenberg."

"Nice to meet you," said the desk clerk at the Newfoundland Hotel. "Are you looking for a room?"

"I like your dress," said Lilly.

"Thank you. I bought it at Bowring's."

"So, it's not bespoke then."

"Unfortunately, I can't afford that."

"Could you afford it if I were to offer you twenty-five percent off a hand-made outfit?"

"Are you a tailor?"

"No, but my father is."

"Where's his place of business?"

"On Duckworth Street, less than a five-minute walk."

"What's it called?"

"Joseph Rosenberg's. We're opening next week. Bring this flyer with you and you'll get a twenty-five percent discount on your first order."

Lilly handed the flyer to the clerk.

"Mind if I leave a bunch of them here on the desk for your customers?" she asked nonchalantly.

"Well, that's not our policy here at the hotel."

"The hotel's clientele can also get a twenty-five percent discount on their first order if they bring this flyer to the shop." Lilly put on her biggest smile. "It would mean a lot to our family."

"Leave them with me. I'll see what I can do."

"Make sure you drop by next week. I'll see you get special treatment."

"My name's Rebecca."

"Nice to meet you, Rebecca."

Lilly handed her a packet, took one look around the lobby and left.

She stopped at pretty well every place of business along Duckworth Street and did the same thing. Then she proceeded onto the side streets. She placed a flyer through every mail slot she could find.

⸻

The day everyone had been waiting for had finally arrived. During the previous few days, Ruth had forbidden Joseph from visiting the shop. She wanted it to be a surprise. Ruth

181

and Lilly put on their Sunday best and headed for Hannah's. When they arrived, Joseph was standing in the front room looking more like his old self. Hannah had put everything into making him presentable. They all agreed that a glass of sherry was in order. Then they stepped gingerly into the open air.

They had a quickness to their step. Before they turned the corner just west of the new shop, Ruth and Lilly demanded that Joseph close his eyes. Ruth took one arm. Lilly took the other. They turned the corner onto Duckworth Street and stopped in front of Joseph's new place of business.

"You can open your eyes now," said Lilly.

The first thing that caught Joseph's attention was the balloons swaying in the early afternoon breeze. Next, he saw bunting above the front door with a Newfoundland flag on either side. Then his eyes began to focus on the sign extending from one corner of the building out onto the sidewalk. He moved farther ahead to get a better look. It read: 'Joseph Rosenberg & Family – The First American Ladies' Tailor'. A tear came to his eye. Hannah walked up and put her arms around him.

"Do you like it?" asked Ruth.

"I never thought I'd see this day again," said Joseph.

"I'm very proud of you," said Hannah.

"Well, don't just stand there," shouted Lilly. "Let's go inside!"

When they entered, they saw that Jacob was already there. He had arrived earlier in the morning to set up things. Along one counter, he had lined up platers of sandwiches, cheese, fruit, plates, cutlery and napkins. On the other, he had placed juice, water, sherry, rum and glasses.

He addressed all present. "The table is laid. Now all we need are patrons."

And patrons they got. One by one would-be customers peeked their heads around the open door and peered inside.

They were each welcomed by either Ruth, Lilly or Hannah. Joseph stood to one side and surveyed the proceedings. He couldn't believe what he was seeing. There were neighbours, friends, total strangers and even curious competitors. Simon Goldstein, who owned the jewellery shop next to Joseph's short-lived delicatessen, walked in, as did other business owners Joseph knew on Water Street. Some of his staff from the Wonderland Theatre and his tailor shop were also there. Even members of Joseph's synagogue showed up to pay their respects. They each held a flyer in their hand. Aiden, Sami and Zane also graced the proceedings with their presence.

Joseph was in his glory. He shook all proffered hands, showed people around and answered any questions that came his way. The afternoon flew by. When all the curious had left, Joseph and party could finally relax.

"Where do we go from here?" asked Lilly excitedly.

"Jacob and I had a chat last night and decided that if everything went well today, we would invite all of you back to our place," said Ruth.

"That would be lovely," said Hannah.

"Lilly and I might even be talked into playing the piano," said Ruth.

Lilly addressed Aiden, Sami and Zane.

"Do you think you guys would be up to playing?" she asked.

"We'll grab our instruments," said Sami.

"Sounds like a party!" said Lilly.

"Do you have anything to drink?" asked Zane.

"I'm sure we can figure something out," said Jacob.

The festivities at Ruth and Jacob's place were in full gear. Ruth had made a pot of moose stew and everyone had had their fill. The band had set up in the corner. Before they started playing, Ruth announced that there was a song she wanted to sing. She sat at the piano and nodded to Hannah, who left the room and returned shortly carrying a violin case.

"Where did you get this?" Joseph asked.

"From your closet," said Hannah. "Ruth asked me to bring it along."

"I hope you're not expecting me to play."

"I'm not going to budge until you do," said Ruth.

"I haven't played in years," he protested.

"Why don't you begin by opening the case," said Jacob.

The violin inside sparkled as it always had. He took it out, gently plucked the strings and then removed the bow. After a brief tuning, he put it to his chin. All leaned forward in anticipation. He looked towards Ruth seated at the piano.

"You start," said Joseph.

The emotion in the air was palpable as Ruth and Joseph lovingly revisited the tune they had so often played and sung many years ago. At the end, they felt not merely gratified, but exalted.

Ruth rose from the piano and walked towards her father. They took hold of each other's hands.

"I knew that you'd never forget how to play, 'The Sidewalks of New York', said Ruth, her throat catching. And everyone applauded.

Next it was Lilly's turn. She took Ruth's place at the piano, removed two sheets of paper from the stool and placed them in front of her. She played, but didn't sing.

When she had finished, she turned towards Ruth.

"That's a lovely tune," said Ruth. "Who wrote it?"

"I did," said Lilly. "Would you like to hear me sing it with the lyrics?"

She played the song through again. But this time, she also sang it.

"I can't believe you wrote music to my poem," said Ruth.

"I didn't. I lied. Ali wrote it."

"You shouldn't have done that, Lilly," Ruth said, with anger in her eyes.

She rose from her chair and hurried out of the room. All present looked at each other, not knowing what to say. Lilly got up and followed after her. She found Ruth sitting on her bed.

"Ruth, it's time you forgave Ali," she said gently.

"You should have asked me first," said Ruth.

"I did. But you weren't ready."

"And I'm not ready now, either."

"You can't harbour resentment for the rest of your life. It'll eat away at you. It takes all the joy out of life. In the end, you'll be the one who gets hurt most."

"Don't lecture me, Lilly."

"But it's true though, isn't it. You have to get over feeling sorry for yourself, Ruth. You're stronger than this."

Ruth lay down on her bed.

"It's Jacob I really feel sorry for," she sighed.

"How so?"

Joseph knocked on the open door and came to sit on the bed next to Ruth.

"It takes courage to forgive, Ruth. Be true to the love you two once had and forgive him."

Downstairs, one by one, the partiers made their excuses and proceeded out the door. After they'd gone, Ruth undressed and got into bed.

Not long afterwards, Jacob came into their bedroom. Ruth lay with her back to the door. He thought she was asleep. He gently lifted back the covers and got into bed. She rolled over and faced him.

"I'm sorry about tonight, Jacob."

"That's okay. I understand. You know, forgiveness does as much for the one forgiving as it does for the one being forgiven."

Ruth felt blessed to have Jacob in her life. He had been more patient with her than she deserved. Whether or not she could actually face Ali and tell him she forgave him was another story.

———

The next morning – their first real day of doing business – Joseph and Hannah were already at the shop when Ruth and Lilly arrived. Ruth was still upset with Lilly for having given her poem to Ali, but had decided to put as good a face on it as she could muster.

It had been quiet for most of the morning, and Joseph was starting to get anxious that they might have made the wrong decision to open a shop again, when the bell over the front door sounded and a young lady walked in.

"Is Lilly here?"

Lilly came over.

"Rebecca, right?"

"You remember me?"

"Newfoundland Hotel! How could I forget?"

"Is that discount still on offer?"

"Of course. Come, meet my father."

Joseph had his first actual customer. Measurements were taken, design decided upon and cloth chosen. No sooner had Rebecca left, than Hannah set about cutting and sewing. They were so excited to finally be back at work and by the thrill of it all, they forgot to have lunch. Ruth offered to take care of the store while the rest went for something to eat.

She felt a little nervous there by herself. After all, it had been a long time since she had worked in her father's shop. A few people stopped by while the others were at lunch, and said they would come back when Joseph returned.

She was in the office at the back tidying up the desk when she heard the front door open again. When she saw who it was through the office door, she turned away.

"I know you're back there," said Ali. "I saw you when I came in. I was going to bring a hatchet with me and see if we could find somewhere to bury it."

Ruth walked behind one of the counters and faced him.

"I'm probably the last person you expected to see here today," said Ali.

"Why are you here?" Ruth asked coldly.

"I'm glad to see Joseph has his business back."

Ali walked around the shop for a moment and examined various items on display. Ruth stayed behind the counter.

"I hear Tommy was arrested for the fire," said Ali.

"Apparently," said Ruth with a detached tone in her voice.

"I met your sister, Lilly. She and Aiden seem to be getting along well. She reminds me of you."

"You might not realize it, but I'm busy. I can't stand here all day listening to you make small talk."

A serious look came across Ali's face.

"We've known each other for a long time, haven't we. It's hard for me not seeing you."

"Poor you," said Ruth.

"I didn't handle things very well...."

"A master of the understatement."

"I have no one to blame but myself."

"You should leave."

Ali moved forward. He was not as poised as Ruth at first thought he was. He was actually trembling.

"I have to say it one more time or I'll never forgive myself. I love you, Ruth."

Ruth wasn't ready for that.

"You shouldn't have come here, Ali.

"But here I am."

Ruth turned and headed back to the office. Ali called out to her.

"We can't avoid each other forever, Ruth."

10

Justice Is Blind

On the day of Tommy's trial, the early morning sun that had held such promise quickly turned to oppressive black clouds and freezing drizzle. Everyone who entered the courthouse had bundled up against the ferocious wind and what they were sure would eventually turn to a heavy, drenching downpour.

Ali had wanted to come, but in the end, he decided against it. He didn't want to make things uncomfortable for Ruth.

When Ruth arrived, she found Joseph, Hannah and Jacob standing in the hallway just outside the courtroom. Hannah seemed agitated. Ruth did her best to calm her.

Their brief conversation was interrupted by CC Joe Murphy, who instructed Ruth and Joseph to follow him to the room where the prosecution witnesses were to wait until the trial began. Since Hannah and Jacob weren't to be witnesses at the trial, they entered the courtroom and took their seats.

In the witness room, Ruth and Joseph found Rosie and Skeeter Dunn. There were two other men present as well. One was the owner of a hardware store behind which Tommy lived. The other was the attendant at the gas station close by. The hellos were guarded at best.

In the courtroom, the judge read the charges against Tommy and asked if he understood. Tommy answered in the affirmative and told the judge he intended to plead not guilty.

What followed was three days of back and forth between defense and prosecution attorneys laying out their cases for and against the defendant.

Rosie testified that Tommy had worked for her at her club and was in charge of keeping the peace. She knew he had lent Joseph money. As far as she knew, Joseph hadn't paid it back, which made Tommy furious. She vehemently denied that she had encouraged Tommy to do anything more, but added that she wouldn't put anything past Tommy in his quest to get his revenge.

Joseph told the court that he agreed with Rosie's assessment, and went on to explain the situation with the sealskin coats. He had tried to pay off what he owed. But every effort he had made had, for one reason or another, fallen apart.

Ruth told of how Tommy had threatened her father, telling him he would be thrown off the roof of The Continental if he didn't pay the money back. She also told the court that all their sewing machines and inventory were not found in the shop after the fire.

The owner of the hardware store told the court that Tommy had bought two gas canisters the day before the fire. The gas attendant testified that on the day of the fire Tommy had filled them both.

Skeeter testified that Tommy had planned the whole thing. He had pressured him to help set the fire saying he would take his vengeance out on him next if he didn't co-operate.

Then the defense called its witnesses. Tommy's mother told of how good a boy he was. A man, who described himself as Tommy's best friend in high school, told of the innocent fun they had had together chasing girls. Tommy's landlord talked of him never having missed a month's rent.

When Tommy then took the stand, he said he always tried

to do the right thing. He had taken his job at the club seriously. He acknowledged that he had been incarcerated several times, but was trying to get his life back in order and become an upright citizen. He said he now had a reputation for hard work and dedication to service.

His alibi was that he had spent the night of the fire at home listening to the radio with a couple of girls from the club. They had stayed the night and therefore could have testified that he couldn't have set the fire. Unfortunately, they had since left town for another job somewhere on the mainland. He couldn't remember their names and didn't know their present whereabouts.

By the time the fourth and final day arrived, weariness had set in and all concerned were looking forward to the verdict.

Ali had stayed away from the courthouse, but couldn't resist any longer. He slipped in the back and took a seat.

The judge entered, and the proceedings were called to order. The attorney for the prosecution stood to deliver his summation. He painted Tommy as merely a paid thug who had been in and out of jail almost his entire life. He'd been fired from every job he had ever had. Aside from being a bouncer at The Continental, he had nothing to commend him. He also categorized the character witnesses' testimony as nothing more than vague recollections of a man who no longer existed. He had burned down an innocent man's place of business merely out of spite.

When it was his turn, the defense attorney went through each of the prosecution's witnesses, stressing that all of them had ulterior motives. Their testimonies couldn't be trusted.

He painted Rosie in the worst possible light. There was no level to which she wouldn't stoop. She couldn't be trusted. Joseph, he argued, was a pitiful, chronic gambler, constant liar and fabricator of excuses who would do anything for his next fix. He had it in for Tommy because he wouldn't lend him any more money. Ruth, he said, would do or say anything to protect her father, even if it came to uttering lies or misleading statements. The evidence given by the hardware store owner and gas attendant was nothing more than circumstantial.

He saved his wrath for Skeeter, who he declared had turned state's evidence simply to save his own skin. He even suggested that it could in fact have been Skeeter who set the fire to frame Tommy. Yes, Tommy had made mistakes in the past, but that didn't mean he would do something as heinous as deliberately burning down a man's business.

In one last push, he pleaded with the jury to approach their deliberations with open minds and hearts. If they harboured any reasonable doubts whatsoever, they should return a not-guilty verdict. An innocent man's life was in their hands.

The judge then gave his last instructions to the jury. They were led away by the bailiff to begin their deliberations.

Outside the courtroom, Joseph noticed Ali at the other end of the hallway talking with Rosie. He called out to him. Ali at first hesitated, then relented.

"Ali, so nice to see you here. It's been too long."

"Nice to see you too. Wish it was under better circumstances."

"You here for the verdict?"

"I hope he gets what's coming to him."

The afternoon dragged on. Just as those waiting began to reconcile themselves to the possibility that the jury might adjourn for the day, the bailiff entered the hallway and declared that the jury had arrived at a verdict. Everyone entered the courtroom and took their seats.

The judge took his place at the bench, and the bailiff led the jury into the room. The judge addressed Tommy.

"Would the defendant please stand and face the bench."

Tommy rose, his attorney at his side. The judge turned towards the jury.

"Have you come to a verdict?"

The presiding juror stood and responded.

"We find the defendant not guilty."

The judge thanked the jury for their service. He then dismissed them and called the case closed. Tommy hugged his attorney and then his mother. Ruth and the others sat in dumbed silence. Tommy saw them and walked over.

"I love that disappointed look on your faces," he gloated. "Warms my heart."

"Just keep walking," said Ruth.

"You thought you had me, didn't you," said Tommy. "I'd watch out if I were you. Stay away from dark alleys. Anything could happen."

"Are you threatening us?" asked Ruth.

"Now, would I do such a thing?" asked Tommy.

"One day...." said Lilly.

Tommy turned towards her.

"I don't think I've had the pleasure."

"And I intend to keep it that way," said Lilly.

"Pity," said Tommy. "You and me could have a lot of fun together."

Lilly looked repulsed.

Tommy shrugged.

"See ya 'round."

He walked towards the door. Before he left, Tommy made a point to wave to Rosie and then to Skeeter. Neither returned the gesture.

The house was more silent than usual. Through the front-room window, someone saw her sitting alone in front of the fire reading a book. That was exactly how he hoped he would find her.

He snuck around to the back of the house and found the door unlocked. He entered and made his way softly through the kitchen and into the hall. He took a mask from his pocket and put it on.

He crept through the hall and into the front room, came up behind her, and with one quick motion, wrapped the tape he had brought with him over her mouth. He pushed her onto the floor, turned her over face-down and tied her hands behind her back. Then, as an added precaution, he also put tape over her eyes.

He rose from the floor, made his way to one end of the room and turned off the lights. He walked past her to the other end of the room and closed the window and drapes. Behind him he could hear her frantically struggle to get to her feet. He knew she couldn't get far so he ignored her. Instead, he walked over to the gramophone and turned the volume all the way up.

He rolled her over and got on top of her. She fought him, but in vain.

Then she did something that surprised him. Somehow she had got her hands free. With one hand, she ripped the tape from her eyes and tore his mask off with the other. He punched her hard in the face. She fell into unconsciousness.

When he had finished, he made sure to take the tape, rope and mask with him. The less left behind the better.

He returned to the kitchen through which he had entered, took a quick look around, grabbed an apple from the bright-ly-coloured fruit bowl on the table and softly closed the back door behind him.

Ruth and Jacob found her exactly as he had left her – half-naked, on her back and still unconscious. Ruth shrieked in horror and dropped to her knees. Through her sobs, she tried to revive her.

"Lilly! Lilly! Speak to me!"

Jacob pulled a blanket off the couch and covered her.

"I'll call the hospital," he said hurriedly.

"Lilly, can you hear me?" implored Ruth.

Lilly began to stir. She opened her eyes. Slowly the reality of what had happened hit her. She let out a heartbreaking moan.

"Lilly, who did this to you?" pleaded Ruth.

Lilly didn't respond. Her face had a blank, vacant expression. .Jacob rushed back into the room.

"They're on their way."

Ruth put both arms around her sister and lovingly caressed her.

While the hospital workers were carrying Lilly outside, Ruth quickly set about collecting clothes for her. As she was about to get into the back of the buggy with Lilly, Jacob told her to go on alone. He wanted to see if he could find Aiden.

When Jacob arrived at the hospital, he was accompanied by Aiden and CC Murphy. Aiden approached and took hold of Lilly's hand. Her eyes were open, but with a distant stare.

"Has she spoken yet?" asked Aiden.

"No," said Ruth. "She's been like this since we arrived."

"Have the doctors examined her?" continued Aiden.

"Yes," responded Ruth.

"Who found her?" asked CC Murphy.

"We did," said Ruth. "Me and Jacob. Back at our place."

CC Murphy walked over to the bed, leaned down and whispered in Lilly's ear.

"Who did this to you, sweetheart?"

Lilly remained silent and still.

"Did you recognize him?" he asked again.

Lilly was still unresponsive. Her sister sat down on the bed beside her.

"Lilly, Zane's father is here to help you."

The room went silent. Jacob approached and knelt down on the floor next to her. He held her hand and kissed her forehead. He tried one more time.

"Who did this, Lilly?"

She slowly turned her head towards him.

"Tommy Chan," she whispered.

Part IV

II

Heaven on Earth

Fog wasn't what one would have expected that time of year, but there it was – a thick grey shroud rolling northward from the Grand Banks and covering the entire city on a damp, slushy January day.

Business owners unfurled sailcloth awnings in front of their places of business. Coal men delivered their coal. Milkmen delivered their milk. Icemen delivered their ice. And bleary-eyed tavern regulars traipsed their tipsy ways towards smoke-filled, beer-soaked saloons to meet up with their fellow imbibers and trade stories of wartime bravery and better days gone by.

Erin didn't have the proper footwear for conditions like this – the icy cold seeped through the seams of her boots – but she would not let that deter her. She plowed her way up the hills from downtown, past horses valiantly straining against their reins in a thankless effort to pull long-carts out of ditches.

Christmas had come and gone, but Erin wasn't in a celebratory mood. She hadn't visited her parents for the holidays as was her custom. She didn't think her pious, god-fearing parents and their friends and relatives in Witless Bay were ready to hear about the impending birth of her child. The Blessed Virgin Mary she most definitely was not.

She realized it was about time to face the fact that since she was going to have a baby, she would need help when it came time for the actual delivery.

The steps up to the front doors were icy and slippery, so she stepped carefully. The extra weight she was carrying added to her unsteadiness. The curtains of the two-storey bay windows on either side of the entrance were pulled closed. The building looked mysterious and secretive. She pushed the heavy door open, and entered the vestibule to St. Clare's Mercy Hospital.

St. Clare's was located in a large, white re-purposed mansion surrounded by an iron fence and extensive gardens. It was run by the Sisters of Mercy. Erin had heard that it served the working girls of St. John's, so she was hoping her particular situation would be received with empathy and understanding.

"May I help you?" asked the receptionist.

"Yes, I would like to talk to someone about my pregnancy."

"Have you been a patient here before?"

"No."

"Please have a seat. I'll call you when someone is available."

Erin had never been in a hospital before. The sounds and smells were unfamiliar. What surprised her most was how quiet it was. She expected hustle and bustle and occasional cries of pain. But all she was really conscious of were her cold sodden feet. Eventually, the receptionist called out to her.

"The first door on the left. Go in and have a seat."

Erin did as she was instructed, squishing her way down the hall. The room was large and painted in a drab, nondescript beige. There was a broad mahogany desk in the middle of the room with two straight-backed, wooden chairs in front of it. Behind the desk was an enormous crucifix. The almost life-sized body of Jesus Christ, which hung on the crucifix, was covered in blood. She wondered whose office this could be.

She got her answer when the side door opened and a woman dressed in a full, floor-length black dress walked in. A long black veil covered her head and back, and her forehead was constrained by a wide white band. A large stiff bib covered her entire chest down to her waist, which was encircled by a leather belt from which hung a string of black beads, at the end of which was another crucifix. Her hands were tucked out of sight inside her long sleeves. The only sign that there was actually someone inside all that black and white was an unsmiling face that didn't even acknowledge Erin was also in the room. The black apparition made its way to the desk, sat down and looked at her.

"My name is Sister Mary Louise."

Erin had great difficulty answering. She had never been this close to a nun before.

"My name is Erin O'Shea."

"Please sit down. Tell me why you're here," the nun said.

"Yes ... well.... I'm pregnant, you see."

"Obviously."

"When the time comes, I want to have my baby in a proper hospital."

"And you want our help? Is that why you're here?"

"I hear you take care of working girls in my position."

"And what position is that?"

"I'm not married."

The nun leaned back in her chair and placed both hands firmly on the edge of her desk.

"You are Catholic, are you not?"

"Yes. I'm from the southern shore."

"And yet you carry on in this shameful manner." the nun admonished disdainfully. "You do realize you have committed a grave sin, don't you? A mortal sin?"

Erin dropped her head, crestfallen.

"Yes. Bow your head in shame," said the nun.

"I was hoping you'd understand and...." Erin's voice trailed off.

The nun stood up, walked around her desk to where Erin was sitting and stared down at her.

"The first thing you must do is to go to confession and beg God's forgiveness. The next thing you must do is agree to give the child up for adoption."

Erin jumped up, but the nun continued speaking.

"There are many good Catholic families who..."

"What!"

"A woman in your position..."

"I'm not going to do that!"

"...doesn't have many choices without a man to protect her and provide for her. Besides, it is the best way for you to atone for your sin."

"What kind of woman would ask another woman to do that kind of thing?"

"That's enough out of you, young lady! My advice to you is to go down the road to the Grace Hospital. They deal more with your kind."

Sister Mary Louise turned and walked towards the door.

"May God have mercy on your soul."

The Grace wasn't far from St. Clare's, but the heavy slush and icy sidewalks made walking difficult. The building itself was larger than St. Clare's. It had a magnificent verandah surrounding the entire front and sides, and there was also a similar but smaller verandah around the outside of the second floor. The routine at St. Clare's was followed almost to the letter at the Grace. However, this time it wasn't a nun who walked into the room, but rather a man.

He wore a four-button, dark-blue, utilitarian jacket with matching pants. There were red epaulets on top of each shoulder, two white 'S's inside a red insignia on each short jacket lapel, and a white shirt and black tie. This was topped off by a black cap with a shiny brim and a black peak, on the front of which was another white 'S' inside a red insignia. Wrapped around the cap between the brim and the peak was a wide red band. On the band, in large white letters were the words 'The Salvation Army'. Erin got up to leave.

"Please, sit down. My name is Captain Murdock."

"I think I'm in the wrong place," said Erin.

"Why do you say that?"

"You look like you're in the army or something."

"I am. God's army."

"The nun at St. Clare's told me this is a hospital, not an army base."

"We are a hospital."

"A military hospital?"

"No, a hospital for people like you. For God's children who need his love and affection."

"I could definitely use some love and affection."

"We can't take the place of your husband, but we will do our best to see to your corporeal, and hopefully spiritual, needs."

"What if I were to tell you that I'm not married?"

"It is not our place to judge you or your motives. The sworn mission of The Salvation Army is to help those in need, including unwed mothers. We adhere strongly to Christ's teachings. 'Judge not, and thou shalt not be judged.'"

Erin had found her hospital. She was not alone after all. She got up to leave, but didn't get very far. As if waiting for their chance, the waters chose that very moment to burst from inside her, run down her legs and puddle at her feet.

In her whole life, she had never felt more vulnerable. Captain Murdock walked to her and put his hand on her shoulder.

"Sit down, my child. Don't worry. You are in the hands of God. We will take good care of you."

———

Ali knew Erin had gone looking for a hospital where she hoped she could get the kind of assistance she would need. He had offered his help, but she insisted that it would be better if she did it on her own.

Sami stuck his head in Ali's bedroom. He was smiling.

"Ali, the Grace Hospital is on the phone. They want to talk to you. Something about wanting you to perform brain surgery, I think."

Ali went to the phone.

"Hello."

"This is Dr. Johnson from the Grace Hospital. Are you Ali Abbott?"

"Yes, I am. What can I do for you?"

"Do you know Erin O'Shea?"

"Of course. Is she in trouble?"

"Not anymore. She just gave birth to a lovely baby girl."

Ali had never seriously thought about the day that the baby would be born, and he would suddenly become a father. Even though he had been expecting the news for many months, when he actually heard it, it came as a shock.

"Is she okay?"

"Yes, she's resting now."

"Give her my congratulations, will you?"

"Why don't you give them to her yourself? We asked her who she would like us to notify and she gave us your name and phone number."

Ali grabbed his hat and coat and made his way downstairs. Sami was tending the shop.

"Everything okay?" he asked.

"Erin just gave birth to a baby girl!"

"Uh-oh. Just wait 'til Mom hears about this!"

"I'm on my way to the hospital now."

"Say hello to my first niece for me, will ya?"

Ali left and made his way to the Grace Hospital. The maternity ward was on the second floor. He proceeded with caution.

"Can you tell me where I can find Erin O'Shea?"

"May I ask who you are?"

"I'm Ali Abbott."

"Are you immediate family?"

"Not really."

"I'm sorry. Only immediate family are permitted to visit."

Ali hesitated for a minute.

"I'm the father of her child."

The nurse guided him to the fourth bed on the right. He approached and looked down at Erin. She appeared drawn. Obviously, she had been through a rough time. Thankfully, she was asleep. That gave him time to get his thoughts together.

He couldn't bring himself to leave Erin to fend for herself. Without him, she had no one else to turn to, since her parents refused to see her. He was determined to do everything he could to protect her from his mother. He had to step up. Be a man and not shirk this responsibility.

Erin stirred and opened her eyes. When she saw Ali, she smiled and reached out her hand.

"Thank you for coming."

"I'm so sorry I wasn't there for you to help out."

"It happened so fast. You wouldn't have been of much use anyway. Have you seen my baby?"

"Don't you mean *our* baby?"

"I won't hold you to that. You're still in love with Ruth. I know that."

Ali heard footsteps and looked behind him. A nurse cradled a pink, swaddled bundle in her arms. Erin looked up and smiled when the nurse neared.

"Are you the father?" asked the nurse.

"Yes, I am."

"Mr. and Mrs. O'Shea, here's your baby girl."

Ali bit his tongue. The nurse passed the baby to him.

"She's the face and eyes of her father, that's for sure," said the nurse.

Ali had never held a baby before. He felt so unsure of himself. He looked down at his little girl and grinned. She definitely had his skin colour. He could see her dark black hair peek out from under her blanket. He kissed her and handed her to Erin.

"She's so beautiful," said Ali.

"Just like her father," said Erin.

"Do you have a name for her yet?"

"Alice. Kinda like the female version of you."

"I like that. All she needs now is a sweet little Alice-blue gown and she'll be on her way."

"Pick one up on your way home, will you?"

He smiled. "I hope they have one in her size."

On the day Erin and baby Alice were to be released from hospital, Ali had arranged for a carriage and driver to transport them all from the Grace. He stood on the front steps of the hospital, his excitement growing, until he saw the coach turn the corner onto Lemarchant Road and pull up at the entrance. He waved at the driver and ran back inside the hospital, in his excitement almost knocking over a washerwoman carrying a large load of laundry wrapped in a bedsheet. He was rewarded with a scowl and a "Watch where you're going!"

Erin smiled when the driver took her arm and helped her up the step and onto the back seat. Ali got in beside her. She passed Alice to him.

They took the long route back. Erin found the clack-clack of the horses' hoofs on the pavement soothing. She rolled up the isinglass curtain and waved to a woman hanging her laundry out to dry, to a boy riding in a homemade cart being pulled by a Newfoundland dog, and to a young girl doing her best to keep from falling off her bike while munching on a caramel-covered toffee apple. Then Erin sat back, settled in and let the sights, sounds and smells of St. John's engulf her.

Ali, Erin and baby Alice were met at the shop door by Aiden and Sami. They quickly whisked her upstairs to show her the changes they had made to her room. The bedsheets and blanket had been changed. There were pictures on the walls and a lit candle on the bedside table. There was also a brand-new crib next to the bed. Over the crib were hung brightly-coloured, cut-out wooden animals.

"That's so sweet," said Erin. "I could cry."

"Blubber all you want," said Sami.

Shafeek appeared in the doorway.

"May I hold the baby?"

"Of course," said Ali.

Shafeek sat down on the bed next to Erin.

"Babies are such a blessing," he said, kissing Alice on the forehead.

"How's Mom handling it?" asked Ali.

"She's a stubborn woman," Shafeek answered. "Erin, when

you're feeling up to it, we can discuss you getting back to your role here in the house."

Majedah appeared in the doorway. On seeing her, Erin reached over and took Alice from Shafeek. She held her baby close to her breast.

"Such wonderful news!" declared Majedah.

"You have no idea how happy I am to hear you say that," said Ali.

"Yes, the birth of a child is always wonderful news," said Shafeek.

"Come and meet baby Alice," said Aiden.

"No, I mean it's *me* who has wonderful news," said Majedah.

"The last time you said that, you were trying to marry me off to that girl from Lebanon," said Ali.

"I just heard back from The Salvation Army," said Majedah.

"They were so wonderful to Erin and the baby at the Grace," said Ali.

"I don't care about that," said Majedah.

"Majedah...." Shafeek implored.

She pointed at Erin and the baby.

"Since those two obviously can't stay here with us, I asked The Salvation Army Hostel for Wayward Women to take them in."

"You did what?!" asked Ali.

"They just called. They have room for them. They can move in tomorrow!"

The room went silent.

"It's better than living on the streets," shrugged Majedah. "I thought you'd all be excited. With her out of the house, our family won't have to deal with this mess anymore. That woman won't be able to ruin my son's life and our family's reputation."

"Mother, that's disgraceful," said Ali.

"It's her who has brought disgrace on this family. Not me."

Erin stood up, handed Alice to Ali and walked across the room to face her.

"You've said some horrible things about me, Mrs. Abbott. I've mostly remained silent. But know this. I'm not going anywhere. I'm staying here in this house despite you. You will be forced to see me everyday and it will tear at your very soul!"

Majedah stood there with rage in her eyes. Shafeek walked over, took her by the arm and led her out of the room.

12

Prey vs Predator

First, the devastating fire. Then Tommy's acquittal. And now, Lilly's brutal rape. Ruth was despondent. She needed to concentrate her efforts and see to the well-being of her sister.

They all decided not to tell Joseph and Hannah about what had happened to Lilly. They were afraid of how they might react. The last thing anyone needed at that moment was more drama.

Before Lilly was released to her family's care, Ruth had decided her sister could benefit from a couple of weeks in a convalescent home. There, she hoped she could receive the help she needed to get back on her feet and heal her physical, as well as her emotional, wounds.

Lilly wouldn't hear of such a thing. She didn't need anyone's help. What she did need, was not to return to Ruth's and Jacob's house.

Aiden stepped in and took her to a hotel. As soon as he had opened the door to their room, Lilly grabbed the key from his hand and slammed the door in his face.

When Aiden returned the next day, there was no response when he knocked. He waited in the lobby for two hours before giving up and heading home. He did the same the following day as well.

On the third day, Aiden was beside himself. He told the

clerk at the front desk that he had lost the key to his room and requested another.

The room was a complete mess. The bed was unkempt, dirty clothes littered the floor, and scraps of food and empty beer bottles covered the table. But there was no sign of Lilly. He left the room and headed to Ruth's.

Ruth fell back into her chair on hearing the news. She had worried that something like this would happen. She wanted to rush out of the house and go looking for her sister, but Jacob settled her down. Lilly needed space. She needed time.

The next day, Ruth couldn't take it anymore. She headed to the Court House and CC Murphy's office. Aiden and Jacob went with her. Lilly was a missing-person.

<hr>

Lilly didn't have an exact plan. All she knew was that she wasn't going to wait for the police to determine if her version of events was as she had described them. There was no need for the cops. This was between her and Tommy!

She wandered the streets and questioned anyone who would talk to her.

Finally, she found out where Tommy lived. She followed close on his heels, looking for a weakness – an opportunity to destroy him as he had destroyed her. She waited for him outside bars, and followed him down dark alleyways. She saw him pick up a wayward girl on the waterfront and pull her into a deserted doorway. She watched his every move.

In their search for her, Ruth and Jacob combed the downtown and knocked on doors – to no avail. Aiden asked Ali to help. To increase their chances of finding Lilly, the two men decided to search separately.

It was two o'clock in the morning when Ali stumbled upon

her – crouched in a doorway across the street from what Ali recognized as Tommy's house. She looked pale and gaunt. Her clothes were dishevelled and her eyes were rubbed raw. She had the look of a predator locked onto its prey.

He sat down on the ground next to her. They remained like that for several minutes. Silent.

"Can I take you back home?" he asked softly.

"Leave me alone!"

"Everyone's looking for you."

"He thinks he's going to get away with it. I've got news for him."

"Are you sure he's worth it?"

"I'll get him if it takes the rest of my life."

Ali thought for a moment. Then he reached out and turned Lilly's face towards him.

"He'll pay for this one way or another," he reassured her. "If you need my help, all you have to do is ask."

She looked at him as though for the very first time. Then she laid her head on his shoulder.

"Come with me," he said. "I'll take you somewhere where you can get some rest."

The late-night crowd were making their way home when Ali and Lilly arrived at The Continental. He was surprised but relieved when he found Aiden about to enter. Immediately upon seeing them, Aiden rushed forward and threw his arms around Lilly. She didn't respond to his embrace.

"Where did you find her?" he asked.

"Let's go in," answered Ali.

They found Rosie in her office. One look at Lilly, and Rosie knew she needed help. Ali quickly filled her in on what had happened. Rosie wasn't at all surprised Tommy would do such a thing.

"The poor girl," said Rosie.

"This is not the time to be living alone in a hotel room," said Ali. "Can she stay here with you for awhile. She needs someone to watch over her."

Rosie took Lilly's arm. She knew a woman in despair when she saw one.

"She can have the spare room upstairs."

Lilly fell onto the bed. Exhausted, but not deterred.

Over the next few days, Lilly rested, but was largely unresponsive. Rosie did her best to make her as comfortable as possible. Aiden visited several times, but Lilly preferred to be left to herself.

Ruth visited as well. Still Lilly refused to leave the sanctuary she felt at Rosie's. Ruth knew why. Lilly couldn't bring herself to revisit the house where Tommy had so violently attacked her.

Ruth finally convinced Lilly that it would be best for her to spend time at a convalescent home outside town. Ruth had a friend who lived close to the home. She arranged to stay with her and her husband so as to be close to her sister when she needed her. Lilly was there three weeks.

When Lilly's time at the home was ending, Ruth asked Jacob if he had any ideas as to where Lilly could stay. He suggested that they ask his shipmate, Antonio, if Lilly could live in a furnished house he rented out for as long as she needed to. It was currently vacant. The fact that the house was on Bond Street where Ruth and Jacob lived was a happy coincidence. That put Ruth's mind at rest, at least for the time being.

Aiden suggested that he move in with her, but Lilly refused. He did, however, visit regularly.

———

Having finished interrogating Tommy, CC Murphy asked to see everyone. Lilly didn't feel up to it yet, but Aiden told her that if Tommy were ever to be brought to justice, she would eventually have to participate. He was relieved when she finally agreed.

The next afternoon, Ruth and Jacob walked down the street and into the house where Lilly was now living. CC Murphy arrived shortly afterwards. When they were all seated, he launched right in.

"I'm so glad you're all here. Especially you, Lilly. You're finally back where you belong. With your family...."

"Have you talked to Tommy?" interrupted Ruth.

"We questioned him for a couple of days. He had his lawyer with him most of the time."

"What did he have to say for himself?" asked Aiden.

"His alibi was that he was at the family cabin on the Salmonier Line when the incident occurred. His mother was with him. They didn't get back into town until much later that night. We questioned his mother and she corroborated that. We have our suspicions as to the veracity of her testimony, but no proof."

"They're obviously lying," said Ruth.

"We couldn't find anything to indicate that Tommy was ever in the house," said CC Murphy.

He turned to Lilly.

"You said you pulled his mask off, but we couldn't find it. You said he tied your hands behind your back, but we couldn't find any rope. You also said he taped your eyes and mouth, but we couldn't find any tape either."

"He must have taken that stuff with him when he left," said Jacob.

"His lawyer says that's a sign that Lilly's either lying or exaggerating," said CC Murphy.

"Do you think Lilly's lying?" asked Aiden.

"My opinion doesn't matter. It's what a jury would think that matters. A jury found him not guilty before, didn't they."

"That doesn't mean he didn't set that fire though, does it," said Ruth.

"That's exactly my point," said CC Murphy. "Tommy's lawyer now says Lilly probably didn't see who did it at all. That she blamed Tommy only to get back at him for not being found guilty for the fire. The lawyer's even saying that it could have been consensual and it got out of hand."

"That's preposterous!" said Aiden.

"Lilly, are you one hundred percent certain it was Tommy Chan?" asked CC Murphy.

Lilly looked at him with an icy, chilling stare.

"I hope he rots in hell!"

"Are you going to press charges?" CC Murphy asked.

"Of course we are," said Ruth.

"Remember, we have no hard evidence," said CC Murphy. "It will come down to Lilly's word against his. From my experience with cases like this, the burden of proof will definitely be on Lilly."

"That's so unfair," said Aiden.

"I know," said CC Murphy. "But that's how it is."

"What would you suggest we do?" asked Jacob.

CC Murphy turned towards Lilly.

"You have a stark choice, Lilly. Either you put this whole thing out of your mind and not press charges, or you go ahead and put yourself through what will likely be a long, gut-wrenching trial. Questions will be asked about any previous sexual experiences, real or imagined. Private details of your body will be discussed. Boyfriends past and present will be fair game."

"He'll get off scot-free if we don't press charges, won't he," said Ruth.

CC Murphy rose from his chair and sat on the end of the couch next to Lilly.

"You don't have to decide right now," he said. "We'll talk again in a few days."

"Where's Tommy now?" asked Aiden.

"We had to release him," said CC Murphy. He rose and walked towards the door.

"Someone has to stop him," hissed Lilly.

———

A few minutes after CC Murphy left, Joseph entered. He had heard that Lilly had rented a house close to where Ruth and Jacob lived. He wanted to know if he could help in any way. He had been surprised to see CC Murphy leaving the house.

"I just saw Murphy outside. Is anything going on?"

"Nothing, Pop," said Ruth. "He just had a few questions about a case he's working on."

This raised Joseph's suspicions, as did the uneasy look on everyone's face.

"Are you hiding something from me? If so, I'd like to know what it is."

"We didn't want to upset you with more bad news," said Ruth.

"You've been through enough," added Jacob.

"I'm the head of this family. And demand to be treated as such!" declared Joseph.

"You better sit down, Pop," said Ruth. "This is going to upset you."

"I don't want to sit down!"

Ruth braced herself.

"A few weeks ago, we found Lilly unconscious and naked on the floor in the front room. She'd been brutally violated."

"What?!" gasped Joseph.

"Tommy Chan did it," added Aiden.

Joseph's face turned blood red. Every nerve in his body jolted through him. He made for the door. Jacob stood in his path.

"Joseph...."

"Get out of my way! That bastard can't get away with this!"

Joseph tried to push past him, but Jacob took hold of him.

"If you're determined to do this, at least let me come with you."

Joseph shoved him aside. Jacob followed him out the door. Ruth turned to Lilly.

"Will you be okay here with Aiden for a little while? I'm going to go with them. I want to make sure Pop doesn't get into any trouble."

"I'm not staying here," said Lilly. "That son of a bitch needs to be taught a lesson!"

She walked past Ruth with determination in her step. Aiden followed them both out the door.

On their way to Tommy's, they passed Hannah's house.

"Wait here," said Joseph. He rushed inside.

Moments later, he emerged shoving something into his overcoat pocket. Hannah followed him out of the house.

"Joseph, don't!"

Her call having been ignored, she followed him and the others down the street.

Joseph was the first to reach Tommy's house. He knocked hard. Tommy opened the door. He didn't even have time to speak before Joseph pushed him backwards. The others arrived immediately after.

"You slimy, good-for-nothing bastard!" Joseph was shouting. "You're not going to get away with this!"

"Whatever are you talking about?" asked Tommy with an innocent look.

"Don't play dumb!" said Ruth. "You know exactly what he's talking about."

"So I burned down your bloody business," said Tommy nonchalantly. "Big deal. Anyway, I'm the real victim here 'cause I didn't get much for that crappy machinery and stuff you had out back. You still owe me, Rabbi!"

"You're a loathsome man," said Jacob.

"Shut up, you," said Tommy dismissively. He pointed at Lilly.

"Where have I seen you before?" he asked while rubbing his chin. "Oh, yeah, now I remember."

Lilly tried to run at him, but Aiden held her back.

Tommy, meanwhile, walked over to the table, sat down and resumed the game of solitaire he had been playing.

"Besides, ya got no proof, do ya? The cops hit me with everything they had, but I had answers for it all. She's gonna have to like it or lump it."

"To hell with that," said Joseph. "I don't need proof!"

He reached into his coat pocket and pulled out a revolver. He pointed it at Tommy. Jacob tried to grab his arm, but Joseph pulled it away.

"Pop, what are you doing?" yelled Ruth. "Don't be foolish. He's not worth it!"

Tommy looked up and saw the gun pointed at him.

"Yeah, right. Gonna shoot me are ya? In front of all these

witnesses? Go back where you came from, Jew."

Joseph walked closer to Tommy and pointed the gun at his face. His breathing was shallow and his hand was shaking.

"Look at you," said Tommy. "Ya can't even hold the gun straight. Piss off!"

"Joseph, please give me the gun," said Hannah nervously.

"Don't worry about him," said Tommy. "He don't got the nerve."

Lilly ran up to Joseph and yanked the gun out of his hand. "But I do!"

She pointed the gun directly at Tommy's heart and pulled the trigger. The force of the bullet pushed him backwards. Lilly calmly walked up to him and looked down. She showed no emotion. She slowly put the gun in her pocket and headed out the door.

—

Early the following morning, Ruth received a call from CC Murphy. He wanted to see all of them in his office the following day at four o'clock. They were on edge. All except Lilly, who felt calm. Almost serene.

They had been worried about Lilly since the rape. Now they had a murder to deal with.

They all gathered at Lilly's, where Ruth did her best to settle them down. Despite how distraught they felt, they had to get their stories straight. Lilly must be protected at all costs. There must be no divergence of accounts.

The next day, CC Murphy ushered them into his office. Much to their surprise, Ali was standing just inside the door. Ruth halted in her stride when she saw him, but Jacob guided her towards the seats in front of the desk. There was a uniformed officer, motionless, off to the side.

"I hope you don't mind," said CC Murphy. "I asked Ali to be here as well. I want to get to the bottom of this."

Aiden, for one, was happy Ali was there. He had called his brother the day before and told him what had taken place at Tommy's. Ali was shocked that Lilly had done such a thing. But he understood why.

When they were settled, CC Murphy continued.

"Tommy Chan has been shot. His mother found him in his house the day before yesterday about seven o'clock. Not long after I talked to all of you at Lilly's, actually. The last time he was seen was about four o'clock. Do you mind me asking what you all did after I left?"

"Pop and Hannah arrived just after," said Ruth. "Lilly was upset about what you had said about pressing charges."

"We couldn't leave her alone at a time like that," said Joseph.

"We asked them to stay for dinner," added Aiden.

"Did all of you stay?" asked CC Murphy.

"Till about nine o'clock," answered Aiden.

"So, all of you were together till nine?" asked CC Murphy.

"That's right," answered Hannah.

"You do realize all of you have motives, don't you."

"But not the opportunity," said Ruth.

"Well, that's not exactly true, is it," said CC Murphy. "We have witnesses who said they saw all of you going into Tommy's house around five o'clock."

"That's not possible," said Joseph.

"I'm going to tell you what I think happened," said CC Murphy. "Lilly was traumatized. She left the house and headed to Tommy's. You all followed after her. She confronted Tommy and shot him. Did I leave anything out?"

Everyone was caught off guard. They looked to Ruth for reassurance.

"Your silence speaks volumes," said CC Murphy.

He rose from his chair and went to stand in front of Lilly.

"Lilly Rosenberg, I'm arresting you...."

Jacob jumped up.

"Wait a minute...."

"...for the murder of Tommy Chan," he intoned. "Constable, put the handcuffs on."

Ruth and Joseph rushed towards Lilly, trying to protect her. The constable stood in their way.

Suddenly, Ali spoke up.

"I shot him."

They all turned to face him.

"They're just trying to protect me," said Ali calmly.

"Be careful what you say, Ali," cautioned CC Murphy.

"Joseph and Hannah didn't go to Lilly's alone after you left. I went with them. We all went to Tommy's after. We wanted to get him to confess to the fire and the murder. Unknown to us, Joseph had a revolver. He threatened Tommy at gunpoint. Lilly took the gun from her father and pointed it at Tommy. I rushed towards her. There was a scuffle. I grabbed the gun. But as I pulled it from her hand, it went off. Tommy fell to the floor."

There was silence in the room again. Finally, CC Murphy spoke up.

"Why didn't you come to the Constabulary?" he asked.

"We were scared," said Ali. "None of us have any experience with this kind of thing."

CC Murphy scanned their faces.

"Is that what happened? Would you all swear to that?"

They looked at each other. Joseph spoke up.

"Yes. It was an accident."

One after another, they all nodded.

CC Murphy was sworn to uphold the law, and he took his solemn duty seriously, mitigating circumstances notwithstanding. Everyone, no matter how vile – even someone as vile as Tommy Chan – deserved equal treatment under the law. However, not every case required the same level of urgency. It wasn't that CC Murphy was lazy: just that, in his experience, some cases called for greater circumspection. He began to think this might be one of those cases.

"Stay close to home," he cautioned. "I'll surely have further questions."

As they were leaving, Lilly spoke up.

"Is he dead?"

"Yes, Lilly. He's dead."

CC Murphy couldn't swear to it, but he was fairly certain he saw a Mona Lisa smile come to Lilly's face.

After Joseph and Hannah had made their weary way home, Ruth and Jacob were also about to leave. Aiden was standing at the door. He reached out his hand towards Ruth.

"Why don't you stay a little. I'm sure Lilly would like some time alone with you."

"Aiden's right," said Jacob sympathetically.

He patted Aiden on the back and left.

Aiden said goodnight to the two sisters. Lilly sat down on the couch next to Ruth.

"I didn't want to say this in front of Jacob. But I'm pretty sure I know why Ali did what he did."

"That was very foolish of him."

"So why do you think he did it?"

"To protect you, obviously."

"Think harder."

13

Lay Your Burdens Down

The next morning, Erin returned to the house from her daily constitutional. She had taken to going on walks through Bannerman Park. She enjoyed the quiet time with her baby. The fresh air and open spaces were a welcome change from the charged atmosphere at the Abbotts'. The snubs and chilly reception she often received from the neighbours she would pass along the way had become routine and no longer upset her.

She found Ali in the living room. She had no idea what he had done the day before, so she was in good spirits.

Ali had spent a lot of time thinking throughout the night. Although he felt pangs of guilt for having lied to CC Murphy, his mind was mostly at rest. He knew he had acted rashly. But he also felt he had done the right thing. Lilly would not suffer more than she already had. She could now get her life back in order, as could everyone else.

Ali asked Erin to come in. No sooner had they settled into conversation than Majedah poked her head around the door. She had a big smile on her face. Ali was pleased to see her in such good spirits.

"Ali, have you seen my necklace?" she asked. "The one with the small diamonds and rubies your father gave me for our twenty-fifth wedding anniversary."

Ali replied, doing his best not to let his mother or Erin know the strain he was under.

"Maybe Sami borrowed it," he smiled weakly. "He always said it matched his eyes."

"I'll take another look," said his mother.

Shafeek was in the kitchen putting the finishing touches to a lunch he had assembled for the family. He called out. Aiden and Sami came running down the stairs and into the kitchen. Aiden gave Ali a quick, surreptitious nod. Ali acknowledged. Shafeek walked into the living room where Ali and Erin were seated. Erin had Alice in her arms.

"Lunch is served," said Shafeek. "You too, Erin."

He called upstairs to his wife.

"I'll be down in a minute," she shouted. "Start without me."

The conversation at lunch was mostly about the baby. Erin was heartened by the fact that all four men expressed interest in the minutiae of Alice's daily routine. She took great comfort in that, and felt herself lucky to have such welcome support. Majedah finally came into the kitchen. Aiden fought hard to keep the conversation light.

"Lucky for you there's still food left," he joked.

"Shafeek, do you know where that necklace you gave me last year is?" asked Majedah.

"I suppose you've already looked in all the usual places," he answered.

"I've been searching for it for days," said Majedah.

"Sami, own up to it," kidded Ali, taking Aiden's light-hearted lead.

Majedah pointed at Erin, but didn't look at her.

"Shafeek, ask her if she stole it."

"Majedah, not again," he implored.

She put her hand into her dress pocket, pulled out the

necklace and held it high in the air.

"Look what I just found in her room!"

"This is ridiculous," said Erin.

She stood up, and with her baby in her arms, she made for the door. Majedah blocked her way.

"If you don't leave this house in the next twenty-four hours, I'm going to call in the Constabulary and charge you with theft!"

Erin forcibly pushed her aside and rushed out. Ali went after her. He found her in her room.

"I can't believe Mom would sink that low."

"Ali, I can't continue like this. I thought I could make it work, but...."

"I'll have a word with Mom and Dad. We'll...."

"It's too late for that. God only knows what she's capable of. She won't stop until she gets rid of me."

"What are we going to do?"

"I don't know about you, but I'm going to pack my things. I'm going home to Mom and Dad and throw myself on their mercy."

"You're taking Alice with you?"

"You can't take care of her yourself, can you."

Ali reached out and took Alice in his arms. "I'm going to miss the two of you."

"Not as much as we're going to miss you."

Erin spent the rest of the day packing her things. She said goodbye to Shafeek, Aiden and Sami. They were upset at the thought of her leaving, but knew deep down it was the only alternative. Majedah would never give up.

That night, Erin bundled Alice up in her baby carriage and

headed out the door. She had one more thing to do.

At first, her pace was hurried. Then it turned to a pensive amble. She knew that what she was about to do was the right thing. If she didn't carry through, she was afraid she would regret it for the rest of her life.

Erin paused in front of the door and took a deep breath. She knocked. The door opened.

"I hope I'm not disturbing you," she asked tentatively.

Ruth shut the door as quickly as she had opened it.

The last thing Ruth wanted to see at that moment was Erin and the child she had had with Ali. It only served to remind her of the hurt he had caused her, and how she had dealt with the aftermath. It drove what Ali had done in CC Murphy's office entirely out of her head. Her anger rose to the surface.

Erin knocked again. Ruth flung the door open.

"Of all the gall!"

"I think you and I should talk," said Erin.

"I know what happened. I don't need to talk to you."

"You can hate me all you want, but I would appreciate it if you would just hear me out. Then I promise you'll never hear from me again."

Ruth left the door open and walked into the front room. Erin lifted the baby carriage up over the stoop and into the hallway. Ruth was in the front room sitting on the couch. A low fire in the fireplace tempered the cold drafts seeping through from the outside. It added a welcome soft, warm glow to the surroundings – much in contrast to Ruth's mood.

Erin sat down in an armchair opposite her.

"I'm leaving St. John's for good tomorrow," said Erin. "I'm going home to Witless Bay. But I can't leave without talking to you first."

"Running away?"

"I don't blame you for hating me. I would feel the same way if I were in your position."

"You're not in my position though, are you."

"No, I'm not. I would appreciate it if you'd let me offer something in the way of an explanation."

"What's to explain? He found you easy prey and took advantage of the situation."

"It wasn't that Ali took advantage of me, Ruth. The truth is, I took advantage of him."

"I don't believe that."

"Ali was furious with his mother when she tried to marry him off to that young girl from Lebanon. She wouldn't listen to reason and went ahead with the wedding plans without his approval."

"You're just lying for him."

"I have no reason to protect him. I'm telling you the truth."

Ruth shook her head, but Erin continued.

"When his mother told him that the girl was on her way from Lebanon with her father, he lost it and swore revenge on his mother. I heard everything that happened that night at the house. I saw my chance. I walked into Ali's room and made myself available to him. If he was thinking at all in that moment, he was thinking that if he had sex with a lowly maid such as myself, his mother would be disgusted, and the girl and her father would see him as untrustworthy and unfit as a husband."

"So, you're saying he had sex with you to get back at his mother?" Ruth asked incredulously.

"His guard was down and I took advantage. He was not expecting it. I was the first thing available, and he's regretted it ever since."

"That's hard to believe."

"I made the first move. I seduced him, not the other way around. I'm the one who is to blame, not Ali. I loved him and I saw it as my best opportunity to have him to myself. It backfired. He doesn't love me. He never did. He loved you. He still does."

"And now he's deserting you, just like he deserted me."

"It's not his fault. He has done all he could to protect me and my baby from his mother. But she has made my life miserable since Alice was born. She even accused me of stealing her necklace. She threatened to call in the Constabulary. I can't live there anymore."

"I won't be sorry to see you go."

Erin ignored it. "Ali's a good man, Ruth. He would make a great father and great husband to the woman he loves."

Ruth turned and stared blankly at the fire.

"Ruth, he's devastated by what he did to you."

Ruth turned back to face Erin.

Erin sat forward in her chair and looked directly at her.

"Ruth, I'll say one more thing. Please hear me out. Ali and I made one – only one – very big mistake. I know you are the one who's been hurt by it the most. I don't presume to know how your relationship with your husband is. But, if you were a free woman, my advice to you would be to forgive Ali and give him a second chance."

"I don't need any advice from you, Erin."

Erin rose from the couch and took hold of the carriage.

"If I can't have his love, the woman he truly loves should."

Erin walked to the door, opened it and stepped into the night.

The next morning, Ali and Aiden came to Erin's room. Ali

helped her dress Alice. Aiden carried her suitcases down the stairs.

When they got to the store, Shafeek and Sami were standing at the front door waiting for them. Sami walked up to her and gave her a hug. Aiden did the same. For his part, Shafeek kissed her on both cheeks and surreptitiously stuffed an envelope under Alice's blanket. He whispered in her ear.

"A little something to help with the expenses."

Erin kissed him back. Then she and Ali turned and left.

As they made their way down the street, Ali and Erin failed to notice Majedah standing at the living-room window watching their every step. She got what she wanted. What didn't occur to her was what she might have lost in the process.

As she was about to board the bus, Ali gave Erin one last hug, and kissed Alice goodbye. He tried to accept blame for what had happened. Erin would hear none of it. She kissed him affectionately and sat at the rear of the bus.

As the bus pulled out of the station, she could see Ali getting smaller and smaller. It reminded her of an earlier, more innocent time, when she had seen her parents slowly disappear as the bus took her from Witless Bay to St. John's. However, this time she wouldn't need a hand-written note attached to her jacket identifying her as Erin O'Shea. Where she was going, they knew her, and she knew them. She hoped that her parents would put their love for her above their long-held notions of right and wrong and accept Alice as their own. She wasn't a woman prone to prayer. But if there were ever a time when prayer could serve its purpose, it was then. She held Alice close to her chest and closed her eyes.

One week later, CC Murphy was in his office waiting for

them to arrive. Ruth, Joseph, Lilly, Aiden, Jacob and Hannah walked in. Ali followed a few steps behind. He stood off to one side. The others took seats in front of the desk. CC Murphy took a deep breath.

"About Tommy Chan's murder."

He looked at them for any sign of nervousness.

"I received the final report," he continued.

"What does it say?" asked Ruth.

"I've been a cop for over thirty years and have a nose for this kind of thing."

"And what does your nose tell you?" asked Joseph.

"I don't believe Ali's story. We have two witnesses who say they saw Ali at The Continental at the time of the murder. Instead of all of you covering for him, I think it's him who's covering for all of you. Especially you, Lilly. I think you killed Tommy. And deliberately. All the rest of you are accomplices to a crime. Or, at the very least, gave tacit permission."

"And what are you going to do about it?" asked Aiden.

"Without firm proof, there's not much I can do," said CC Murphy.

"He got what he deserved," said Lilly.

"Yes, maybe so," said CC Murphy. "But taking situations like this into your own hands is not a recipe for a clean conscience."

"My conscience is completely clean," said Lilly.

"I have no doubt it is," said CC Murphy.

"Are we free to go?" asked Hannah.

"Freedom is in the eye of the beholder," said CC Murphy. "And so are mistakes. You wouldn't want to be caught on the wrong side of what you see as right."

"What does that mean?" asked Jacob.

"That's a question you all have to ask yourselves. Not me."

Jacob was heading out to sea again. He packed the usual things. His uniforms, personal clothes, toiletries, binoculars, radio, a few mementos from his parents and his childhood, as well as a photo of Ruth and himself. But he was unusually apprehensive about leaving town this time. So much had happened since the last time he had been at sea. Especially Tommy's death at the hands of Lilly. Everyone's nerves had been on edge at first, but as the days slipped by, so did the memory.

Ruth and Lilly decided they couldn't let Jacob leave without a proper send off. He had been a stalwart and was the levelling force whenever emotions seemed to be getting out of control.

They chose a restaurant directly across the street from the wharf from which Jacob's ship was scheduled to leave. They served local fare, and pan-fried cod was their specialty. The conversation – at first reflective – turned lively and light-hearted. But Ali was the elephant in the room. Jacob and Lilly knew Ruth still hadn't forgiven him. They weren't sure she ever would.

They were enjoying themselves so much that Jacob lost track of time. When he looked at his watch and realized it was almost nine o'clock, he quickly called for the bill and grabbed his duffle bag. They made their way across the street and onto the wharf. Several of Jacob's shipmates were also there saying goodbye to loved ones.

"Be safe, Jacob," said Ruth affectionately.

Lilly gently poked him in the ribs.

"And don't have too much fun, hear!"

Ruth walked up to him and spoke softly in his ear.

"Thanks for always being there for me."

"And for me," added Lilly.

Jacob hugged both of them.

"There's no other place I'd rather be."

A man walked up behind Jacob and nudged him with his shoulder.

"Smarten up, sailor!"

"Hi, Antonio," said Ruth.

"Sorry to drag your husband away from you. The sea's a-callin'."

He blew kisses to Ruth and Lilly and slung his arm around Jacob's shoulder. The two men headed towards the ship.

Ruth and Lilly remained silent for a while. Lilly broke the silence.

"Now ... don't bite my head off, Ruth. But Aiden told me the band has finally got back to playing. They're at Rosie's tonight. He asked us to drop by."

Ruth turned and walked away. Lilly caught up to her.

"I know what you're thinking. Yes! Ali will be there. He and Aiden could use our support, especially after all we've been through."

Ruth turned again. Lilly took hold of her arm. She could feel the tension running through Ruth's body.

"It'll do us good. I can't go there on my own. We'll just stay for one set. Then we'll leave. I promise."

—

Rosie was at a table near the entrance of The Continental deep in conversation with Ali, when there was a commotion at the door. Skeeter was giving Ruth and Lilly a hard time about coming in. Noticing Ruth, Ali made his excuses to Rosie and retreated to the comparative safety of the stage.

"Cool it, Skeeter!" shouted Rosie.

Lilly pushed past him, pulling Ruth behind her. She sat down next to Rosie.

"I was in pretty rough shape the last time I saw you," said Lilly. "Thanks for that."

"Glad to see you on the mend," said Rosie.

She elbowed Lilly in the arm and gave her a knowing look. "I bet you're all broke up about Tommy getting snuffed out like that", she continued.

Lilly shrugged.

Rosie looked around the room, in case someone might be listening, then leaned in.

"I don't suppose you had anything to do with it? Not that I'd blame ya if ya did."

Lilly smiled but didn't take the bait. She stood and took Ruth's arm.

As they moved to an empty table, Rosie called out, "Drinks on me tonight!"

On stage, the band was starting its first set. Ali's heart wasn't in it to begin with, and when he saw Ruth and Lilly chatting at the back of the hall, he became overwhelmed with nostalgia. He thought of all the good times and ignored the bad. He recalled when he and Ruth had first met at Hall's Horse Wagon Repair Shop shortly after she had thrown food to him while he was lying on his bed. They were nine years old. She cared for him even then, as he did for her. He still cared for her. But he couldn't break the barrier she had set up to protect herself from any further harm he could cause her. How had it come to this? He knew exactly how. But was there anything he could do about it?

For her part, Ruth was glad when the first set was over. She was anxious to get home. Lilly wanted to stay for one more drink, but Ruth was determined. Ali's presence had made her tense. She worried that he would take her being there as an invitation to try to smooth things over. She wasn't ready for that yet. She might never be ready.

She rose from her chair and grabbed her coat. Ali saw that as his chance. He jumped down from the stage and approached.

"You're not leaving already?" he asked tentatively. "Can't we be cordial at least?"

"I've said all I want to say to you," replied Ruth.

"Aiden told me you've written a new song, Ali," Lilly interjected. "He said it's very beautiful. You should play it for us."

"Only if Ruth will sing it with me. I can understand why she wouldn't, though."

"Lilly, it's time to leave," said Ruth.

Ali didn't want to push things. He had said what he wanted to say. The rest was up to Ruth. He turned and made his way back to the stage.

Lilly faced Ruth. "Maybe it's time you stopped feeling sorry for yourself, Ruth. You two have been friends for so long. It won't kill you to sing with him."

"Put yourself in my shoes for a minute, Lilly," Ruth said angrily.

"I have. And what I see is a man who stepped up to help your sister when she needed help most. Without him, I'd be in jail right now! Do you understand that?"

She let her words sink in for a moment. Then she continued, with a softer tone.

"If you won't do it for him ... do it for me."

—

Ali was seated at the piano when Ruth and Lilly walked onto the stage. Though he had his back to them, he could hear them approach. The band was milling about. Lilly took a quick glance at Aiden, who pointed towards Ali. She walked over, took the sheet music off the piano and handed it to Ruth.

"It's a duet," said Ali, still with his back to them. He played
a brief intro and then started singing.

I am a man seeking that someone.
You tell me maybe I might as well reach for the sun.
If you looked my way, I'd answer the call.
I would kiss your cheek, and not speak at all.
If you loved me,
you'd see it in my eyes, if you loved me.
If you loved me, you'd feel it in the touch of my hand.
Doubt wouldn't stand a chance if you loved me.

Ali stopped singing. The last chord hung in the air.
Lilly leaned in and whispered in Ruth's ear.
"Come on, Ruth. Show 'em what ya got!"
Ruth took a quick look at the sheet music, drew a deep
breath and started to sing.

I am a woman fumbling for romance.
You tell me maybe I'm striking the wrong stance.
One thing for sure, when love comes to call,
There will be no need to speak at all.
If you loved me,
I'd see it in your eyes, if you loved me.
If you loved me,
I'd feel it in the touch of your hand.
Doubt wouldn't stand a chance if you loved me.

Ali joined in at the bridge. He took the higher harmony.

We're not so different you and I.
We both reach for the sky.

You wear your heart upon your sleeve.
God only knows what we can achieve.

The band took up their lead. Ali rose from the piano, picked up the trumpet sitting on top of the piano and played an eight-bar verse break. Ruth sang the rest with a quiver in her voice. Ali played along on the trumpet.

One thing for sure, when love comes to call,
There will be no need to speak at all.

Ali took his place at the piano. Both he and Ruth sang together again.

For if you loved me, I'd see it in your eyes,
If you loved me.
If you loved me,
you'd feel it in the touch of my hand.
If you loved me, you'd look in front of you,
And then you'd know our love is true,
And I'm the only one for you,
If you loved me.

The audience erupted in applause – including Rosie. On stage, however, there was silence.

Ali turned around and looked at Ruth. It took a while before she spoke.

"Did you have a particular girl in mind when you wrote that song?" she asked.

"Yes, I did," answered Ali carefully.

Ruth turned, descended from the stage, took her coat and left the club. Ali glanced at Lilly and Aiden, then hurried after her. He caught up to her halfway down the street.

"Leave me alone!" she cried.

She picked up her pace. Ali followed, a few paces behind, all the way to her front door, where he caught up again as she was fumbling with her keys.

"I can't live without you," said Ali. "It's tearing me up inside."

"Please don't," pleaded Ruth, with her back to him.

"Do you really love Jacob?"

"Don't ask me that."

"It's time to stop pretending."

Ali grabbed her and spun her around. Facing him, Ruth felt herself yielding.

Ali kissed her. Ruth kissed him back. Then she turned the doorknob and went into the house, leaving the door open. Ali followed and closed it behind him. Ruth calmly took his hand and led him upstairs. She walked towards the bed and slowly laid back. He gently lowered himself onto her until she could feel his full weight pressed against her.

She hadn't realized how much she'd been waiting for this moment. Jacob had given her all she could have ever hoped for, except the passion she so desperately needed.

———

Lilly and Aiden spent a lot of the night talking about Ruth and Ali. Lilly worried that she might have pushed Ruth too far in encouraging her to sing with him, though it did warm her heart. Aiden was more concerned about what had happened after Ali ran after Ruth when she rushed out of the club.

The next morning, Lilly rose early. She decided to have breakfast with her sister down the street.

She let herself into Ruth's house. To surprise her, she set about making breakfast. She was about to lay bacon in the frying pan when Ruth came in and sat at the table.

"Mornin', sis," Lilly said. "I got bacon and eggs coming up. Wanna a cup of tea?"

"Lilly, about last night...."

"I hope you're not upset with me about the song."

"I have something to...."

They heard the stairs creak. Lilly turned towards the hallway.

"Didn't Jacob leave last night?"

Ali entered, quite obviously having just got out of bed. Lilly looked at each of them in turn.

"So ... does this mean what I think it means?" she asked.

Ruth and Ali silently looked at each other.

Lilly walked over and sat next to her sister. Ruth rested her head on Lilly's shoulder.

"What will we do about Jacob?" she sighed. Lilly could hear the sadness in her voice.

"The real question is ... do you love him?"

"Lilly, I love Ali. And he loves me. We've always loved each other and always will."

"It's better to live the truth than live the lie, Ruth," said Lilly.

"I've been a foolish woman, Lilly. I married Jacob to get back at Ali. I knew I didn't love him. The truth is ... I took advantage of the love he had for me."

"Does Jacob know that?" asked Lilly.

"I hate to say this, Lilly, but Jacob and I have never had sex. Even though we were husband and wife, I couldn't bring myself to consummate our marriage."

"How is that possible?" asked Lilly in astonishment.

"He never put pressure on me. He left the decision to me."

"What are you going to do when he comes back?"

"We haven't thought that far ahead," said Ali.

"Maybe it's time," said Lilly.

Lilly needed something to take her mind off everything. She had promised her father and Hannah that she would help open the shop that morning, and she didn't want to disappoint them. She had to collect her composure and be her usual self, or her father would suspect something. She called Aiden and told him about Ruth and Ali. Aiden wasn't surprised. But, like Lilly, he was concerned about the implications.

Joseph and Hannah were in the shop getting ready for what they hoped would be a busy day. They had kept a low profile since the day in CC Murphy's office when he had deduced what had really happened the night Tommy had been shot.

It had been a very trying time for Joseph and Hannah. In his heart of hearts, he knew that if he hadn't brought his gun to Tommy's, the whole thing wouldn't have turned out the way it did. He blamed himself for what Lilly had done. If there hadn't been a gun, there wouldn't have been a shooting. Hannah refused to let him dwell on this. She had no intention of spending her days sopping up spilled milk.

Joseph was cutting patterns and Hannah was sewing in the back room when Lilly arrived.

"Isn't Ruth with you?" asked Joseph. "She said she'd be in early."

Lilly fidgeted with a pattern on the counter.

"She told me to tell you she isn't feeling well and is going to sleep in," said Lilly. "She'll probably be in this afternoon."

"Can you go to the back room and help Hannah?" asked Joseph. "She's got her hands full."

Ruth never did show up that day. She stayed home with Ali talking through what the effect might be on everyone when they discovered what she and he had done. Jacob was loved by all. No one would ever want to see him hurt, including them.

They feared that those who loved him might judge them too harshly and have trouble accepting it as just and righteous. They understood the nature of the love they had for each other. But would everyone else?

Part V

14

Strength in Adversity

It was a quiet afternoon at The Continental. Rosie was in her office. Ali was seated at the piano. He found solace in letting himself drift off in thought. He hadn't seen his mother and father since Erin had returned to Witless Bay.

Since the night Ruth and Ali had reaffirmed their love for each other, Ali had taken to living at the club. He was appreciative of the fact that Rosie didn't ask too many questions – mainly because she wasn't really looking for answers.

The front door opened and Aiden entered.

"You're early," said Ali. "Band practice isn't until tomorrow."

Aiden climbed onto the stage and came up to the piano.

"Lilly told me about you and Ruth," he said.

"I figured she would. It's a lot to unravel."

"I'm here for you if you need me."

"Thanks, Aiden."

Rosie walked out of her office.

"Hey, Rosie," called Aiden. "Don't know if it's appropriate, but condolences about Tommy."

"Tell that to someone who cares."

Aiden handed an envelope to Ali. "A telegram came to the store for you."

Rosie approached the stage. "What's it say?" she asked. "World War Two has erupted in Europe?"

"It's from Jacob," said Ali. "He'll be back tomorrow."

"You better tell Ruth," said Aiden, with urgency in his voice.

"It says here he doesn't want me to tell her. He wants it to be a surprise. He asked me if I'd be free to meet him at the wharf."

Rosie addressed Ali. "You can tell me to mind my own business. But how are things going between you and Jacob's wife? You know, that old girlfriend of yours?"

"You're right," said Ali. "Mind your own business."

Ali arrived shortly after Jacob's ship had docked. Since Jacob had put to sea, Ali had dreaded the day Jacob would come face to face with what had happened between himself and Ruth. Ali and Ruth had talked about it several times. They couldn't find a solution that wouldn't result in Jacob being hurt. Neither of them wanted to do that.

When he saw Jacob walk down the gangplank and come his way, Ali put on his best smile.

"Great! So you got my telegram," said Jacob. "Thanks for coming."

"Wouldn't miss it for the world," said Ali.

"Does Ruth know I'm here?"

"I didn't say a word. Let me help you with your bags."

They started their walk towards Jacob's house.

"How's Lilly?" asked Jacob intently.

"She's got her revenge. Now she can get on with the rest of her life."

"That was an amazing thing you did, Ali. Protecting her like that. You're the best friend anyone could ever hope for."

Ali changed the subject.

"How was your voyage?"

Jacob recounted stories of life at sea and of how he had missed everyone. Ali wasn't listening. His focus was on not giving any hint of his new relationship with Ruth.

Jacob's pace picked up as he saw his house come into view.

Lilly and Aiden were visiting Ruth. She had invited them for dinner in Jacob's absence.

Jacob had intended to walk right in, but decided it would be more dramatic to knock instead. Lilly answered the door. Jacob was beaming.

"Surprise!"

Lilly's eyes popped wide open. She leaned back in disbelief. "What are you doing here?"

"I live here!" said Jacob. "Surely you haven't forgotten."

Lilly turned to Ali.

"Did you know about this?"

"Where's that wife of mine?" called Jacob.

He moved past Lilly, catching Ruth as she came into the hall.

"What are you doing here?" she asked, hoping that Jacob wouldn't notice her nervousness.

He dropped his bags and gave her a bear hug.

"Glad to see me?"

"Of course. But ... you should have let me know."

"He told me not to tell you," said Ali.

"So you knew?"

"He wanted to surprise you."

"Well, he got his wish," said Ruth.

"How's everyone holding up?" asked Jacob. "I wish I could have been here to help out."

"Why don't I leave you guys to it?" said Ali. "You've got a lot to talk about...."

"No, stay!" said Ruth and grabbed Ali's arm.

They all made their way to the front room.

"Stay here," said Jacob excitedly. "I want to go upstairs and change first. I have something for all of you."

The rest remained seated in the front room, lost in thought.

"Ruth, are you going to tell him about you and Ali?" asked Aiden.

"Of course," said Ruth. "But he just got back."

"No time like the present," said Lilly.

"Let him settle in first."

"It should come from you," said Lilly.

"It'll break his heart," said Ruth.

They heard Jacob coming down the stairs. He walked into the room. He was still in uniform.

"I thought you were going to change," said Ali.

Jacob extended his hand towards Ruth. He was holding something.

"What's a man's razor and shaving brush doing in our bathroom?" he asked, and held them up.

There was complete silence in the room.

"Well? Someone say something!"

"Jacob, sit down," said Ruth.

Jacob's eyes pleaded with Ruth.

Ali spoke up. "Ruth and I wanted to tell you but...."

"Are you trying to say what I think you're trying to say?" asked Jacob.

"We didn't plan this, Jacob," said Ruth.

"Ruth, how could you?"

"Whatever you do, please don't blame Ruth," said Ali.

"Who should I blame then?" asked Jacob.

Again there was silence.

"Maybe I should blame myself," said Jacob.

He sat, put his hands to his face and wept. Lilly hurried

over, knelt beside him and hugged his knees. Ruth came to sit beside them.

"I know you don't love me, Ruth," he said. "But this?"

The full impact of what she had done overcame her.

"I should never have done this to you," said Ruth. "You've been the kindest and most understanding husband a woman could ever hope for."

"And in return I get this?"

"I wouldn't blame you for hating me," said Ruth.

"That's the problem, Ruth," he said. "I don't hate you. I never will. I love you."

He looked over at Ali.

"You might find this hard to believe, Ali, but I don't hate you either. I knew all along you two loved each other. Ruth only married me to get back at you for what you did."

He looked back at Ruth.

"You need to be in love, Ruth. And if I can't have your love, then Ali should. There's no need to say anything further right now. I'm tired and need some time to myself...." His voice drifted off.

He got up and moved towards the door. Aiden nudged Lilly in the side.

"Jacob, wait!" she called. "I'll come and help you unpack."

She followed him out of the room. Aiden made his excuses too, wanting to give Ruth and Ali some time together. Ali took Jacob's place on the couch beside Ruth, where they remained in silence. Along with the love they felt for each other, they now felt shame. Jacob had shown himself to be a better person than they had shown themselves to be. He had refused to strike back at them. Instead, their actions had sharpened his focus.

Although the bus was crowded, Ali was able to find a seat at the back. It had been quite some time since he had been out around the bay. He missed those wonderful ocean views he remembered so fondly. He hadn't visited this part of the Avalon Peninsula before. His anticipation mounted.

However, as the bus left St. John's and made its slow, bumpy way southward, all he could see out of the window were black spruce, balsam fir, the occasional birch and an overabundance of rocks.

As he was about to abandon all hope, it appeared. At first, it was merely the occasional sparkle of light, then a quick glimpse of a bay. Finally, the full grandiose expanse of the ocean revealed itself before him – beautifully blue and exceedingly comforting. The scene at Ruth's the day before, when Jacob had learned the truth, lay heavily on his mind. A few hours away from St. John's was exactly what he needed. He could feel his tension begin to melt away.

At the foot of the hill, the bus made a left turn and pulled to an abrupt stop. Ali grabbed his bag and left the bus. Then, as quickly as it had pulled to a stop, it sped away. He was left standing alone.

He looked around. Not a soul was to be seen. The narrow road in front of him wound its way down towards the sea, where he could see several tree-covered islands of various sizes scattered throughout the bay and beyond. Then he realized he wasn't alone after all. Puffins, in an abundance he had never dreamed possible, flew overhead and crowded the harbour on the way to their island homes. He was enchanted.

He walked down the hill and stopped in front of one of the houses. He examined it closely. It was two storeys high. The first storey consisted of a front entrance with two rectangular windows on either side. The second floor was concealed within a mansard roof which sloped off on all four sides. Three second-storey dormer windows dominated the roof. In front of the house was a small flower garden surrounded by a low, picket fence. Ali leaned over and opened the gate. On the front porch, he paused. He had no idea what to expect, but he hoped for the best. He knocked.

Erin opened the door. On seeing her, he quickly realized how much he had missed having her around. He had known her for most of his life. She was also the mother of his child.

"Do you mind if I give you a hug?" he asked hesitantly.

"I was hoping you would," smiled Erin. "Come in."

In the front room, Erin walked him to a baby carriage. "Recognize anyone?"

Ali looked down. "She's gorgeous!" he gushed. "Takes after her old man."

"Pick her up. She won't bite. But she might spit up on you."

"I can take it."

Ali picked Alice up and held her close to his chest. He could feel her warmth and smell the sweetness of her breath. It felt good.

Ali wanted to know all about Alice and how she was adapting to life back in Witless Bay. Erin was more than happy to oblige. He was relieved to hear that she was adjusting well to being a mother and that her father had finally come to accept things as they are. His love for his daughter had proven to be stronger than he had realized.

"I wasn't sure you'd come," said Erin. "It was such short notice."

"I've been meaning to visit you, but I wasn't sure you'd want to see me."

"Have you seen Ruth since I left?"

"We've gotten back together."

"I can't say as how I'm surprised. Does her husband know?"

"He's been at sea. He only found out yesterday."

"Is she going to leave him?"

"It's a very complicated situation."

"It sounds like no matter what happens, someone is going to get badly hurt."

"We all might. There's no winner here."

—

While Ali was visiting Erin and Alice in Witless Bay, Ruth was making her way back home. She had spent the night at Joseph and Hannah's. They were happy to have her, but had no idea what was happening between her and Ali, nor how things had played out when Jacob had returned from sea.

Ruth had spent a lot of the morning mulling over how to address the current situation with Jacob. He was her husband, and she had made a vow to him when they got married. The thought of breaking that vow didn't sit lightly with her. But she realized that things had to change.

She found Jacob sitting in the kitchen, a cup of tea in front of him.

"Jacob, about yesterday," said Ruth. "I'm sorry you had to learn about it like that."

"It's true I wanted you to forgive Ali for what he had done, but I didn't really think it would go that far."

"I was going to tell you when you got back, but you surprised me. I wasn't expecting you until...."

"Why did you leave me alone last night?"

"I thought you wanted it that way."

"I never want to be left alone without you."

"That's what we have to talk about, Jacob."

"You're not going to leave me, are you?"

"But we can't just go on like nothing happened."

"Why not? Nothing has really changed."

"Do you really believe that?"

"Of course I do."

"Jacob, Ali and I love each other."

"I know that. You've always loved each other."

"And we want to be together."

"I wouldn't have it any other way. All I want is for you to be happy."

"I want you to be happy too. But I can't be happy without Ali and he can't be happy without me."

"And I can't be happy without *you*."

Ruth looked at him with sadness in her eyes.

"Don't leave me, Ruth. I don't want to live without *you*. I can't live without you."

"Oh Jacob...."

Ruth stayed with Jacob that night, knowing he needed her. However, when morning came, she left and went straight to Rosie's looking for Ali.

"We need to talk," said Ruth.

"I've been thinking...."

"Ali, I can't leave Jacob."

"But I love you, Ruth, and you love me...."

"He needs me, Ali."

"I need you, too."

"I owe it to him. He has never hurt me. I can't bring myself to hurt him more than I already have. He told me he wouldn't want to live without me. This is very hard on everyone. We should take a step back. I don't want anyone to suffer anymore. I can't just up and leave him."

"Does Jacob know you and I want to be together?"

"Yes. He said he wouldn't want it any other way."

"Even us sleeping together?"

"I couldn't leave him entirely...."

"Ruth, here's the thing.... I've been saving this for the right moment, and I think this is that moment."

He leaned over the table and spoke with determination.

"I can't live at my parents' place anymore. And I don't want to stay here with Rosie either. So ... I've been looking."

"At what?"

"At a place to rent. I found one over in the other end of town. It's a little flat on the second floor. It comes with a storefront. I can set up in the grocery business like Mom and Dad. I know the trade. It can be very profitable if I do it right. There's even an old stable out back that would be perfect for band practice."

"You're not expecting me to live there with you, are you?"

"Why not?"

"No, Ali!"

"You just told me Jacob doesn't mind us being together."

"I also told you that I couldn't leave him entirely."

"Exactly! Half your time with Jacob. Half your time with me. Problem solved!"

"It's not that simple, Ali."

"Yes it is! Jacob would understand."

"Sounds to me like you're trying to take advantage of that."

"I would never take advantage of Jacob."

"But that's exactly what you're proposing. That's so heartless of you. He's your friend."

"Yes, he is. But you're my love."

—

Ali was relieved his relationship with Ruth was out in the open. When they finally got up the nerve to tell Joseph and Hannah, Joseph was furious. Jacob was like a son to him. Eventually, though, he had to admit that he suspected as much all along. He wasn't particularly happy with it, but he knew it was fruitless to fight inevitability.

Shafeek had also taken the news in his stride, although he avoided telling his wife. It wasn't so much that he didn't want to tell her. It was more that he didn't want to be around her when she found out.

Ali had borrowed money from his father for the first two months rent on the apartment and storefront. After much deliberation, he came up with a suitable name. He would call his store Ali Baba. And the sign he would hang on the door would read: 'Open Sesame'.

Aiden, Sami and Zane loved that idea. What they loved even more was the stable out back. The name of the store, the stable out back and the 'Open Sesame' sign on the door inspired them to change the name of their band. From thence on, they were to be called Ali Baba and the Forty Thieves. The only thing left to do was somehow to incorporate the *Thousand and One Nights* into their act.

Shafeek was certain Ali's store would be a success as there was little competition in that part of town. He showed his son where to source the inventory he would need. As well, he suggested that they combine much of their wholesale purchases and thereby wrangle better prices from the suppliers. That appealed to Ali. He had, however, underestimated the amount of commitment it would take to open and maintain a store.

One evening, Ali was about to put his 'Close Sesame' sign on the door when he saw his father and mother peering through the window.

Majedah had been stewing in her own juices ever since Erin had left. Although she was glad to be rid of the woman who, in her eyes, had almost ruined her family, she was less pleased about not having seen her son since.

What made things worse were the rumblings she heard that Ali and Ruth had gotten back together even though Ruth was still married. She confronted her husband and forced him to tell her all he knew. Although reluctant, Shafeek relented. She was livid. Majedah had insisted they visit Ali and try to beat some sense into him.

Ali braced himself for what he knew would be an awkward conversation as his parents entered his store.

"So, this is where you've been hiding yourself?" said Majedah.

"You're the only one who would see this as hiding," answered Ali.

"Let's not get this off on the wrong foot, shall we," Shafeek cautioned.

Majedah walked around the shop inspecting the various items on display.

"So ... when are you going to come home and stop this silly sulking of yours?" she asked.

"You miss me, do you?"

"You are my eldest."

"You should have thought of that before you kicked Erin and your grandchild out."

"That's not my grandchild."

"Why don't you show us around, Ali?" interrupted Shafeek.

"I hear you're seeing that married Jewish girl again," said Majedah.

"Her name is Ruth, in case you've forgotten," said Ali.

"How could a son of mine sink so low? I don't know who's more stupid, you or her."

"Dad, get that woman out of here, will you," said Ali.

"Show us your apartment upstairs," suggested Shafeek. "I'm sure your mother would love to see it."

"I've seen enough," said Majedah.

She left and closed the door behind her. Before he followed his wife out the door, Shafeek addressed his son.

"Please don't give up on her, Ali. She needs you more than she realizes."

"She's got a funny way of showing it."

Ruth was torn between her desire to spend as much time as possible with Ali and her inability to completely turn her back on Jacob. At first, Ali hadn't been able to convince her to move in with him. But eventually they came to an *ad hoc* compromise that resulted in satisfying none of them entirely, but each of them partially.

Ruth divided her time between the two men in her life. The nights Ali was playing with his band, she spent with Jacob. The nights Ali wasn't playing, she spent with Ali. It wasn't anyone's idea of perfection, but it worked for the time being. Her hope was that Jacob would eventually come to the realization that that arrangement couldn't go on forever. She also hoped that someday he would be able to find his independence and realize it would be best for him and her to go their separate ways.

Ruth and Ali were stretched out on his front room couch.

"How was he last night?" Ali asked. "This arrangement must be taking its toll on him."

"Especially when he hears my news."

"You're moving in permanently?" he asked excitedly.

"Not exactly. I'm pregnant."

Ali had heard that same phrase before, but this time was different. His jaw dropped.

"Are you excited?" asked Ruth expectantly.

"Of course I am!"

Ruth threw her arms around him and squeezed him tight. He kissed her.

"This changes everything, you know," said Ali.

"I know. I have no idea how Jacob is going to react. We have to go see him. I can't keep this from him."

"Now?"

"Are you up for it?"

"I guess it's best if he hears it from both of us. How far along are you?"

"I'm due in March."

"Paddy's Day would make a great birthday. There would always be a built-in celebration."

"For the Irish."

"Don't you know that on St. Paddy's Day everyone's Irish?"

"Even the child of a Lebanese and a Jewess?"

"We'll just have to call the baby Seamus.

"Or Colleen," grinned Ruth.

Jacob was in the basement of his house, working. The arrangement between himself, Ali and Ruth had been hard on him. He knew he had put Ruth in a difficult position. To make things easier on her, he had made no objection to her spending as much time with Ali as she wanted. His sole concern was that she not leave him completely.

On their way to see Jacob, Ruth insisted they pick up Lilly, and then Aiden. She felt that they should hear the news at the same time as Jacob. They were going to find out one way or another anyway. She and Ali having a baby would definitely change the family dynamic. They were going to need all the moral support they could get.

At the house, Ruth called out to Jacob to join them.

"Ruth tells me your store is doing well," said Jacob to Ali.

"Slow, but getting there," he replied, and began to talk about his latest shipment of salt cod.

Lilly couldn't wait any longer.

"So, Ruth," she interrupted. "What's all the mystery about?"

"All of you probably thought in the back of your minds that sooner or later this day might come," said Ruth. "Well, it has."

"Surely you're not converting to Catholicism," joked Aiden. "Joseph would be furious."

Ruth turned to Jacob.

"Ali and I are going to have a baby."

Lilly didn't wait for the details. She jumped from her seat, ran towards Ruth and threw her arms around her. Aiden was more circumspect. When things settled down, all eyes turned to Jacob.

"Is that something you want, Ruth?" he asked.

"Yes, but I'm concerned with what you want," she answered.

"What I think Ruth is trying to say, Jacob, is do you want an annulment or something," said Ali.

"I would never do that," said Jacob. "I think it's wonderful news you're going to have a baby. It's probably the closest thing I'll ever get to having one of my own."

"Jacob, you never cease to surprise me," said Ali. "Any other man would have kicked his wife out and taken a swing at me long ago."

"I'm not any other man," said Jacob. "You must have noticed that by now."

"How do you see this working out?" asked Ruth.

"I'd like to be as much involved in the child as you two," said Jacob. "Isn't my wife's child my child as well?"

"Things are definitely going to get interesting around here," said Aiden. "The busy-bodies will be out in full force."

"I don't give a hoot," said Jacob. "This is our life, and we'll lead it as we want."

"I wonder how it will feel to be an auntie," said Lilly.

Later, as everyone was preparing to leave, Ruth held back and took Ali's arm.

"I'm going to stay here tonight if you don't mind. I'm sure he'd like that. Be patient, Ali."

The next few months were relatively calm as everyone settled into their own routines. Shafeek stood by Ali and Ruth, and offered whatever advice he saw fit whenever called upon. He couldn't bring himself, however, to tell his wife about the pregnancy.

Lilly had become more involved in her father's shop, especially as Ruth began to spend less and less time there. She and Aiden had shown themselves genuinely attached to each other, so Aiden finally moved out of his parents' place and in with her. He also found time to help Ali with his store, for which Ali was grateful.

Ali split his time between Ruth, his new business and the band. He, as well as Jacob, had encouraged Ruth to return to performing, but she couldn't see how that would be feasible in her condition. She was, however, enormously grateful that they would even consider the possibility. She missed singing with Ali. That would have to wait for another day.

As it turned out, Joseph and Hannah had shown themselves to be surprisingly sanguine when they heard of Ruth's pregnancy. That was not the case, however, when it came to Ruth and Jacob's neighbours. Not much was said in front of them. They showed their vehement disapproval in other ways.

One evening Jacob was relaxing and listening to the radio. Ruth was on the phone talking to Ali. Their conversation was interrupted by someone who shared the same party line as they did.

"We know what's going on over there," said the voice. "It's disgusting!"

"Are you talking to me?" asked Ruth.

"You should be ashamed of yourselves!" said the voice.

"Who is this?" asked Ali.

"Cats and dogs," shouted the voice. "That's what you are!"

"Those who live in glass houses...." said Ruth.

"You got some nerve!" said the voice.

"It's none of your business!" said Ali.

"Don't you worry," said the voice. "You'll get what's coming to you. All of you!"

Jacob called out from the front room.

"Who are you talking to?"

The front door swung open and something was thrown into the hall. Jacob left the front room to see what was happening. The fumes from the stink-bomb almost choked him. He cupped his nose and mouth with his hands and stomped on the packet. That made the smoke even worse. He kicked the burning film wrapped in newspaper out the door and slammed it shut.

He was coughing uncontrollably when Ruth ran over to him. She grabbed his hand and rushed him into the kitchen. As she was washing his face in the sink, she could hear Ali shouting over the phone line.

15

God Bless the Mark

On St. Patrick's Day around nine o'clock, it began to snow. It was the heavy, wet kind with which anyone living in St. John's at that time would be all too familiar.

Ali Baba and his Forty Thieves were about to take the stage at The Continental for Rosie's party to commemorate the day. Appropriate for the occasion, the Gaelic sign outside the door read: *Lá Fhéile Pádraig sona duit,* below which were the picture of a pint of beer and the supplication: *Sláinte! Come, wet yer shamrock.*

Since Ruth was a couple of weeks overdue from the actual due-date her doctor had given her, Ali had been reluctant to play that night. Jacob, however, stepped in and encouraged him to go enjoy himself. He would, as always, stay by her side.

Inside the club, Rosie had excelled herself. The stage was encircled with Irish-green shamrocks as well as the proud salute to Ireland: *Éirinn Go Brách.* The patrons sported bunting-like 'wearin' o' the green' shamrocks on their lapels, and Rosie's girls were provocatively dressed as sexy little leprechauns who would suggestively tap the male clientele with their shillelaghs whenever the fancy struck them.

Ali and the rest of the band had also risen to the occasion. Instead of playing their usual instruments, they took up the more suitable fiddle, tin whistle, bodhran, concertina squeeze box, *uilleann* pipes and *cláirseach* harp.

Traditional Irish songs reigned supreme: 'When Irish Eyes Are Smiling', 'The Rose of Tralee', 'Rocky Road to Dublin', 'Sweet Rosie O'Grady', 'That's an Irish Lullaby', 'Brennan on the Moor', 'Molly Malone', 'My Wild Irish Rose', 'Galway Bay', 'Foggy Dew', 'The Minstrel Boy', 'By Killarney's Lakes and Fells', 'So Abroad As I Was Walking', 'A Little Bit of Heaven', 'The Harp that Once Through Tara's Hall', 'Off to Tipperary in the Morning', and 'I'll Take You Home Again, Kathleen'.

Unsurprisingly, the highlight of the night was when Ali – doing his best imitation of Ireland's-own, John McCormack – sang 'Danny Boy'.

During the course of the evening, the temperature started to drop and the weather took a nasty turn. No one noticed and the party carried on.

Shortly after the 'Come-warm-yer-cockles' midnight meal of corned beef and cabbage, however, word started to spread that if everyone stayed any longer they might not be able to get home. The crowd started to thin out.

Around one o'clock, the band decided to join the exodus.

Outside, the weather was brutal. The snow was already knee deep, which made trudging through the drifts exhausting. When Ali finally reached home, he immediately collapsed into bed and quickly fell asleep. Ruth was staying at Jacob's, as she always did when Ali was playing.

Ali didn't hear the phone the first time it rang. He didn't hear it the second time. He did, however, hear it ring the third time. He couldn't remember ever having received a phone call at two o'clock in the morning. Who would have had the audacity to wake someone at that hour?

The conversation was brief and to the point.

The drifts were even higher, and the going was slow and

arduous. Ali had one thing he had to do on his way. The detour delayed him, but it was necessary.

He had to knock on the door several times before it opened. The two men had a brief conversation and quickly left together. The second door Ali knocked on was opened immediately.

"Oh, Ali," said Jacob. "I'm so glad to see you!"

"Where is she?" asked Doc Harrison.

"Upstairs," said Jacob. "Thank God you could make it! The doctor at the hospital couldn't get here because of the snow."

The three men ascended the stairs and found Ruth and Lilly in the bedroom. Jacob had awoken Lilly shortly before to tell her Ruth would need her.

Doc Harrison looked at Ali.

"When is she due?"

"Two weeks ago."

"Oh, I see," he said, while rubbing his chin.

He quickly turned to Jacob.

"What's your name?"

"Jacob Arenberg."

"Jacob, you go get some hot water and towels," said Doc Harrison. "Ali, do something about the heat. It's freezing in here."

Doc Harrison turned to Lilly.

"What's your name?"

"Lilly. I'm Ruth's sister."

"Have you ever seen a baby born before?"

"No," she answered nervously.

"You need to be my nurse for a day. There's nothing to be scared of. It's as natural as breathing."

When Jacob came back with the hot water and towels, Doc Harrison told him to go back downstairs and wait with Ali.

He'd call them if he needed anything.

The next couple of hours were excruciating. Every scream unsettled them. They looked at each other whenever they heard any movement whatsoever from upstairs. They hardly spoke. Doc Harrison finally came downstairs.

"Doc, how is she?" asked Ali.

"Don't be alarmed," he answered. "These things happen all the time."

"What's going on?" asked Jacob.

"The baby is in the right position and Ruth is fully dilated. She's pushing fine but the delivery isn't progressing. The size of Ruth's pelvis is a factor as well. I'm concerned she will have trouble delivering without some form of intervention."

"What kind of intervention?" asked Ali.

"I'll have to use forceps to help guide the baby's head out of the birth canal. Ruth's blood pressure is rising. I'm concerned about the baby's heartbeat. I can't wait any longer."

"Sounds like we don't have any choice," said Jacob.

"Do what you have to do, Doc," said Ali.

"If there's anything we can do to help, let us know," said Jacob.

"You can help by staying out of my way. She's a strong young woman. She'll be fine. Don't worry."

The minutes ticked by, emphasized by the grandfather clock in the hallway. Jacob was seated on the couch, lost in thought. Ali went to the window. The snow had stopped falling and the clouds were breaking up. With the sun slowly showing above the horizon, he felt his spirits lift. At any minute he and Ruth would have the baby they'd been expecting all these months. She was having a hard night. He was certain she must be exhausted. He was also certain their baby would smooth all that out.

The cry of a newborn baby shook them out of their stupor. Lilly walked into the room.

"Doc wants to see you upstairs."

"How's Ruth?" asked Ali.

"Come see for yourself."

Ali and Jacob both hurried upstairs and poked their heads around the door.

"Which one of you is the father?" asked Doc Harrison.

Ali and Jacob looked at each other.

"I am," said Ali.

"And I'm the husband," said Jacob.

"Wonders never cease," said Doc Harrison. "Come meet the latest addition to your family."

Ruth was awake, but pale and drained. Doc had laid the baby on her breast. That soothed her considerably. Ali and Jacob walked to the bed. Ali sat beside Ruth, and Jacob smoothed her forehead. She looked at them both.

"It's a boy," she whispered. "His name's Ramon."

"After Ramon Novarro?" asked Lilly.

Ruth nodded.

"The other love of her life," smiled Jacob.

"She'll need lots of rest," said Doc Harrison. "Give St. Clare's a call in the morning. They may send a wagon as soon as the streets are clear. Mother and baby should get a thorough hospital checkup. Just don't mention my name!"

⸺

All of them were all exhausted. Ali stayed in the room with Ruth and caught a few winks on the armchair by her bed. Lilly laid her head down by her sister. Jacob made himself as comfortable as he could on the couch in the front room.

Ali was the first one to rouse himself. He went immediately to the phone and called St. Clare's. They told him someone would be there to take Ruth and the baby to the hospital as soon as they could. Since he was already awake, he decided to make himself busy in the kitchen and prepare breakfast for everyone.

No sooner had they finished eating than they heard a knock on the door. Two men had arrived with instructions to take Ruth and Ramon to the hospital. They were shown to Ruth's room. Ruth and the baby were brought down the stairs on a stretcher and placed in the back of the hospital wagon.

At St. Clare's, Ruth and her baby were whisked away. Ali, Jacob and Lilly were told to wait in the visitors' room. After what seemed like forever, a nurse arrived. She looked at Ali.

"Are you Ruth's husband?"

"No, I am," said Jacob.

The nurse turned to face him.

"I'm so sorry. It's just that baby Ramon seems to have more of the other gentleman's colouring. My mistake. Please follow me."

Ali followed the others into Ruth's room.

Ruth was asleep. Ramon was in a crib next to her.

After ten minutes or so, a doctor walked in.

"Hello, my name is Dr. Lindsey. I'll be Ruth's doctor while she's here in St. Clare's. First, I would like to say that Ruth is fine. As for Ramon, that is a slightly different matter."

Lilly drew in her breath.

"I had a chat with Ruth a little while ago and filled her in on what is happening," said the doctor. "Tell me, did you have help with the delivery?"

Ali, Jacob and Lilly looked at each other. None of them

wanted to be the first to speak. Dr. Lindsey knew what that meant.

"Was he a doctor?" he asked.

"We couldn't get Ruth to the hospital because of the storm, and they couldn't get to us," said Jacob.

"We had no other choice," said Ali.

"You're not going to tell me who it was who helped you, are you."

No one replied.

"If Ruth had been here at the hospital, we could have avoided what has happened," said the doctor.

"What are you getting at?" asked Lilly.

"Did any of you notice those bruises on the sides of Ramon's head?" asked Dr. Lindsey.

"Not really," said Ali.

"Well, it looks like whoever delivered the baby used high forceps in the delivery. That procedure can sometimes cause damage to the baby's skull. I'm afraid this might be one of those times."

Lilly's head drooped. Ruth remained motionless.

"There's a very real chance Ramon's brain has been damaged," said the doctor. "We won't know for sure, or how serious it might be, until we do more tests. You should brace yourselves for the possibility that Ramon could not develop as you might expect ... mentally. Also, if the test confirms what we suspect, he might never be a normal child and could possibly have a shortened life span."

The nurse crossed herself.

"God bless the mark."

Lilly threw herself onto Ruth's bed and cried uncontrollably.

—

Shafeek was uncomfortable. In the past, he had left such things to his wife. In this case, however, he thought it best he undertake the task himself. The saleslady felt his unease and offered to help. He gladly accepted. She took her time and slowly described the various options available to him. She didn't show any real preference. But if she were to be pushed, it would be the large one on the top shelf. That was good enough for Shafeek. He paid his bill. And with his magnificent acquisition tucked securely under his arm, he sauntered out of the store.

Half-way home, he realized he had forgotten to ask the saleslady to gift-wrap it. That meant he would have to stop by the local news stand and buy some wrapping paper. The choice was considerably short of spectacular. He decided that the blue paper with the silver edges would have to do.

When he got home, he went straight to the living room and set about the task at hand. Majedah saw him enter and noticed that he seemed more preoccupied than usual. She also noticed he was carrying a large parcel, which he appeared to be trying to hide. She didn't address him directly. Instead, she decided to follow him and see what he was hiding.

She heard the rustling of paper coming from the living room and took a quick peek. If it were a present for her, she was determined to find out. She hated surprises.

When she saw that Shafeek was wrapping a teddy bear, she knew she wasn't the recipient. But who could it be for? And why was he trying to hide it?

As quickly as Shafeek had come in, he left, teddy bear in hand. Majedah put on her hat and coat and followed him at a distance.

The house where Shafeek stopped was unfamiliar to her. He knocked. The door opened. Majedah saw the young woman who answered the door, but didn't recognize her. Her mind began to spin out of control.

———

It had been only a few days since Ruth had given birth. The news Dr. Lindsey had delivered in the hospital the day of Ramon's birth had hung like a dark cloud over all of them. She had never for a moment considered the possibility that her baby would be anything less than perfectly healthy. She couldn't see past the heartbreak and dread of what might lie ahead for her and little Ramon.

Her worst fears were confirmed when earlier that morning, Dr. Lindsey made a house call. Everyone had gathered to offer whatever assistance they could, including Shafeek. The doctor verified what he and the other doctors had suspected. Ramon's temples had been compressed and his brain had been severely damaged. He would not develop normally. And it was probable he would not live beyond the age of thirty.

Ruth was devastated. No amount of consolation could compensate for the fact that her lovely little baby boy had been damaged so egregiously.

That was when Majedah burst into the house. She pushed Shafeek aside.

"Majedah, did you follow me?" he asked.

Majedah pointed at Lilly. "Who's this?"

"Ruth's sister, Lilly," said Shafeek. "Lilly, this is my wife, Majedah."

"Tell me this child isn't your girlfriend!" demanded Majedah indignantly.

"Excuse me!" exploded Lilly.

Jacob came into the hallway.

"What's going on here?" he asked.

"Shafeek, what are you up to?" asked Majedah.

She pushed past Jacob and strutted into the front room, followed by Jacob and Lilly.

"Mother, what are you doing here?" asked Ali.

Majedah looked around the room.

"Aiden, do you know all these people?" she asked.

"Hello, mother," he answered.

"I presume you're Ali's mother," said Jacob.

"Who are you?" asked Majedah dismissively.

"My name is Jacob Arenberg. I'm Ruth's husband. This is my house."

"So, you're the one she married," said Majedah. "You Jews are all alike."

She pointed at Ramon.

"Whose baby is that?"

"Mine and Ruth's," said Ali. "His name is Ramon."

Majedah stared at her son. "You have another child with yet another woman? A married woman?" She crossed herself.

"And you, Aiden. I thought you would have more sense."

"With a mother like you, I'm surprise he has as much sense as he does," said Lilly.

"This is a house of sin!" declared Majedah.

She glared at Jacob.

"What husband would allow this? And under his own roof? What kind of man are you?"

"You wouldn't understand even if I told you."

Majedah turned to Joseph next.

"And you, her father, you knew about this all along and didn't do or say anything?"

"You can't trust a Jew, can you," Joseph mocked.

Majedah faced Shafeek last.

"And my so-called husband. How can I ever trust you again?

You're no better than the rest of them!"

"That's quite a wife you have there, Shafeek," said Lilly.

"And who are you sleeping with, may I ask, young lady?" Majedah demanded.

"Your son Aiden, if you must know."

Majedah fumed and crossed herself twice.

"You are all sinners in the eyes of the Lord!"

"Majedah, please...," Shafeek pleaded.

She stiffened and looked at all present with disgust in her eyes. Her gaze finally rested on Ruth. She raised her arm towards heaven. Then pointed directly at Ruth.

"May God Almighty condemn you to hell!"

She then pointed at Ramon.

"And take that child of Satan with you!"

Ali got up and came up to his mother.

"Mom, the doctors told us today that Ramon's skull was partly crushed when he was delivered. His brain has been damaged. He will never be a normal child and could possibly never reach full adulthood."

"Serves you right!" shrieked Majedah. "God Almighty, in his infinite wisdom, has wreaked his vengeance upon you!"

"Rather than being a child of Satan, as you so horribly referred to him, he is a child of God," said Ali. "You might not understand, but the Almighty has a special place in his heart for children such as Ramon. He will hold him close to his breast for all eternity."

Majedah stared at her son. Her whole body shook. She turned. And with all the dignity she could muster, she left the house and slammed the door behind her.

After Majedah's exit, Joseph, Hannah, Shafeek, Lilly and

Aiden didn't stay long. It had been a difficult day for everyone. And Majedah calling God's curse down on Ruth and her baby hadn't made things any easier. Ruth, Ali and Jacob remained in the front room.

"Things aren't going to get any easier, you know," said Ali.

"I can handle anything your mother, or anyone else for that matter, throws at me," said Jacob. "That kind of stuff doesn't bother me."

"You have to realize Ramon is going to need special care," said Ruth.

"I want to be involved in Ramon's upbringing as much as possible," he insisted.

"Are you really up to all that entails?" asked Ali.

"I know you might see my view of things as untenable," said Jacob, "but I don't. I will take Ramon as my very own and love him as much as you and Ruth do. He will be my little boy too."

Jacob looked at Ruth. She could see the hint of a tear in his eyes.

"Till death do us part, Ruth."

16

The Angels Wept

In some ways, Ali was right. Things did not get any easier.

The neighbours knew that Jacob was Ruth's husband, but clearly he wasn't the father of his wife's son. The gossip was ear-shattering.

But although Jacob realized what was being said behind his back, he loved his little boy, and would show him off whenever and wherever the opportunity presented himself. He took him shopping, on walks, to visit friends, to his office and even onboard ship. Ramon was amused, though not entirely engaged.

What did excite him was parades. Jacob would push his way to the front of the crowd, lift his little boy up and place him high on his shoulders. It was one of the few times Jacob would see the beginning of a smile on Ramon's face.

Not only was Ramon slow to smile, he was also slow to laugh, to turn over, to crawl, and to stand. He also had noticeably slow eye movement and would strike out randomly for no apparent reason.

While Ali and Ruth found this worrying, they were thrilled when Ramon began to display a wonderful sense of rhythm. While his attempts to sing along to a song he liked resulted in a garbled monotone, he took great pleasure in swaying his body back and forth to the pulse of the music. When Ali pointed this out to Ruth, her heart rejoiced. There was a place for Ramon in the world of music.

Lilly, meanwhile, had enrolled in college classes. She had decided she wanted to be a teacher. In her spare time, she worked in her father's shop, where she had become quite an accomplished saleswoman. She was in high demand, which made her father proud.

She continued to write to her mother in New York. Although Sarah still pleaded with her to return home, Lilly had no intention of complying. She liked her life in St. John's, and now had a history there, albeit a painful one.

For his part, Aiden had become more involved in his parents' expanding business and spent most of his days there. At night, he and Ali, Sami, Zane and Woody continued to play at various dance clubs around the city. Ali Baba and the Forty Thieves were still thriving.

Joseph and Hannah were immersed in their tailoring business and were grateful for any assistance Ruth could provide. With Ramon to take care of, however, her time was limited.

Ali continued to be hopeful his mother would come to her senses, but he wasn't holding his breath. Shafeek had become despondent and worried that it would never happen. The thought of his son being estranged from his mother still kept him up at night.

One day, Jacob's superiors told him they wanted to recommend he be given his own ship. It was an opportunity he could previously only have dreamed of. There was still one more assignment at sea to undertake before he was to start the rigorous training he would need to captain his own vessel. He was on pins and needles waiting for the call.

When it finally came, he packed his bags and headed straight to the harbour, with Ramon planted firmly on his shoulders and with his arm around Ruth.

On the wharf, Ruth held Ramon's hand and hugged Jacob, telling him how proud she was of him.

As Jacob was heading up the gangplank, he turned and waved. Ruth bent down, straightened Ramon's sailor's hat and whispered in his ear.

"Do that thing Daddy taught you."

Ramon saluted his father.

Jacob grinned and proudly returned the gesture.

Everyone was present. Joseph had called the family together. He wanted to share some wonderful news with them. Despite the many questions fired at him, no more details were given.

Ruth offered to host the event. She had prepared several of Ali's favourite Lebanese dishes, one of the few positive things that had come from knowing his mother.

Lilly had tried her hand at a New York take on codfish. Instead of frying it, she squeezed on lemon juice, sprinkled cheese on top, worked in caramelized onions and baked it. Hannah had prepared Joseph's beloved oven-roasted brisket, over which Joseph was ecstatic, and Ali had assembled his *tour de force* – cabbage salata with lemon, salt and lots of garlic. For his part, Aiden had brought Turkish baklava and coffee from his parents' store. Even Ramon had a contribution: a Cherry Blossom chocolate bar. After everyone had had their fill, Ali stood and addressed the family.

"I would like to propose a toast to our dear, and absent, friend, Jacob, who is now at sea training in his quest to be captain of his own ship. Captain Arenberg has a nice ring to it, don't you think."

They clinked glasses in Jacob's honour.

"Now, Joseph," said Ali. "Why all the secrecy? What's this wonderful news you've been keeping to yourself?"

Joseph rose from his chair. All eyes and ears were focused on him. He smiled and looked at Hannah.

"It's time."

Hannah stood and turned her back to everyone. She reached into her dress pocket, turned back around and stretched out her hand.

Just as she had hoped, the diamond on her ring finger caught the light from the chandelier over the dinner table and glistened in all its splendour. Cheering broke out.

Ruth jumped up and, almost knocking her chair over in the process, ran to embrace Hannah. Ali and Aiden stood and madly shook Joseph's hand.

"You old scalawag!" said Ali.

"How long have you been keeping this from us?" asked Aiden.

Joseph simply grinned.

Ruth held Hannah's hand even closer to the light and turned it this way and that in order to maximize the sparkle from the solitaire.

"This is so exciting!" gushed Ruth.

"That's quite a rock," said Aiden. "You know, the size of the diamond tells the woman how much you love her."

"You must love Hannah an awful lot," said Ruth.

"Have you set a date yet?" asked Ali.

"There's no hurry," said Hannah. "There's so much to do at the shop."

"When that settles down a little, we'll see," said Joseph.

"Don't leave it too long, Hannah," said Ruth. "Don't want Pop getting cold feet after fifteen years."

Lilly hadn't had much to say since Hannah had revealed

the engagement ring. A little later in the evening, while everyone's attention was elsewhere, she rose from her chair and stood next to her father. She spoke in a hushed tone.

"I didn't want to say this in front of everyone, but have you forgotten you're still married to Mom?"

"That was ages ago," said Joseph. "Besides, there'll be lots of time to figure that out later."

Lilly could only laugh.

"Okay then, Pop."

The celebration continued. Everyone was unconstrained. So much so, they didn't hear the knock on the door. They did, however, hear the knocking on the window of the front room. Ali looked outside and saw two men standing there. He waved them to the front door. When he opened it, he saw that both men were wearing uniforms.

"Is Mrs. Arenberg at home?" asked one of the men.

"Ruth, there's two guys standing here who want to talk to you," called Ali.

Ruth came to the door.

"Mrs. Arenberg, my name is Captain Withers. This is Chief Mate Cummings."

"Hope we're not disturbing you, ma'am," said Chief Mate Cummings.

"We work with your husband, Jacob," said Captain Withers.

"He's not home right now," said Ruth. "He's at sea."

"We know, Mrs. Arenberg," said Chief Mate Cummings. "That's why we're here."

Ruth clutched the doorframe.

"There's been an accident, Mrs. Arenberg," said Captain Withers. "Your husband has been injured. He's being transported to St. Clare's."

Ruth's hand went to her mouth.

"We are here now to take you to see him," said Chief Mate Cummings.

Ali came up behind Ruth.

"Is it serious?" he asked.

"Our car is out front," Captain Withers said.

Euphoria is a fickle thing. It can blindside you when you least expect it. One minute you can be as happy as is humanly possible. The next, it could seem as though your world had come to an end.

Joseph heard voices at the door and came to see what was happening.

"Joseph, Jacob has been injured," said Ali. "Ruth and I are going with these gentlemen to St. Clare's. Tell the others."

Joseph clasped his shoulder.

"We'll be right behind you."

At the hospital, Joseph, Hannah, Lilly and Aiden joined Ruth and Ali in the lobby. Ali held Ramon's hand. The two officers led them directly to Jacob's room and identified themselves to the nurse.

Jacob was in bed. A doctor and nurse were hovering over him. Ruth approached the bed. Jacob's shipmate, Antonio, was sitting next to the bed. He'd been crying.

"He's resting now," said the doctor, in a hushed voice.

"What happened?" asked Ruth as she approached the bed.

Chief Mate Cummings began.

"Jacob was aboard ship and...."

"This is all my fault," Antonio interrupted.

Cummings continued.

"Antonio fell overboard. Jacob threw him a life preserver, grabbed another one and jumped in after him."

"He was so brave...," sobbed Antonio. His voice trailed off.

"Antonio took hold of the life preserver and swam over to where Jacob was."

"Jacob was obviously in trouble," added Captain Withers. "When he jumped in after Antonio, he hit his head on one of the lifeboats. He..."

Antonio didn't let him finish. He had trouble controlling his voice as he looked up at Ruth.

"We had an argument at breakfast because he told me he would never leave you. I overreacted. I climbed the rail of the ship and threatened to jump off. I slipped and fell."

There was an audible gasp in the room.

Ruth sat on the side of the bed. She looked into Antonio's eyes. He looked lost.

"I loved him," sobbed Antonio. "I never did truly know how he felt about me, but whatever it was, he couldn't bring himself to return my love. He would never permit it. It broke my heart."

He took both Ruth's hands in his.

"He loves you, Ruth, more than he could ever love me. More than anything else. I know that now."

He paused for a moment. Ruth reached out to sooth him. He took her face in his hands and looked into her eyes.

"He said he was born to be with you. He put his love for you above all other forms of love. His love for you is pure..., true love. You're a very lucky woman, Ruth."

Ruth burst into tears. Ali walked over and sat beside her.

Antonio turned to the doctor.

"Tell me Jacob will be alright," he pleaded.

"There's been a lot of damage to his heart," said Dr. Sweeney. "The shock was too much for him. He's getting weaker by the minute."

At that moment, Jacob began to stir. Ruth leaned over and kissed him on the forehead. He turned towards her and tried to smile.

Antonio reached over and took his hand. Jacob looked back and forth between them.

"I'm sorry I didn't tell you about Antonio, Ruth," Jacob said weakly. "He's a very sweet man."

"Don't try to talk," said Ruth.

"I have things I want to say to you," said Jacob.

He looked at Ali.

"And to you."

He spoke slowly.

"Ruth, I have loved you more than I ever thought I would love another human being. My love for you will last through the ages."

Ruth laid her head next to Jacob's.

"Ali, I leave Ruth and Ramon in the hands of someone who I know loves them, and will take care of them."

"That I will promise with all my heart," said Ali.

Jacob's eyes closed.

The funeral procession wound its stately way along Duckworth Street. The hearse was flanked by the Merchant Marine honour guard. That was followed by twenty merchant marines in full dress. Behind them walked family and friends. Ali held Ramon's hand. Ruth held Antonio's. Along the way, people stopped what they were doing and bowed their heads. Women pulled their children to them. Men doffed their caps.

The procession stopped in front of the Jewish synagogue. The coffin was carried inside. Joseph led the service and read from the Torah and Prophets.

Captain Withers spoke of Jacob's sense of honour, his courage and his commitment to duty. He was loved by all. In closing, he announced that Jacob would be awarded a post-humous Merchant Marine Captaincy.

Ali spoke of his friend who had never lost sight of what was most important in life. He loved his wife and his son more than he loved himself. He was never one to pass judgement on another. He would be sorely missed by all who were fortunate enough to have known him and to have called him friend.

Antonio then walked to the lectern.

"What I am about to say might be difficult for some of you to grasp. It might make you feel uneasy. Even shocked. Or appalled. But it has to be said."

He paused to steady himself.

"The fact is ... I loved Jacob. I always will. And not merely as a friend or as a shipmate. In the way that Ruth was the love of Jacob's life, Jacob was the love of mine. He understood the love I had for him. But he was steadfast. Wise. Wiser than I am. The thought of never seeing him again would have brought me to despair, except for the example he set for me."

He left the podium and walked to stand by Jacob's coffin. He spoke through his tears.

"Jacob ... you are, and will always be, the love of my life. You are my sailor's delight. My red sky at night."

Ruth rose and gently guided Antonio to his seat. She then took his place at the head of Jacob's coffin.

She reached into her pocket and took out a sheet of paper. She attempted to read from it, but couldn't get her words out. The thought of Jacob not being there for her and their son lay heavily on her heart. Something had died within her.

Lilly, sensing Ruth's distress, rose and stood by her side. She steadied her sister's trembling hand.

Ruth read:

A letter to my husband, Jacob.

There are husbands. There are loving husbands. There are husbands to be admired and emulated. There are husbands who come to you in your hour of need. And then there is you, Jacob.

You once said to me: "You know, Ruth, you and I have never argued. We have never fought. And we have never had an angry word spoken by either of us towards the other." I must say, I had never thought of our relationship in quite that way before. But thinking back, I now realize you were absolutely right.

And there was your love for your son, Ramon. Is it possible for a father and son to be any closer? I think not. Not a day passed that you didn't eagerly spend as much time with him as possible. You were inseparable and devoted to each other. You were as close to Ramon as a flower blossom is to its petals.

But now the unthinkable has occurred. Ramon and I will have to face life without you. Fortunately, we have Ali to love us as you loved us, fiercely and devotedly.

You once told me – "Love will out." How right you were.

I'll keep a light burning in your memory until I see you again.

You are my hero. I am your loving wife.

Ruth

Jacob was laid to rest in the Jewish cemetery at Mundy

Pond. The wording on his tombstone would have made him proud.

Captain Jacob Arenberg
Merchant Marine
Chivalrous Knight in Shining Armour

Epilogue

The day Ali and Ruth were married was a joyous celebration. She arrived at Cape Spear in a horse-drawn carriage seated next to her father. Her two bridesmaids, Lilly and Hannah, were sitting opposite her. Ramon was seated between them – a bouquet of flowers on his lap, and a big smile on his face.

Upon their arrival at the foot of the hill leading up to the lighthouse, Joseph helped Ruth step down from the carriage. She was clothed in a white satin dress he had made for her. Her head was adorned with a matching lace cap and a long, flowing veil.

They made their way slowly up the hill to where the light-house held dominion. At the head of the gently sloping path, Ruth could see Ali. He was dressed in a black single-breasted, one-button tuxedo with a red carnation in his lapel. His groomsmen, Aiden and Sami, stood by his side.

Ali gave Ruth his arm and led her to the foot of the light-house where – with the ocean waves, distant Europe and humpbacks and minkes as their backdrop – they stood hand in hand.

When Ali saw his mother and father standing at the back, he smiled.

Joseph presided over the ceremony. He took his place in front of Ali and Ruth and the assembled guests. Hannah nudged Ramon towards his mother. He bowed and handed her his bouquet of roses. Ali bent down and shook his hand. Ramon scampered off and hid among the guests.

"It is not often a father gets to join his daughter in holy

wedlock to the man she has loved all her life. Ali and Ruth were meant for each other from the moment they first met. Life has thrown many obstacles their way. But they remained steadfast. They always knew they loved each other above all else."

He addressed himself to Ruth.

"It's time for me to admit I've been keeping something from you, my daughter. Now don't blame me. It was my other daughter's idea.

"When you and Ali announced you were going to marry, Lilly suggested we make this as special an occasion as possible. But what she had in mind was quite a doozie.

"At first, I was skeptical. So much water has passed under so many bridges over the years that I couldn't get my mind around what Lilly had suggested. However – and you know how persuasive Lilly can be – in the end, I relented. And I'm so very glad I did.

"Enough with the chatter. Ruth, and all those assembled here, I would now like to introduce to you ... just off the boat from New York City ... the one ... the only ... Sarah Rosenberg! Ruth and Lilly's mother!"

Ruth wasn't sure she had heard her father correctly. She looked at him for clarity. He simply nodded. The door to the lighthouse burst open and Ruth turned around.

Out stepped Ruth's mother. She ran towards Ruth and threw her arms around her. Ruth tried to step back to see if what her father had said was in fact true – that this woman was indeed her mother. But Sarah wouldn't let her go.

"My darling little girl! I can't believe what my eyes are seeing!"

Ruth was dumbfounded.

"Say something, sweetheart. Aren't you glad to see me?"

Ruth finally regained her composure.

"Mother, after all these years...."

Lilly rushed up and took Ruth's hand.

"You knew about this all along?" Ruth asked incredulously.

"Aren't kid sisters a pain in the ass sometimes," laughed Lilly.

"My God, Mother," cried Ruth. "I can't believe you're actually here."

"There's been a hole in my heart since the day I sailed back to New York," said Sarah. "Since the day I last saw you."

Ruth put her arms around her mother and wept. Sarah and Lilly wept.

"Now look what I've done," said Sarah. "I've ruined all our makeup."

Hannah walked over and stretched out her hand towards Sarah.

"Hello, again."

"I'm sorry. Do we know each other?"

"I'm Hannah Epstein. Remember?"

Sarah racked her memory.

Hannah continued.

"Joseph hired me to take care of Ruth when she was a little girl. The last time I saw you, you were boarding a ship back to New York.

Sarah reached out and took Hannah's hand.

"Of course. Hannah. So nice to see you and Joseph have remained friends."

"More than that. We're engaged."

Sarah pulled her hand back.

"You're what?!" she bellowed.

A ripple of unease swept through the wedding guests.

"Joseph! Get over here!" Sarah shouted.

"Keep your voice down," he pleaded. "There's a wedding going on here."

"Are you still my husband, or aren't you?!"

The guests began to murmur louder.

Joseph stumbled over his words.

"Well ... that was a long time ago, and..."

"Up to no good as usual, are you, Joseph?" scolded Sarah with her hands on her hips.

"I thought that since...," Joseph stammered, his eyes pleading with her.

"We're only engaged," interrupted Hannah. "We're not married. Technically he hasn't done anything wrong."

"Yet!" said Sarah.

Lilly took her mother's hand. Ruth followed suit. Sarah looked from one to the other.

"Mother, this is Ruth's wedding day," implored Lilly. "Can't this wait till later?"

Sarah looked at Joseph. Then she looked at Hannah. Her face softened.

"Well ... husband of mine. As you say ... that was a long time ago. I suppose it's past time we finally got that divorce, don't you think?"

Ruth hugged her mother again.

Ali walked over, Ramon squirming in his arms.

"Sarah, I would like you to meet your grandson. Say hello, Ramon."

At the back, Majedah jumped up and glared down at her husband.

"I knew I shouldn't have let you force me to come here."

Shafeek attempted to reassure his wife.

"Majedah, it's a special day...."

"Do you really need any more proof? You can see, they're

all sinners and bigamists. The lot of them!"

She turned and trudged off. Shafeek started to go after her, but stopped, turned back and resumed his seat among the other guests.

Joseph, meanwhile, was struggling to regain control of the proceedings.

"Would everyone just settle down? I've got a ceremony to conduct here! Please! Return to your places!"

Eventually the hubbub died down and he was able to make himself heard.

"Where was I? Oh, yes.... I'm sure you'll all agree I would be remiss if I didn't mention our precious Jacob. He was, and will always remain, part of Ruth's and Ali's family. He loved each of them dearly. May God hold you tenderly in this loving embrace, Jacob."

Ali squeezed Ruth's hand.

"And now it is time for Ruth and Ali to proclaim their love."

Ali and Ruth turned, faced each other and took the other's hands in theirs. They proclaimed their vows in turn.

Passion is not for the faint of heart.
It consumes as much as inspires,
And lives in all of us.
It can whittle away at our self-esteem,
But it can also raise us to heights
Our imagination can only dream of.
My passion is yours,
And yours is mine.
It is our responsibility to discover its place in our lives.
I promise to walk that road with you,
Until we find our palace among the stars.
I kiss you as you do me.

I caress you as you do me.
You will be mine,
And I will be yours
Until our hearts no longer beat
And eternity calls us to its timeless breast.

Joseph once again addressed all those present.

"Ali and Ruth, by the powers invested in me by this beautiful country of Newfoundland – this country that we have chosen as our home – I now pronounce you man and wife. Ali, you may now kiss your bride!"

Applause rang out and echoed off the rocks below them.

When they descended and took their places among the lichen, spring-green moss and boulders that buffered them from the breaking tide, they feasted on the ocean's bounty and drank champagne. A gloriously-tiered wedding cake followed. They celebrated their many blessings.

As the sun revealed the very last of its majesty and was quietly setting over the darkening hills behind them, Ali sang his love song to Ruth.

Later that night, they gently undressed one another, layer by layer, and fell into each other's arms. Their passion knew no bounds, and they slept the sleep of lovers in love.

Acknowledgements

The last thing I thought I would ever do is write a novel. Well, maybe not the last thing, but pretty close.

It's all Wendy O'Brien's fault. Without her incessant persistence to "Write! Write! Write!", I would never have started down that precarious path. Instead, I would have continued blissfully tending my garden, merrily singing my song, and wistfully whistling into the wind.

But all caution aside. Thanks, Wendy!

I must also thank Beth Oberholtzer and Grant Boland for their exquisite cover design and artwork; Jane Warren, Wendy O'Brien, and my son, Christopher Michael, for their insightful editing wizardry; and Kathleen Metcalfe and Alex Bolduc of Inglewood Press for their patience. Isn't it wonderful when one's expectations are so magnificently exceeded.

And of course, Helen, my one-and-only, beloved life-partner of fifty years. How she has continued to put up with me after all this time, I'll never know. But God love her for it. Can I count you in for another fifty?

Photo by Katherine Michael

The Author

DAVID MICHAEL was born in the Dominion of Newfoundland, six years before it became Canada's tenth province.

Before pursuing an M.A. in 20th Century French Literature at Sorbonne Université in Paris (thanks to a scholarship from Memorial University of Newfoundland), he did his undergraduate work at Iona College in New Rochelle, New York.

His many pursuits have included teacher, choirmaster, singer-songwriter, musician, recording artist, TV host, businessman, and co-owner of the highly-successful Toronto pub, Brass Taps.

David and his wife, Helen, have three children: Katherine, Lesley and Christopher, as well as five grandchildren: Lucy, Elliot, Marlowe, Alden and Greydon.

He currently lives in Toronto, where, when not writing or composing, he assiduously tends his rose-infused, English-cottage garden. *Love Will Out* is his first novel, and the first of a trilogy.